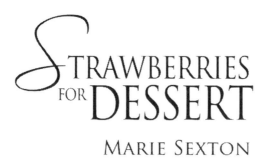

STRAWBERRIES FOR DESSERT

MARIE SEXTON

Dreamspinner Press

Published by
Dreamspinner Press
4760 Preston Road
Suite 244-149
Frisco, TX 75034
http://www.dreamspinnerpress.com/

Strawberries for Dessert

Cover Art by Anne Cain   annecain.art@gmail.com
Cover Design by Mara McKennen

ISBN: 978-1-61581-550-0

Printed in the United States of America
First Edition
August, 2010

eBook edition available
eBook ISBN: 978-1-61581-551-7

Troy and Julie: Thank you for your support and encouragement.

Scarlett: If he ever turns, he's all yours!

Wendy: Thanks for the ongoing workshop chats. This book would not be what it is without you. And thanks for giving me the naughty half of our brain!

Sean: As always, thank you for your never-ending love and support.

And last but never least, Kendall: One of these days you may be embarrassed by the books your mother writes, but for now, I'm glad you find it so exciting. And because it means so much to you, I will include the words you added to the manuscript when it was less than ten pages long: tim   jim lim dim7975   6781

I love you!

THE flight was six hours long. Six hours to contemplate all the ways this could end.

I had flown more times in my life than I could possibly count, but only one other flight had ever caused me this much anxiety. That flight had ended with me voluntarily throwing myself out of a perfectly good airplane. I had known then that I might be about to experience the thrill of my life—or I might come to a very messy end on the ground below.

This didn't feel much different.

Every minute was an exercise in patience. Pre-boarding made my heart pound. Finding my seat made my palms sweat. The takeoff almost caused me to hyperventilate—there was no turning back now. I was given a bag of pretzels (because peanuts were no longer allowed) and a tiny shot of Sprite on the rocks. What I really needed was a Valium, but I was pretty sure the stewardess didn't have those on her rickety little cart.

Every choice I had ever made had led me here, to this airplane. Everything I wanted in the world was at the other end of this unbelievably terrifying cross-country flight. What if it all went wrong?

Finally we began our descent, and I could not stop my hands from shaking or trepidation from growing in my chest like some kind of parasite. The fear was almost overwhelming. It might even have been crippling, if not for one simple thing: underneath it all was something stronger. Something pure. Something that drove me on.

It was hope.

EIGHTEEN MONTHS EARLIER

Date: April 10

From: Jared

To: Cole

Cole—We were in Vegas a few weeks ago and ran into a friend of Zach's. He lives in Phoenix, and he said you should look him up. Good looking guy and he seemed nice enough as long as you're not the one dating his ex. I think the two of you might hit it off. His name is Jonathan Kechter.

Jared

Date: April 11

From: Cole

To: Jared

Hey Sweets! It's good to hear from you, even if your email is dreadfully short. What happens in Vegas doesn't really have to stay in Vegas, honey. Would it kill you to give me some juicy details?

So, you think I should look up this Jonathan fellow? I'll take your word on the good-looking part. After all, you do have fabulous taste in men, even if that big pissed-off cop you're with now isn't exactly my type. As long as I'm "not the one dating his ex"? That's terribly intriguing. I suspect there's a good story to go along with such a cryptic statement. You never were much of a gossip (you really should work on that, Sweets). I'll be in New York for the next few days, but when I get back home, maybe I'll give him a call. God knows Phoenix has been awfully dry lately—and sugar, I'm not talking about the weather!

THE flight from LA to Phoenix took about an hour. One hour that I had a perfectly legitimate excuse for turning off my cell phone.

What did it say about my job when the commute was the fun part?

I'd just spent a week in LA helping our newest hotel client transition their accounting data into my company's software. Next week, I would be doing the same thing for another client in Vegas. Between those two cities and Phoenix, I was currently juggling six different clients in various stages of the transition process. All of them seemed inclined to call me at all hours.

And then there was my boss.

The calls started at six a.m. and usually ended by ten at night. Although I was skeptical that my simple cell phone really posed any threat to modern aviation equipment, I was quite happy to abide by the FAA's rule that it be turned off during the flight. But all too soon we were on the ground in Phoenix, and my reprieve was over. As I walked from the gate to the baggage claim, I turned my phone back on and was immediately informed that I had four voice mail messages. Four messages in one hour?

I bit back my annoyance. Another year or two in this position, and I would be eligible for a promotion. I tried to keep my eye on the prize. Still, four messages waiting for me was a definite sign that my arrival home in Phoenix was not going to be the end of my work week, even if it was Friday afternoon.

Before I could even listen to the first one, my phone rang. Shit. Here we go again. "This is Jonathan."

"Jonathan! Where the hell are you?" It was Marcus Barry, my boss.

"I'm at the airport. Is there something wrong?"

"That woman from the Clifton Inn has been trying to reach you for the last hour." I had only left the Clifton Inn four hours ago. What could possibly have come up in that time that was so urgent?

"I was on the plane," I said, trying not to let him hear my frustration.

He sighed. "Well, she's driving everybody here nuts. She wants answers *now*."

"I'll call her right away."

"Good," he said, and hung up without saying goodbye. Not that I minded.

I made it to the baggage claim carousel and confirmed that my bag had yet to be spit out onto the conveyor belt. I stood there watching for it while I called Sarah, the accounts manager at the Clifton Inn. It went directly to her voice mail. I left her a message saying that I was now back in Phoenix and for her to call. Before I could even hang up, my phone buzzed again.

Five voice mails now. Great.

I saw my bag spill out of the chute, and I shouldered my way to the front of the crush of people so that I would be able to grab it when it got to me. I was just about to reach for it when my phone rang.

"This is Jonathan."

There was a half a second of silence, and then a voice I did not recognize said, "So formal, aren't you darling? I wasn't expecting that. This is Cole." The voice was light, the tone mocking. Definitely a man's voice but with a very feminine quality.

"I'm sorry," I said. "Who—*shit!*" Because I realized at that moment that, in the process of answering the phone, I had missed my bag and would now have to wait for it to make another circuit on the conveyor before I could retrieve it.

"Is something wrong?"

"No." My phone buzzed in my hand. Six voice mails. I at least managed to keep my obscenities silent this time. "I'm sorry," I said, trying not to let him hear the annoyance in my voice. "Who are you?"

"I'm a friend of Jared's. He gave me your number, darling."

Darling? Really? "My name is Jonathan."

"Yes. You said that already," he said with obvious amusement.

I managed to not sigh audibly. "I only meant—"

"I know what you meant," he said, interrupting me. There was a lilting cadence to his voice, which only amplified my perception of him as overly feminine. "Jared led me to believe you would be expecting my call."

"He did. I mean, I am. I *was*." I stopped short and took a deep breath. I hated being flustered, and I was a little annoyed that he had managed to make me that way so easily. I made myself count to five. Ten would have been better, but I had learned that people rarely gave me enough time to make it that far. "Jared did mention a friend in Phoenix," I said, feeling calmer, "but he never actually told me your name." And to be honest, that brief exchange between Jared and me, made in a busy Vegas casino more than four weeks ago, had completely slipped my mind.

"So it's okay that I'm calling?"

"Of course. You just caught me off guard, that's all."

"You're at the airport."

It wasn't even a question, and I asked in surprise, "How did you know?"

"I can hear it. I'm quite familiar with that particular brand of chaos."

"Oh," I said, because I really couldn't think of an intelligent response. My bag was headed my way again, and I was determined not to miss it this time.

"Is this a bad time, darling? Are you getting on a plane?"

"Getting off," I said. "I just got back into Phoenix."

"Perfect timing, then. Are you busy tonight?"

"Tonight?" I asked in surprise, and my bag rolled past me again. "Shit!"

"Would you like to join me for dinner?" he asked, ignoring my outburst.

"I... well... I have to unpack, and—" I was stalling, trying to decide if I really had the energy for the conversational gymnastics a blind date would require. It sounded exhausting. On the other hand, the thought of what would probably come after was of course appealing. I hadn't had time in LA for any type of sexual encounter that involved anything more than my own hand. In fact, I hadn't had time for anything more gratifying in more than three weeks. Still, there was no guarantee he had the same agenda, and it seemed rude to ask.

Like he was reading my mind, he said, "Darling, it's a yes or no question, and it's only dinner. Let's leave the rest open for negotiation, shall we?"

My phone buzzed again. Seven.

Jesus, what the hell did I have to lose? "That sounds great," I said.

THE greater Phoenix area sprawls over more than five hundred square miles. Where other cities build up, we build out. Cole and I were lucky to both live on the north side of the city. He named a restaurant, and I agreed to meet him there at six.

I wasn't sure what to expect. This was a friend of Jared's, and Jared and his partner Matt were both strong and masculine. They were both football-watching, beer-drinking, outdoorsy guys, and my first assumption was that Cole would be cut from the same mold. Just hearing his voice, though, had changed that. Then there was the restaurant. I hadn't been there before, but I knew it was one of the more expensive establishments in the Scottsdale area.

I didn't have enough time after work to drive home and change, although that meant that I arrived at the restaurant early, still wearing the same suit I had been wearing since six o'clock that morning. The only thing that saved me was that in mid-April, Phoenix temperatures were peaking in the seventies rather than the low hundreds. Thank goodness for small favors.

The restaurant was small, quiet, and incredibly busy. They told me it would be at least forty-five minutes before they had a table for us. I decided to wait for Cole in the bar. I was about to order a drink when my phone rang. I halfway expected it to be Cole, calling to say he was running late or wasn't coming, but it wasn't. It was my father. My father also lived in Phoenix. He and I weren't exactly close, but since the death of my mother nine years earlier, we made an effort to stay in touch.

"Hello, Dad."

"Jon! Where in the world are you now?" I was out of town as often as I was in Phoenix, and he seemed to find it amusing to start our conversations with that question.

"I just got back into Phoenix tonight."

"That's great! How about dinner?"

"I can't, Dad. I have…" I hesitated over the sentence. It wasn't as if my dad didn't know that I was gay, but he never seemed to be very comfortable with it. "I have a date."

"A date?" he asked, as if the term was completely foreign to him.

"Yes, *a date*. You know: dinner, drinks, small talk"—sex, if I was lucky, but I didn't say that to him—"with another person."

"Oh," was all he said, and I wondered if he was fighting the urge to ask if it was with a woman. He still did that sometimes, as if I might suddenly surprise him by announcing that I had changed my mind about the whole male/female thing. I decided not to give him the chance.

"Listen, Dad, it's good that you called. I'll be out of town again next week. I have tickets to a show. I wondered if you wanted them." I had season tickets to the theater, but I rarely got to use them anymore.

"I don't know, Jon," he said reluctantly. He didn't share my love of the theater. He preferred baseball. And that pretty much summed up our entire relationship. "What show is it?"

"*West Side Story*."

"No, thanks, Jon—"

"You might like it."

"I already know how it ends. The Capulets and the Romulans—"

"The Capulets are *Romeo and Juliet*—"

"Same story, different music."

"—and I assure you there are absolutely no Romulans in either story."

"More's the pity, too. That probably would have livened things up a bit."

I made an effort to not sigh. I hadn't really expected him to be interested in the show, but I hated to see the tickets go to waste. Maybe I could give them to my neighbor, Julia.

My phone started to buzz in my hand, signaling another incoming call. "Dad, I have to go."

"Okay, Jon. Good luck on your date."

I knew it took a certain amount of effort for him to say that, so I said, "Thanks, Dad," before hanging up and answering the new call.

It was my boss again.

"Jonathan, did you get that Clifton Inn issue resolved?"

"Not exactly. Their records were a mess. They were using two different systems to—"

"I think you're going to need to fly out there on Monday."

"I leave for Vegas on Monday," I said, although I felt that he should have known that already. "Franklin Suites. Remember?"

He sighed. "You may have to cut that short. The Clifton should be your top priority right now."

Deep breath. Count to five. "I suppose I could leave Vegas on Wednesday and fly directly to LA. Assuming that Franklin has their books in order—"

"Let me look into it and call you back."

I hung up the phone and checked my watch. It was exactly six o'clock. Cole wasn't late yet, but he could very well have arrived while

I was on the phone. I looked around but didn't see anybody that seemed to be looking for anybody else. I wondered how I would identify him when he arrived.

I shouldn't have worried.

There are more stereotypes about gay men than I could even name—bears, twinks, leather-clad bikers, fairies. The list went on and on. Most of the men I knew didn't fit neatly into any of those categories. But when Cole walked into the restaurant, the word that jumped into my head was "flaming." He was about five nine, shorter than me by two or three inches. His body was thin, his features slightly feminine. His hair was almost the same color as mine, light brown, well cut, but with a long fall of bangs that tended to hang in his eyes. His clothes were obviously expensive but slightly eccentric—black, tight-fitting pants that might have been suede, a close-fitting lavender sweater that was probably silk, and a light scarf around his neck.

I've never been into effeminate men, but I certainly couldn't leave now. And he didn't necessarily need to be my type if it was only one night.

He walked up to the podium where the hostess was taking names, and she seemed to recognize him. She immediately smiled at him, and it looked genuine. He tilted his head, causing his bangs to fall over his eyes. He smiled at her flirtatiously, and I thought maybe he was even batting his eyes at her. I couldn't hear what he said, but she laughed and then pointed my way.

There was a slight sway to his walk when he came over. "I think you're waiting for me."

"I think so too." I held my hand out and he shook it. I expected his grip to be weak and limp, but that wasn't the case. His hands were slim and incredibly soft, but his handshake was firm. "I'm Jonathan Kechter."

He tilted his head again, but to the right this time, so that his bangs fell away from his eyes, and smiled at me in a way that made me think he found me incredibly amusing. "Cole Fenton," he said, in a somewhat sarcastic tone. He cocked his head back toward the hostess, who was waiting with menus in her hand. "Come on, then. Our table's ready."

"They told me it would take a while," I said in surprise.

He was already walking away, and he glanced at me over his shoulder, smiling. "Darling, I *never* have to wait."

They seated us, and Cole handed his menu back to the hostess without even opening it. He leaned back in his chair and regarded me with his head tipped to the right so his hair was out of his eyes. His skin was almost a caramel color—a shade too dark to be called white, but too light to be called anything else. I couldn't see his eyes well enough in the low light to determine their color—I thought brown—but I could see his expression. It was mischievous, almost mocking, as if he took nothing seriously, and it annoyed me for no good reason. "So, you're Zach's ex."

It wasn't even a question, and I tried not to act too surprised. Zach and I had been apart for more than ten years now, and I had spent those years thinking of him as the one that got away. I hadn't ever stopped loving him. A chance encounter in Vegas had made me remember all the ways we had been good together… and all the ways we hadn't. "Jared told you that?"

"Not exactly. But it wasn't hard to figure out, darling."

I bit back my irritation at both him and Jared. "My name is Jonathan."

"I *know*. You've told me four times now."

I debated briefly whether there was any point in asking him outright to stop calling me "darling." I had a feeling he would only laugh. "And you're a friend of Jared and Matt? Do you know Zach and Angelo too?" I asked.

"I'm sure Matt would object to being classified as such. The only one of them I *really* know is Jared. I've known him for nearly twelve years now. We've been friends since college. The others I've only met once or twice."

The waiter arrived then. "Hello, Mr. Fenton. It's good to see you again. I assume you don't need to see the wine list?"

"It's wonderful to be back, Henry. You're correct, of course, I don't need the list. I'm not sure quite yet what we'll be drinking though." He looked over at me. "Do you know what you're ordering, darling?"

I swallowed the urge to tell him my name again and said, "I was thinking the lamb chops."

He smiled. "Excellent." Then to the waiter, "I'll have the same. And a bottle of the Tempranillo Reserva, please."

"Of course."

A Spanish red—Zach's favorite. What were the chances Cole would pick that? Not many restaurants even carried Spanish wines. Zach was always bemoaning the fact when we ate out.

"Did I say something wrong?" Cole asked suddenly, interrupting my thoughts. I realized I had been staring absently at the tablecloth, and shook myself out of it.

"No. Just the wine you chose—it reminded me of Zach."

"Then you shouldn't have ordered the lamb, darling."

I had no idea how to respond to that.

The waiter brought the wine. As he was pouring it, my phone rang. It seemed impossibly loud in the hushed dining room, and everybody around us turned to look at me. I felt myself blush. I pulled my phone out and hit the button to turn off the audible ring. I looked over at Cole and found him looking slightly amused.

"I'm sorry," I said, pointing to it. "I really have to—"

"Be my guest," he said, and I answered.

"This is Jonathan."

"Jonathan, it's Sarah!"

"Sarah, can I call you back?"

"Jon, we put in all of the charges for the spa products we sell, but when we try to enter the state tax—"

"You don't do that until checkout." I was certain I had already told her that, but it was a common mistake.

She sighed in frustration. "I'll never figure this out!"

"Sarah, you'll be fine. It's Friday night. Go home and get some rest. You'll do better if you wait until morning and look at it with fresh eyes."

"Maybe you're right," she said, but I knew she wouldn't take my advice.

"I'm a little busy right now, Sarah. Can I call you first thing in the morning?"

She sighed again. "Sure. All right. Good night."

I hung up and said to Cole, "I'm really sorry about that."

He smiled. "Duty calls?"

"Always. I'm sure you know how it is."

His smile got bigger. "Not really."

"What do you do?"

His haircut was perfect. If he cocked his head to the right, his bangs fell to the side, allowing him to make eye contact. But if he looked down, or cocked his head the other way, as he did now, his hair fell in front of his eyes, making it harder to read his expression. "Such a predictable question, darling. What do *you* do?"

"I'm the Senior Liaison Account Director for GuestLine Software, Incorporated."

His mouth twitched into a smile. "That's *quite* the title. What exactly *is* GuestLine Software, Incorporated?"

"We write software for large hotels and resorts. Reservations, spa services and room charges, payroll and staffing. We put it all in one place so that—"

"I don't own a hotel, darling. You don't have to sell it to me. Is that why you were in Vegas when you ran into Jared?"

"Yes. We have three new clients there."

"And what exactly does a *Senior Liaison Account Director* do?"

There was a mocking tone to his voice, and I tried not to be annoyed. It had taken a great deal of time and hard work to achieve that position in such a short time. "I help our new clients transfer the bookkeeping portion of their records into the GuestLine software."

"I see," he said. "How long have you worked for them?"

"Eight years."

"Eight years. Tell me, darling"—and now he tipped his head again so I could see his eyes— "are you *happy* being the Senior Liaison Account Director?"

"Well, ultimately I would like to travel less. Another year or two, and I should be able to move up and start doing more of the in-house accounting. Another few years after that, and—"

"Is there a position you're aiming for, or do you just climb and climb until you can't climb anymore?"

The question seemed odd to me. Of course promotion was always the goal. "What do you mean?"

"I mean, will there ever be a point where you're happy with what you have and you can sit back and relax?"

I wasn't sure how to answer him, but it ended up not mattering because my phone rang. Again. And once again, everybody at the surrounding tables looked my way. I answered as quickly as possible.

"This is Jonathan."

"Jonathan!" It was Marcus Barry again. "I've arranged for Lyle to cover Franklin Suites. I want you on a plane to LA Sunday evening."

"Of course."

"Let's get this one wrapped up before they drive us both to drink."

I couldn't have agreed more. "I'm sorry," I said to Cole as I hung up. "It's a new client, and—" He waved his hand at me dismissively, although it was obvious he found it less amusing the second time. "I don't think he'll call again," I said as our food arrived. I turned my phone to vibrate and put it on the table next to me. We ate in silence for a while. The wine really did complement the lamb chops perfectly. I broke the silence by asking again, "What do you do?"

He looked up from his plate, tilting his head so that his hair fell into his eyes again. I couldn't tell if he was annoyed or amused by my question. "Is it so important?"

"No," I said, although I found it odd that he seemed unwilling to answer. "I was just curious."

"You're curious, because somehow your image of who I am is all tied up with my profession?"

"Well…" Wasn't it? "Yes."

"What if I told you that I was a hustler?"

"I—umm—" I realized I was stammering and stopped short. Was he serious? Had Jared given my number to a hustler? I had no idea how I was supposed to react. "I would tell you that I'm not paying you for anything tonight," I finally said. On the other hand, it would mean that I could quit trying to make conversation with him. "Are you?" I asked.

"Of course not," he said, grinning at me, and I figured it was a good sign that I was relieved to hear it. "But the thought that I might be changed everything, didn't it?" I had no idea what I was supposed to say. I felt like I was caught in some strange game of twenty questions. He laughed at me, and I tried not to be irritated by it. "You're still *dying* to know, aren't you?" he asked as he flipped his hair out of his eyes.

Of course I was. His reluctance to answer only made me more curious. "Yes. It's a simple question: what do you do?"

He seemed to consider for a moment, drinking his wine, and then he said, "I travel."

"You *travel*?" I asked. I was racking my brain in an effort to figure out what in the world he meant. "I don't understand."

"Is it a word you're not familiar with?" he asked, and I could see in his eyes how amusing he found it all. I felt like he had been quietly laughing at me ever since we had introduced ourselves, and for better or worse, it was starting to annoy me.

"Of course I'm familiar with it," I said, "but don't see how you can make a career out of it."

"I never said that I did, darling."

"But you just said—"

"I like to cook, too."

"So, you're a chef?"

"I guess you could say that. But I don't do that for a living either, if that's what you mean."

"*Of course* that's what I mean!" I said, and even I was surprised by how angry I sounded. Several of the people at nearby tables had turned to look at me, and I felt myself blushing again. I closed my eyes and made myself count to five.

"Have I upset you somehow, darling?"

"No!" I said, calmer now, although I was still irritated at him.

"So quick to apologize about the little things," he said lightly. I finally opened my eyes again and found that he was still smiling at me, although his expression was far less mocking than it had been earlier. "How long were you and Zach together?"

The sudden change of subject completely caught me off-guard. I was still confused and annoyed over the last conversation. But the look he was giving me now was open and honest, rather than condescending, and I answered, "Three years."

"How long ago was that?"

"It ended ten years ago. Why do you ask?"

He smiled at me apologetically. "I was only making conversation, actually. But it was a terrible topic to choose, wasn't it? I guess what I really wanted to know is, are you seeing anybody?"

"Obviously not, if I'm here with you."

"Does that make it obvious? I have to admit, I've met plenty of men who felt it was acceptable to be vague about their relationship status."

He had a point. "No, I'm not seeing anyone, in any capacity." Occasionally I would go to clubs to pick somebody up, or go to the bathhouse, but I hadn't actually dated anyone in months. "Are you?"

"I have many friends, but no commitment of any kind."

I couldn't help but laugh a little. "It seems that *you're* one of those men who chooses to be vague."

He smiled back, just barely. "Suffice it to say, I haven't had dinner with anybody in a very long time."

We were interrupted then by a familiar voice saying, "Jonathan!" I looked up to find Julia beaming down at me. Julia was my next-door neighbor. She was a few years older than me. Her husband Bill was in real estate, and Julia spent most of her days shuttling their three kids around town.

"Hey, Julia."

She turned to Cole meaningfully. I was about to introduce them, but my phone rang again. At least with the ringer off, the only people who noticed were Cole and Julia.

It turned out Cole didn't need me to introduce him anyway. He had already stood up from the table and was shaking her hand. I actually thought for a moment he was going to kiss it. I was on the phone with Sarah again, talking her through another software glitch, so I didn't hear their conversation, but I watched them. Something about Cole's manner was respectful yet still flirtatious, and Julia was eating it up.

I was just ending the call when Julia's husband appeared. "Looks like our table is ready," she said. "It was nice meeting you, Cole." She looked pointedly at me. "I'll talk to *you* later, Jonathan."

She left and Cole sat back down, watching me with a sly smile on his face.

"What?" I asked, although I couldn't help but smile back.

"I get the feeling my ears will be burning later."

I had to laugh. "I have a feeling you're right."

"How do you know her?"

"She's my neighbor. She takes care of my house whenever I'm away on business. She feeds my fish and brings in my mail. And I dated her brother Tony for a couple of years before he moved to California."

"Are you and she close?"

"I guess so. I don't know. We have been known to drink a bottle of wine together. Or two." He looked even more amused now, and I asked again, "*What*?"

"Nothing *really*, darling—"

"It's *Jonathan*."

"—I was just thinking: it's terribly cliché, isn't it? For a gay man to be friends with a straight woman?"

"Would it be *less* of a cliché if *all* of my friends were gay men?"

He smiled at me, and it was a genuine smile. For only the second time all night, I didn't feel like he was mocking me. "I suppose you have a point."

Next to me, my phone started buzzing again on the table.

"Shit!"

"Is it always like this, darling?" he asked, and this time, the irritation in his voice was obvious.

"Not always. Just—" *Buzz, buzz, buzz.* "I'm sorry. I really have to get this." He looked away but flicked his hand at me in a way that seemed to indicate I should answer. "This is Jonathan."

"Jonathan!" Marcus again. "That Clifton woman will be the death of me. Forget about Sunday. I want you on a plane tonight."

"Tonight? Marcus, I've been home for less than four hours."

"I know that. But if she's not taking the weekend off, neither are you. You may as well work there, where you can actually do some good."

I counted to five, then said, "I can leave at six tomorrow morning. Will that be good enough?" Please God, just let me sleep in my own bed tonight!

He sighed. "It will have to be."

"Thank you, sir." I was already apologizing to Cole again as I hung up. "I'm really sorry—" I started to say, but then I looked over to find him pulling his wallet out of his pocket. "Are you leaving?" I asked in surprise. He didn't answer, but took four one-hundred dollar bills out of it and tucked them under the candle holder on the table between us. "You don't have to—" I was going to say he didn't have to pay for my dinner, and he certainly didn't have to leave such a giant tip, but he interrupted me.

"Listen, darling, you're completely adorable, really. But the truth is I rather like being the center of attention. *Especially* when I'm on a date."

"You don't have to go—"

"I'd like to try this again sometime though." He handed me a business card. It was completely blank except for his name and a phone number. He let his hair fall in his eyes and batted his eyelashes at me. "Call me. Preferably some night when you can leave the phone *at home*."

He walked away, and I was left to finish my dinner alone.

My phone didn't ring once the rest of the night. It didn't ring again until five-thirteen the next morning. I was already back at the airport.

Date:	April 17
From:	Cole
To:	Jared

Oh Sweets, I have such a bone to pick with you! I called Jonathan like you suggested, and he obviously had no clue who I was. If you're going to set me up, at least give the poor fool my name first, won't you love? I suppose I'll have to forgive you. I would say that you owe me, but I know your big bad boyfriend will never allow you to make it up to me properly. Such a shame, too....

So Jonathan and I met for dinner, and honey, it was a disaster. I'm quite sure that I'm not his type. And although he is terribly cute, he's also uptight, has no sense of humor, and is completely obsessed with his career. Just for the record Sweets, those are things that should be mentioned when you're setting up the blind date. I'm afraid I didn't handle it well, and suffice it to say, things in Phoenix are still depressingly dry. I gave him my number, but I suspect it will be a rather cold day in hell before he calls. Good thing I'm loaded, because the way things look at the moment, I may have to fly all the way back to Paris just to get laid.

THE next weekend, my father took me to a Diamondbacks game. I wasn't much of a baseball fan, but he insisted that we go together a few times a year. We would buy overpriced hotdogs and cheap-ass, mass-produced beer that still cost eight dollars a cup. My father would talk about RBIs and the batting lineup, and I would pretend to care, even though we both knew I didn't. Likewise, I would spend half of the game fielding phone calls from my office, and he would pretend he didn't care, even though we both knew he did. It was a ridiculous arrangement, but it kept the peace.

It was early in the second inning, and I had just finished a call with my boss when my dad asked suddenly, "How was your date?"

My mind was still on the phone call—Marcus had informed me I would be leaving for LA again on Monday—and my response was to ask stupidly, "My what?"

My dad gave me the *father* look—it was the same look I used to get from him when I failed to do my chores. "You know," he said sarcastically. "*A date*: dinner, drinks, small talk. With another person."

I hated it when I gave him an opportunity to throw my own attitude back in my face, and I knew my cheeks were turning red. "It didn't go well."

"Why not?"

I didn't want to tell him what had happened. He was always scolding me for letting my work run my life. I wished I could lie. But I'd never been able to come up with untruths in a timely manner, and he would have been able to see it on my face anyway, so I braced myself and admitted the truth, although I couldn't look him in the eyes while I did it. I looked out at the field instead. "I was getting a lot of phone calls that night, and it annoyed him. So he left."

I expected him to start haranguing me right away, but he didn't. He was silent, and when I looked over, I found him watching me with a sad look on his face. "I'm sorry, Jon."

"It doesn't matter," I said, with feigned nonchalance, because it did still bother me a little that he had walked out on me. "He wasn't my type anyway."

"Are you seeing anyone else?"

"No, not at the moment." Not for a depressingly long time, in fact.

He was quiet for a minute, and when I looked over at him, I saw that his ghosts were with him. Not literal ghosts. Not like in the movies. These were only in his mind. But I had learned to identify when he was being haunted by his past.

I had a sister once. I had no memory of her—only hazy images that I probably formed afterward by looking at her picture. She was six years old when she died, and I wasn't even two. She drowned in our swimming pool one day while my mother and I were napping and my father was on the phone with the air conditioning company. My dad had the pool filled in after that, and anytime her name was spoken in our house, it was in hushed tones. More than thirty years later, the guilt of her death still followed him around like a shadow. It wasn't always visible, but when the situation was right, you would see it there in his eyes.

And then there was my mother. I knew he still missed her all the time. She had died nine years earlier of pancreatic cancer. My dad and I hadn't spoken much in the years leading up to her death. He was uncomfortable with my sexuality, and I was young and unaware of the fact that my family wouldn't always be there. Her death hit us both hard. We realized then that, although we may not have been close, we were all each other had. That was when I left Colorado and moved back to Phoenix.

I was still waiting for him to speak. I knew he had something he wanted to say. He was just trying to decide how to say it. "Jon," he said hesitantly, "there's a girl at the office—"

"No."

"I know how you feel—"

"Then why bring it up?"

"What could it hurt, Jon? You're not seeing anybody right now. Why not meet her? Why not see where it goes?"

"No."

"I just...." He trailed off, and I could see the weight of the ghosts upon him. His shoulders slumped. His face was sad. I thought maybe he was fighting back tears. "Families should grow, Jon," he said quietly. "Not shrink."

And that was the true heart of the matter. It wasn't that he disapproved of me being gay. It was simply that he longed for more. He longed for the family that had been taken from him and for the grandchildren he would never have. I couldn't blame him for that.

"I know, Dad," I said softly. I looked back out at the field so he could wipe his eyes without being embarrassed.

We didn't talk again until the bottom of the fifth, and although we stayed until the very end, I had no idea who won the game.

I CARRIED Cole's number around with me for the next two weeks. It took me a while to admit to myself that I wanted to see him again. He was arrogant and obnoxious and flamboyant and most definitely not my type. On the other hand, he was also smart and funny and cute and undeniably intriguing. Plus, there was the simple fact that he had shown interest and I had absolutely no other prospects at the moment. In the end, I told myself that if nothing else, I really did owe him an apology.

When I called, he answered the phone in French. "*Allô?*"

"Hello, Cole. It's Jonathan."

"Well *hello*, sugar. What a pleasant surprise. How have you been?"

For half a second, I considered reminding him of my name, but then decided against it. I had a feeling I would have to get used to the pet names. "I wanted to apologize—"

"Don't worry about it a bit, sugar. I think it's fair to say neither of us was on our best behavior. Just water under the bridge, really."

"I wondered if you would like to try again."

"I would love to. Will it be just the two of us this time?"

"I can't *not* bring my phone. But none of my clients are in crisis mode right now, so it shouldn't be as bad as last time."

"I suppose that will have to suffice then," he said with obvious amusement. "Were you thinking of tonight?"

"No. I'm actually in LA at the moment."

"Well, that would make it more difficult, wouldn't it? When do you get home?"

"Tuesday afternoon."

"Your timing is dreadful, sugar. I leave for Paris on Wednesday."

"Really? Are you going on vacation?"

"No," he said in an off-hand manner that made me curious. "So are we on for Tuesday then?"

"Sure."

"What time does your flight get in?"

"At four, but I have to go straight to the office and meet with my boss. I should be home a little before six."

"That's perfect, sugar. I'll see you then."

"Wait—what?" But I was too slow. The line was already dead. I debated calling him back, but figured I would only end up looking like a fool.

MY FLIGHT home was delayed by an hour, and I had to rush to get to my meeting with Marcus Barry on time.

Marcus was in his forties, and although I wouldn't quite have called him a friend, he was fair and easy to work with. He was the type of man who could be expected to drop dead of a heart attack long before he reached sixty. He was overweight and overworked. He smoked too much, drank too much, and lived off of fast food. He was also incredibly successful. He reported directly to the CEO of the company, made more than five hundred thousand dollars a year, and drove a Porsche. I hoped to follow in his footsteps, minus the trans-fat and imminent cardiac arrest.

"I'm sorry I'm late, Marcus," I said as I rushed into his office and closed the door behind me.

"Where have you been?"

"My plane was late—"

"I've been trying to call."

"You have?" I pulled out my phone and looked at it. "Shit. I'm sorry, sir. I guess I forgot to turn it back on when I got off the plane. I was in such a hurry."

"Never mind," he said. "Leave it off so we're not interrupted."

"Do you want to hear about California?"

He waved his hand dismissively at me. "No, Jon. You know your job." That was the closest thing to praise I would ever get from Marcus. "There's something else I wanted to talk to you about."

I sat down in the chair opposite him. "I'm listening."

"Monty called a meeting yesterday." Montgomery Brewington was our CEO, and Marcus was one of the only people in the entire company who could refer to him by his first name. "He's talking about restructuring."

"Restructuring, how?"

"He wants to have Account Liaisons in each state, to cut down on travel expenses."

"That makes sense, I suppose. What does it mean for me?"

"Keep in mind, Jon, that this is all conjecture at this point. No decisions have been made. But if it happens," he shrugged, "there are several possibilities."

"Such as?"

"There are seven major areas he's talking about having to cover: Arizona, LA, San Diego, San Francisco, Vegas, Colorado, and Utah. The problem is we currently have ten of you covering those areas."

"So you're saying three of us will lose our jobs?" I asked, trying to fight the panic that was suddenly blooming in my chest.

"Nobody's losing their job, Jon."

"Then what?"

"Three of you will probably be demoted."

"*What?*"

"Don't get too upset yet. The good news is you're fifth in line, so there's no reason to believe that you would be one of the three."

That *was* good news. I counted to five, felt myself relax a little. "In which case, I have a one in seven chance of having to relocate?"

"Yes. What I'm asking is, how do you feel about that?"

I had to think about that for a minute. I wasn't attached to Arizona. I hated the idea of moving, simply because I knew it would be a pain in the ass. And my dad was in Phoenix. I would definitely miss seeing him if I had to move. But there was no reason to fight it. "I'll do whatever you need me to do, Marcus. You know that."

He smiled. "Good man." He stood up, which told me our meeting was over, and I followed suit. "Go home and get some rest. I'll see you in the morning."

I LEFT the office with my head full of visions of moving to another state and the possible promotion that might come along with a new position. I drove home in a bit of a daze. My first indication that something strange was going on was the Saab parked in my driveway. When I walked in the front door, I found Julia sitting on the couch with a glass of wine.

"How was your trip?" she asked.

"Uneventful," I told her as I dumped my luggage just inside the door. "What are you doing here?"

"Your boyfriend asked me to let him in—"

"My *what?*"

"—and I wasn't going to at first. But somehow he talked me into it, and—"

"What are you talking about?"

"—it's so sweet, wanting to surprise you with dinner—"

I didn't wait to hear the rest. I crossed the living room and pushed through the swinging door that led to the kitchen. Cole was at the stove, and I snapped at him, "What the hell are you doing here?"

He didn't even turn to look at me. "I'm making dinner, sugar. Isn't it obvious?"

"You just decided to break into my house and make dinner?"

"There's no need to be dramatic," he said, turning to face me. "I didn't *break in*." He was dressed like before: dark, slim-fitting pants and some kind of lightweight sweater in a pale shade of green. It accentuated his eyes, which I could see now weren't brown but hazel. He was barefoot, and for some reason I found my gaze drawn to his slender feet. "Look, I'm sorry if I upset you. I really am." And he did sound more sincere than usual. "But I know how it is when you're traveling, eating at restaurants all the time, and I thought you might appreciate a home-cooked meal. That's all, sugar. I tried to call, but it went straight to voice mail." Of course. My phone had been turned off since I'd boarded the plane in LA nearly five hours earlier. "I'm sure it was terribly inappropriate, coercing poor Julia into letting me in. But if I waited until you got home to start cooking, we wouldn't be eating until after eight. So I decided to take a chance."

And to be honest, my anger was fading. It really was a thoughtful gesture. I couldn't remember the last time somebody had made any kind of effort for me. After ten days in LA, eating out for every breakfast, lunch, and dinner, the idea of a quiet meal at home was infinitely more appealing than a crowded restaurant. The mouth-watering aroma of whatever it was he was making wasn't hurting his cause any either. Maybe the way to a man's heart really was through his stomach, because at that moment, I really could have kissed him.

"Thank you," I said quietly. He turned away from me quickly, but I still saw the blush that had appeared on his cheeks. "What are you making?"

He glanced at me over his shoulder quickly before turning away again. "Sautéed pasta with lobster."

"It smells amazing."

He turned back to me with a flirtatious smile. "It ought to, doll. I'm an *excellent* cook."

"Do you need any help?"

"Cooking? No. But you could set the table. Tell Julia there's plenty if she wants to stay."

Julia! I had forgotten all about her. After my entrance, I had no doubt she was expecting me to be angry with her for letting him in. I went back into the living room and found her pacing.

"Jonathan, I'm so sorry!" she said as soon as I walked into the room. "I shouldn't have—"

"It's fine, Julia. Really."

She looked skeptical. "I promise not to do it again."

"It's okay. He caught me off guard, but it's really not a problem. I'm glad you let him in."

"Okay. If you're sure...."

"I am. He says there's plenty, if you want to join us."

She grinned at me. "And crash your date? Not a chance."

"It's just dinner," I said as she turned to leave.

"You know, Jon," she said as she opened the door, "I think he's a keeper."

"*It's just dinner*," I said again. But she was already gone.

NOT only had he made dinner, he also brought a bottle of white wine. "I usually drink red," I told him as he poured it.

He tipped his head so his bangs fell in his eyes. The light in my living room was better than it had been in the restaurant, and I realized it had a hint of red in it. It reminded me of cinnamon. I found myself wondering if he smelled like cinnamon too. "You're not one of those deluded souls who thinks that Merlot goes with everything, are you sugar?" he asked me dryly.

"Well," I stammered, feeling myself blush, "I usually buy Chianti."

He smiled knowingly at me. "Trust me. The Viognier will be *so* much better."

I wasn't sure about the wine, but his comment about being an excellent cook turned out to be no idle boast. The dinner was amazing. "Where did you learn to cook like this?" I asked him when we were finished.

He had a habit of sometimes keeping his head down when he talked, so that his gaze on me was shadowed beneath long lashes and the fall of his hair. "I have a lot of free time."

"Really?" I hesitated for a second, not wanting to rock the boat, but I finally gave in to my curiosity and asked, "What do you do?"

He rolled his eyes at me. "That *again*, sugar? Don't you get tired of asking?"

"I might, if you ever actually answered."

He shifted uncomfortably, fidgeting with his flatware. "The truth is I don't really *do* much of anything."

"You must be employed."

"Why do you say that?"

"You obviously have money—"

"I do."

"—so how do you make it?"

"I don't."

I waited for him to elaborate, but after a few seconds, it became clear he wasn't intending to. "So," I said with slow, deliberate cynicism, "are you saying you're independently wealthy?"

He tipped his head back, let his hair fall to the side so he was looking directly at me. The affect was somehow coy and earnest at the same time. "I am, actually."

I wasn't sure what answer I had been expecting, but that certainly wasn't it. "Oh," I said stupidly, because I didn't know what else to say.

"I don't like to tell people too early, sugar. I learned at a very young age how many of them would choose to be with me simply because I might foot the bill."

I could certainly imagine that might be true. "Did you win the lottery or something?"

"No," he said. "I inherited it. It's all terribly predictable, I'm afraid. My father had an obscene amount of money. Some of it was family money, and some he made himself. He had several marriages but no children. About the time he turned fifty-five, he started to contemplate his own mortality, I suppose. He decided he needed an heir, so he found himself a wife. She was twenty-two and beautiful and not incredibly bright."

"A trophy wife?" I asked, and he smiled.

"Exactly. He made her sign a prenup, of course, but once she produced an heir, he cut her loose with a generous stipend. She lives in Manhattan now, actually."

"So you're the heir?"

"Of course, sugar." He stood up, and I thought he was leaving the table. I pushed my chair back and stood up too, but then he just stood there looking at me, so I sat back down. "My father died when I was fifteen. The money was all left in trust. I had to meet a few requirements."

"Like what?"

He started walking around to my side of the table. "I had to graduate from a major university with at least a three-point-oh GPA. I had to agree to continue supporting my loving mother." And I knew just by the way he said it that she was anything but.

"Exactly how much money do you have?" I asked as he reached my chair. I knew it was a rude question, but I had a feeling he wouldn't mind.

"I don't know exactly. Chester takes care of it all. Although he keeps threatening to retire, and I have no idea what I'll do then."

"You *don't know* how much money you have?"

"Not exactly. I know it's enough that I can continue living the way I do and still have plenty left over for the heir I'll most *certainly* never have." He straddled my knees and sat down in my lap, facing me. He unbuttoned my shirt, then trailed his slender fingers through the hair on my chest. The conversation suddenly seemed incredibly unimportant. He had beautiful, full lips, and I couldn't take my eyes off of them. "So tell me, sugar: would you like to discuss my trust fund all night?" He let his hair fall away from his eyes and gave me a wicked, lascivious grin that went straight to my groin. "Or are you ready for dessert?"

I discovered quickly that he didn't really like being kissed on the lips. It didn't matter to me. There were plenty of other areas on his body that he *did* like to have kissed, and I stuck to those. We left a trail of clothes from the dining room table to the bedroom. I found a condom, and offered it to him.

"Do you have a preference?" I asked him. "I'm versatile."

He pushed it back toward me. "I never top, sugar. It's terribly cliché for a guy like me, isn't it?"

I smiled at him. "I don't mind."

His body was slim and beautiful. He was only a couple of inches shorter than me, but he felt small and fragile underneath me. I discovered quickly, though, that he was anything but. He was a very enthusiastic lover.

The only body hair he had was under his arms. Even his groin had been shaven clean. His hair was silky soft, and it didn't smell like cinnamon at all. It smelled like strawberries. There was a small birthmark on the back of his neck, just right of center, where the skin was a few shades darker than the rest of his body. It was triangular, and it reminded me of a butterfly. I found my lips drawn to it over and over again.

Afterward, he didn't lie in my arms or cuddle against me. He moved to the other side of the bed and stretched out languorously, not touching me. "You're not going to make me drive all the way home in the middle of the night, are you, sugar?"

"No. You can stay."

"I knew I liked you," he said. If he said anything else after that, I didn't hear it. I was already sound asleep.

HE WAS still sleeping the next morning when I left for my daily run, but when I arrived back home I found him in the kitchen, making bacon and eggs. He was already fully dressed, but still barefoot.

He indicated the pile of dirty dishes in the sink and said without looking at me, "I don't clean, darling, but I can have somebody come and take care of the mess, if you don't want to do it."

"Are you serious?"

"Of course. I pay Rosa double for the messes I make in other people's homes."

"Does that happen often?"

He smiled, but still didn't look at me. He kept his eyes on the bacon and eggs sizzling on the stovetop. "Not as often as you probably think."

"Do I have time to shower before we eat?"

"If you make it fast."

By the time I was ready for work, breakfast was on the table. "Do you usually cook breakfast the morning after?" I asked.

"It depends."

"Did you cook for Jared?" Of course I didn't actually know that he and Jared had ever been lovers, but I was curious.

He smiled. "I would have if he'd ever had anything in his house *to* cook. I'm pretty sure that man subsists on nothing but Pop-Tarts and beer."

When I finished, I looked over to find him watching me. "I hate to be rude," I told him apologetically, "but I have to work today. I really need to get going."

"I didn't think you put that suit on for my benefit, darling. I can go now and leave the mess in the kitchen for you to clean up, or I can wait for Rosa and have her lock up when she leaves. It's your call."

"I didn't mean for you to rush out. I just didn't want you to be offended when I did."

"I understand."

"You leave for Paris today?"

"My flight is at two."

"How long will you be gone?"

He shrugged. "I don't know yet, darling. Until I feel like coming home, I suppose."

"Do you go there often?"

"Several times a year."

"For vacation?"

"I own a condo there."

"Really?" I asked, unable to keep the awe and envy out my voice.

He cocked his head at me, obviously amused. "Yes. And one in Vail, as well as a house in the Hamptons—well, just a cottage, really, by Hampton standards—and another house in Kapoho."

"Wow."

He smiled. "Indeed. So darling, shall I call Rosa or not?"

"I feel ridiculous having you pay somebody to clean my house."

"And why is that, exactly?"

"It seems childish."

He shrugged. "Suit yourself." He looked down at his plate for a minute, and when he looked back up, his expression was guarded. "Tell me: would you prefer this be a one-time thing? Or would you like to discuss other options?"

"What are the other options?"

"My lifestyle isn't conducive to committed relationships. On the other hand, I've never been all that intrigued by the idea of sex with random strangers. I prefer something in between."

"Is that what you had with Jared?"

He was obviously amused by the question, but said, "Exactly. It was fun and casual and completely uncomplicated."

"And that's what you're proposing?"

"If you're interested," he said, smiling flirtatiously at me. My type or not, he really was incredibly cute. And our time in the bedroom had been a lot of fun. Not that sex was ever *not* fun. But things between us had been easy and natural. Why in the world would I not be interested in what he was suggesting?

"That sounds perfect," I said.

"Good. Then I'll call you when I'm back in Phoenix."

Date: May 3

From: Cole

To: Jared

Have you heard, darling, that global warming is actually nothing more than a myth? That's the only explanation I have for the fact that there apparently was an unusually cold day in hell last week. And let just me say, thank goodness! Dry spell over, and none too soon. I'm back in Paris now, but at least I have something to look forward to when I get home. It's all thanks to you, Sweets. I would kiss you for it, if that big bad boyfriend of yours would let me.

I WASN'T surprised when Julia showed up at my house that afternoon.

"So," she asked teasingly as I let her in the door, "how was dinner?"

"Really good. He's an amazing cook. You should have stayed."

"Yeah right," she said as she sat down on my couch.

"How's Tony?" I asked. The thing was, I didn't actually care how her brother Tony was, and Julia knew that. It was a weak attempt to change the subject, and she didn't bite.

"Cole seems like a keeper!" she said.

"Julia, it's nothing like that. Dinner and sex, yes, but it's not like we're dating."

"Let's see," she said, ignoring me. "He cooks. He's thoughtful." She was ticking the points off on her fingers as she talked. "He's super cute."

"He's really not my type."

"And he's rich."

"How did you know that?"

"Only a guess," she said, and I rolled my eyes at her. "That's like the trifecta. *Plus one.*"

"So what?"

"*So*, you'd be an idiot to let him get away."

IT TURNED out not to matter that Cole was out of town. The next few weeks were so busy I wouldn't have had time to see him anyway. I only managed to spend a handful of nights in my own bed. The rest of the time, I was in Vegas, converting a major casino to our software. I owned a condo in Vegas, which was a little more personal than a motel room. But it still wasn't home.

It was almost a month before I heard from him. It was seven o'clock in the morning, and I was just headed out the door of my condo for another long work day when he called.

"Hello, muffin. How have you been?"

I couldn't help but smile. "*Muffin?*"

He ignored me. "I'd like to see you. Are you free any time this week?"

I sighed. "No. I'm stuck in Vegas."

"You're working? Isn't it the weekend?"

"There are no weekends in the hotel industry."

"You're such a killjoy. How long will you be there?"

"Several days, at least. Are you back in Phoenix?"

"I am, actually. But it will be terribly boring here without you."

"It's pretty boring here, too."

He was silent for a moment, and then he said, "I could change that, you know."

"You could make transitioning accounting data more interesting?"

"Goodness, no. I'm fairly certain that's not even possible. But I could at least make your evenings worthwhile."

"Are you saying what I think you're saying?"

"I'm sure I don't know, muffin. I dare say I can't read your mind when we're in the same room, let alone when you're two hundred miles away."

"Are you offering to come to Vegas?"

"Yes, if I won't be in the way."

"I'll be working during the day."

"I believe that's already been established. I assure you, I'm quite capable of entertaining myself until you're free."

I found myself smiling again. The idea of a few more days in Vegas suddenly seemed infinitely less dreary. "I would love to have some company."

"Good," he said, and I could hear the smile in his voice. "I'll be there in time for dinner."

He called me a few hours later, when his flight got in, and I gave him the address to my place and the key code to get in. I wasn't able to get away from the casino until after six. When I arrived back at the condo, I found him waiting. He was barefoot, wearing slim dark pants and some type of loose-fitting white shirt that accentuated the rich tone of his skin. He was setting plates of food on the table.

"I didn't have time to cook, so I ordered sushi."

It was an enormous relief to not have to fight the crowds at a restaurant again. "I think I love you," I said lightly.

He winked at me. "What's not to love?"

"I didn't even know it was possible to have sushi delivered."

"Well this *is* Vegas, honey. Anyway, when you're as rich as I am, you can have anything brought to your door." He finished putting the food on the table and looked up at me. And then he stopped. His eyes slowly moved up my body, and his smile turned from casual to lecherous.

"What?" I asked.

He shook his head at me, still smiling. "There's just something about a man in a suit, isn't there?"

"Don't get too attached to it. The first thing I'm going to do is take it off."

His eyes narrowed, and he winked at me through the fall of his bangs. "My thoughts exactly."

It was after eight by the time we got around to eating. We were great together in bed, but once we were out of it, he kept his distance. He flirted with me incessantly, but there were no random caresses or spontaneous kisses. It was a casual companionship that was friendly, sometimes awkward, but not at all intimate.

After dinner, we sat on the couch. I sat at one end with my laptop, watching the news and catching up on work. He wrapped himself in a blanket and curled into a ball on the other end, reading a book. I couldn't see what it was, but I was pretty sure it was in French. By the time I turned off the TV, he was sound asleep. I nudged him awake, and he followed me into the bedroom, but like before, he didn't curl against me like a lover. He stretched out on his own side of the bed and fell back to sleep without saying a word.

He was still sleeping when I woke up the next morning. When I was at home, I jogged almost every morning, but I hated to jog in Vegas. Something about exercising in the middle of all that decadence just seemed absurd. Instead I made do with the treadmill in my building's fitness room. I went back to my condo to shower, and when I emerged from the bathroom, dripping wet with a towel around my waist, I found him still in bed but awake.

"How much time do you have?" he asked as he sat up on the edge of the bed.

"I have to leave in forty minutes."

He reached over and grabbed my towel and used it to pull me closer. He opened it up and dropped it on the floor, which was more than enough to get my full attention. His lips brushed my stomach. "Just enough time for a blowjob or breakfast, but not both, I'm afraid." The tip of his tongue moved slowly up my shaft, causing me to shiver.

"Who needs breakfast?" I managed to say, although my voice came out hoarse and breathy.

He smiled up at me. "Good choice, sugar."

Date: June 8

From: Cole

To: Jared

You'll never guess where I am, Sweets. I'm in Vegas with Jonathan. Strangely serendipitous, isn't it? I would love to give you the dirty details, but what comes around goes around. You'll just have to use your imagination.

I WASN'T surprised to find him in the kitchen when I got home that night. The table was already set. "I hope you don't feel obligated to cook," I told him as he put a big bowl of étouffée on the table.

"Love, I don't feel obligated to do *anything.* You should try it sometime."

I couldn't even imagine how it must feel to be so free. "What did you do today?" I asked.

"I read. I napped. I wandered around."

"Did you go to the casinos?"

"Yes, but only for the shopping. I abhor gambling."

"Then why come to Vegas?"

"I don't know, love," he said, giving me a sly smile. "It must be the all-you-can-eat bacon." I laughed at that. "You're here a lot?" he asked.

"Enough to buy a condo here."

He let his cinnamon hair fall forward so I couldn't see his eyes. "And what do you *normally* do for company when you're here?"

"Find somebody at the club or go to the bathhouse." He shuddered dramatically, which made me laugh again. "Does it bother you that much?"

"I admit I've only tried a bathhouse a few times, but I was never overly impressed with the selection."

"So what do *you* do when you're traveling?"

He tipped his hair out of his face and said with a smile, "I have friends."

"Friends like me, you mean."

"Of course."

"'A girl in each port'?" I asked, smiling.

"Not a girl in the bunch, love, I assure you."

"So who do you have in Paris?"

"Arman and Jori. Arman is *infinitely* more fun, but he's perpetually in and out of relationships."

"And when he's 'in,' that makes him off-limits?"

"Absolutely, love. His relationships never last, but I won't be the one to break them up."

"And Jori?"

"Jori is the most beautiful man I've ever met." He stopped short and winked at me conspiratorially. "Present company excluded of course."

"Of course," I said, laughing. I was fairly average. I had no misconceptions as to who was probably better looking.

"But Jori's mostly in the closet," he went on. "He only divorced his wife a couple of years ago, and we can't *ever* go out in public. It's *such* a bore."

"Hawaii?"

"There's a club in Hilo, but I don't have the energy for that kind of thing. I find it terribly dull. It's mostly college students anyway, and suffice it to say, love, those boys get a little younger every year."

"It does seem that way."

"But there's a bartender there named Rudy. He's not exactly an Adonis, but he's funny and good in bed."

"Vail?"

He rolled his eyes. "Vail isn't *nearly* as entertaining since Jared started seeing that big, pissed-off cop."

"The Hamptons?"

"There are a few options there, but mostly I choose to spend time with my gardener, Raul."

"Your *gardener*?"

"Well, he's not just *my* gardener. He works for several families in the neighborhood."

"That's awfully cliché, isn't it?"

He grinned at me. "It may be, but honey, if you saw Raul, you'd understand."

I laughed. "Okay. So what about Phoenix?"

"There are a couple of men I see occasionally. But the truth is, things in Phoenix had been *dreadfully* dull for the last year or two. You came along just in time."

"Glad I could be of use."

"Me too, love," he said with a perfectly straight face. "As soon as we're done with dinner, I'll see what I can do to show you my appreciation."

THE next two evenings were the same. He cooked dinner both nights, and the food was always amazing. I fell into the habit of doing the dishes afterward. It seemed like the least I could do. But on the fourth night, there was no food on the table and no incredibly tantalizing aromas filling the condo when I got home. He came out of the bedroom wearing nothing but slim dark pants.

"I'm sorry I didn't cook tonight, sweets. I lost track of time."

"You don't need to apologize," I said, trying not to sound too disappointed. "I'd offer to cook for you, but my repertoire is pretty limited."

He smiled. "How limited?" he asked, although I knew he was only asking so he could laugh at me.

"Tacos, sloppy Joes, frozen pizzas, and spaghetti. Assuming I have a jar of Prego in there somewhere." I grinned at him. "Any of those sound good?"

He laughed. Like his voice, his laugh was slightly feminine but very quiet. "Not even remotely."

He walked closer to me, and the look in his eyes was slowly changing from mockery to something else—something I had learned to recognize very quickly. "Do you want to go out?" I asked, although that heat in his eyes was giving me other ideas. My pulse was speeding up and my voice came out a little husky.

"I do, actually," he said. He was right in front of me now, but he kept his head down so that all I could see was his hair. It was a little bit damp, and I could smell the shampoo he used. "There's a restaurant over at Wynn that's supposed to be amazing. I made us a reservation."

"That sounds great," I said.

"But first," he pushed my jacket off of my shoulders, and I let it fall to the floor behind me, "let me help you take this suit off."

WE FINALLY got dressed again and headed for Wynn. My condo wasn't far off-strip, and we decided to walk. Not counting our disastrous first date, all of our time together had been spent in private, either at my house or at my condo. In that time, I had all but forgotten my first impression of him—but I remembered now.

He was flamboyant. There was no other word for it. It was the way he walked: too light somehow, with too much movement in his hips. It was the way he stood with one hip cocked out. It was the cadence of his speech and the gestures he made and the way he held his head so that he was looking at me through his hair. Somehow, when it was only the two of us, it was less obvious. Less ostentatious. Less obnoxious. Yes, he still flirted with me incessantly. He batted his eyes at me—but only in jest—and he called me sugar or darling. But somehow, when we were alone, the full force of his affection was dampened. Now that we were in public again, it hit me head-on. It seemed overblown and exaggerated. I felt as if the man I had been spending my time with and sharing my bed with was suddenly gone and there was a complete stranger in his place. Even in Vegas, some people were turning to watch him pass, smiling in amusement as they did. I found that I was slightly embarrassed to be seen with him, and I hated myself for it. It made me feel unbalanced and a little bit uncomfortable.

"Is everything all right, love?" he asked me, as we waited for our table to be ready.

"Of course," I said, making myself smile.

"Mmm-hmm," he said, watching me, and I felt a blush start to creep up my cheeks.

"Everything's fine," I said.

"You don't have to lie to me," he said, giving me a sad smile. "I know that I'm embarrassing you."

"No! Absolutely not!" I said, and then immediately wondered if I had protested a bit too vehemently.

He continued to smile at me. "It's nothing new to me, love. Some people get flustered, and some get offended. Some find it amusing." He shrugged. "It's okay to admit it."

"It's not that," I said, wishing even as I said it that I was telling the truth. "I promise—"

"Don't worry about it," he said, turning away from me. "You'll either get used to it or you'll decide I'm not that good in bed anyway."

I didn't know if I should deny it more or try to apologize or just let it go. I stood there cursing myself—first for being such an ass and then for being so transparent about it. I had never minded before if people knew that I was with another man. Why should it be any different now?

Once we were seated, I got my bearings back. Yes, we were in public. But sitting together at the small table, it felt more like we were alone again. There were still the flirting looks and the singsong, mocking cadence to his speech. Those I was used to. But all the rest of it seemed to fall away, and I felt myself relax again.

"I really am sorry," I told him, although I couldn't stand to meet his eyes.

"Don't apologize to me, love," he said. "Just don't expect me to apologize either."

Whether he felt awkward for a while after that or whether it was only me, I didn't know. We of course had to order dinner *before* we ordered wine. My half-joking suggestion that we simply order a bottle of Chianti was met with mocking disdain, especially after I ordered salmon.

"What do you think of the food?" he asked me halfway through dinner.

"It's delicious," I said, winking at him, "but your cooking is better."

He looked quickly down at his plate, and I suspected it was to keep me from seeing the blush on his cheeks. "You're so good," he said. He kept his eyes hidden from me, but I could tell he was smiling. "Somebody in your past trained you very well."

I laughed, although only a little. "Yes, he did," I admitted, thinking of Zach. "And then he let me go."

The waiter eventually brought the check, and we had one of those ridiculous moments that I thought only happened in movies where we both reached for it at the same time. We each had one hand on the little faux-leather folder, but neither of us picked it up.

"You know I'll get it," he said.

"I know you *will*," I told him, "but I don't want you to."

"Really?" he asked, looking amused. "I picked the restaurant. It only seems fair that I pay."

"You paid last time." And paid way too much to boot, but I didn't say that part. "I want to get it this time."

"Sweetie, I'm not trying to brag here, but we both know I have a ridiculous amount of money—"

"That's not the point," I said, feeling my cheeks turning red again.

"*Really?*" he said again, but this time he sounded genuinely surprised, rather than amused.

Of course he had more money than me. *Way* more money than me, and that was putting it mildly. But I wasn't exactly broke. I made a very good living and had few expenses. I had always thought of myself as being on the lucky end of middle class. He, on the other hand, literally had millions. Even though it was an expensive restaurant, I knew the cost of our dinner was a mere drop in the bucket to him. Still, it bothered me to think of him paying for everything. My pride wouldn't allow it.

"I know it seems silly to you," I told him, "but you paid to fly here just to keep me company. And you've cooked every night. I owe you this."

He still looked amused and a little bit baffled. "This is important to you," he said. It wasn't a question, but I could tell he didn't understand either. He was trying to puzzle it out.

"Yes," I said. He sat there looking at me, waiting for something— whether it was for me to change my mind or to offer some type of an explanation, I didn't know. But then, slowly, he took his hand away from the folder.

It was late by the time we left the restaurant. He was quiet most of the way back to the condo. We got ready for bed in silence and got in on opposite sides. He didn't seem inclined to initiate anything, and I didn't want to be pushy. He curled up on his half of the bed, and I stretched out on my back on mine. I was almost asleep when I suddenly felt the weight of his thin body on top of me. I opened my eyes to find him looking down at me. The lack of light in the room made it impossible for me to read his expression.

"I've been thinking about it," he said quietly, "and I can't actually remember the last time anybody bought anything for me."

I was surprised. "Not *anything*?" I asked.

He shook his head. "Not even dinner."

My insistence on buying dinner had been nothing more than my own pride. I had never expected it to mean anything to him. But hearing him now, I realized it did. "What about Christmas?" I asked.

He shook his head again. "No."

I realized then, for the very first time, how lonely his life must be. His father was dead, his mother apparently estranged. He had no siblings. He had nothing but a handful of casual lovers, scattered across the world from Paris to Hawaii.

My first instinct was to hold him—to apologize and try to make things better—but I also suspected that he would never allow that. I put my fingers into his silky soft hair and said only, "You're welcome."

Date: June 28

From: Cole

To: Jared

Hey there Sweets. I knew you would be intrigued by that last email.
Well, that was the point, wasn't it? But honestly, I only did it to tease
you. It was nothing special. Jonathan was in Vegas on business, and I
just went along for the ride. And honey, that was a sexual innuendo.

HE SPENT two more nights with me in Vegas before returning home. I
called him when I got back into town several days later.

"Hello?" he answered, and it sounded like I had woken him up.

"It's Jonathan. I wanted to let you know that I'm back in
Phoenix."

"That's fascinating, darling, but I'm not."

"Where are you?"

"In Tokyo."

"*Tokyo?*" I asked, flabbergasted. "What in the world are you
doing in Tokyo?"

"Sleeping," he said, and hung up without saying goodbye.

I was a little bit worried that I had seriously annoyed him, but two
weeks later, I came home from work to find him cooking dinner in my
kitchen.

Over the next few months, we fell into an easy, albeit completely
erratic, relationship. We were both out of town so often that it was hard
to find time for each other, and he didn't seem to like to plan anything
in advance. I also learned that it did me no good to call him beyond

simply informing him that I was back in town. Asking to see him only caused frustration. He might give me a flimsy excuse. He might say no but show up at my house later anyway. But no matter what, he never did *anything* that was not his own idea. So I waited for him. And eventually, he always called.

Our time together out of bed had grown less awkward. I gave him a key to my house—not because things were that serious between us, but because it was the only logical thing to do. He hated to wait for me to get home to start cooking, and it was ridiculous for him to have to rely on Julia to let him in. Often when we were both in Phoenix, he would call me only to say that he was busy. But then I would come home to a house that smelled like heaven and him barefoot in my kitchen. I quit trying to predict him at all, but I was always happy to see him.

I was still getting used to what we had together. I knew this type of relationship wasn't new for him, but it was for me. I had been in long-term relationships before, and of course I had been involved in casual hook-ups. But this strange area in-between was completely foreign to me. In my experience, when you kept seeing somebody, it was with the understanding that you were moving toward something more serious. I had always believed that relationships had to move forward or end. But Cole made it quite clear that becoming more intimate was of no interest to him. We had sex, yes. Often. But once we were out of bed, any attempts I made to touch him or kiss him were countered by him pushing me away, playful, but absolutely firm. It was a strange relationship—not lovers, not quite friends even—and I didn't always know how to handle it.

It was September fifteenth, and I had just finished a four-day stint in LA. I landed back in Phoenix at ten o'clock in the evening. I called Cole when I got home.

"This better be an emergency," he said sleepily, without even saying hello.

"It's me."

"I know, love. I have caller ID. I take it you're home now?"

"I am. Why? Did you miss me?"

"Not a bit," he said.

"Good. I didn't miss you either."

"I'm glad you woke me up to tell me that," he said. And then the line went dead. I couldn't help but laugh. I was getting used to his temperament by now, and I knew better than to be offended.

I wasn't surprised when my phone rang the next morning as I was driving to the office. I smiled when I saw Cole's name on the display. "Hello?"

"Hey sugar. I've decided to forgive you for waking me up last night."

"I knew you would."

"How's your weekend looking?" I knew what he was asking: would I be free, or would my clients be calling nonstop?

"Everything's wrapped up at the moment," I told him. "I'm all yours, if you want me."

He was quiet for a moment, but when he spoke again, I could hear the smile in his voice. "I think maybe I do. Why don't you come spend the weekend with me?"

"Where?"

"At my house."

He had never invited me over before, and I was curious about how he lived. "Where do you live?"

"Paradise Valley." Of course. I should have known. Paradise Valley was the most affluent area of Phoenix. "I know it's not as convenient for you during the week," he said, "but it's so much easier to cook in my own kitchen."

"That sounds great," I told him. "Do you have a pool?"

"Of course I do. And a hot tub too. But whatever you do, sugar," he said, his tone turning flirtatious, "*don't* bring a swimsuit."

By the time I left work, drove home to pack a bag for the weekend, and made it to his place, it was close to seven. He lived in a gated community, although his house was one of the smaller ones in the neighborhood. It was a Spanish-style home: white with a red roof, all on one level.

"Hey sugar," he said when he opened the door. "Take your shoes off." He didn't wait for me, but turned and disappeared deeper into the house.

I knew he would be cooking, so I took the opportunity to put my bag in his room and wander around. The house had big, open rooms and high ceilings. Most of the decor seemed to be shades of white and cream. There were a few paintings on the wall, but otherwise the house felt half-bare. There were only three bedrooms: one that was obviously his, one that was filled with bookshelves and a desk, and a third that was outfitted for a guest, although it felt like a tomb. The living room was incredibly formal and obviously not often used. There was a family room that was more lived-in, with a large cushy couch and several luxurious throws. I remembered how he had curled up in a blanket to read in my condo in Vegas and imagined that was how he spent many of his evenings at home.

I wasn't surprised to find that the kitchen was the most comfortable room in the house. It was huge, and although I was no expert on the subject, I suspected a great deal of money had been put into it. The countertops were dark marble. There were two sinks, a giant refrigerator, and a stove that would have put some restaurants to shame.

He was at the stove, of course, stirring something. His feet were bare. His hair had grown out longer than he usually allowed it to get, and it covered half of the butterfly mark on the back of his neck. I found myself wanting more than anything to touch him and to put my lips on that tiny spot, but I knew it would be a breach of protocol.

"Nice house," I said.

"Thank you," he replied, not looking at me. "Of all the homes I own, this is the only one I purchased myself."

"The rest were bought by your father?"

"Or his mother. Or my mother. Or one of the wives who preceded her."

"What made you pick Phoenix?"

"I rather like the heat."

"Are you crazy?" I asked in surprise.

He shrugged. "Something about roasting in the desert makes me feel both rebellious and mundane, all at the same time." I wasn't sure how those things were actually connected to sweating one's ass off in hundred-degree weather, but as the pampered but forgotten son of millionaires, I could see why feeling rebellious yet mundane might appeal to him. "Would you like something to drink?" he asked, turning back to the stove. "Help yourself."

I opened the fridge, which was huge and completely full. "I'll have some wine," I told him as I scanned the shelves.

"Sugar, we're drinking red tonight. It won't be in the refrigerator."

But I had already spotted what I assumed was the wine and pulled it out, although upon closer inspection I saw that it had a screw top instead of a cork. "What's this then?" I asked. I turned it so I could read the label and laughed out loud when I saw what it was. "Arbor Mist Island Fruits Pinot Grigio?"

I looked over to find him staring at me with a look of sheer horror on his face and his cheeks bright red. "I forgot that was in there."

"Do you drink this stuff?" I asked him in surprise.

"No."

"Then what's it doing in your fridge?"

"Rosa must have put it there."

"Your housekeeper? Why? Is she under the age of twenty-one?"

"No. Why?"

"Because only teenagers drink this stuff."

"Not *only* teenagers," he said defensively.

"So you *do* drink it?" I asked, and I could barely keep from laughing at his obvious embarrassment.

His blush deepened, which I wouldn't have thought possible if I hadn't seen it myself. "Well, I...."

"Yes?" I asked, and I really couldn't keep the smile off of my face now.

"I...."

"I'm waiting," I prodded sarcastically.

"Fine!" He grabbed a potholder off of the countertop and threw it at me. "I drink it. Are you happy now?" He turned away from me, back to the stove, but I could see that he was smiling. "Now you know my dirty little secret. I have a penchant for cheap, fruity wine."

"You scold me for drinking Chianti with fish—"

"Of course I do, darling. It's a terrible choice."

"—but you have a secret stash of Arbor Mist. Tell me, Cole, what exactly goes with Mixed Berry Pinot Grigio?"

He was silent for a moment, but then he said with obvious mirth, "Not much, I admit. But sugar, the Blackberry Merlot is to die for. I'm fairly certain it goes with everything."

I laughed and gave up on keeping my distance from him. I crossed over to him and wrapped my arms around his waist from behind, kissing the back of his head. He tensed noticeably but didn't pull away. "I love that you drink five-dollar-a-bottle wine," I said.

"Well for goodness' sake, don't tell anyone. I have a reputation to uphold, you know."

"Oh really?" I asked, laughing.

"No, not really." He pushed me playfully away. "But at least allow me the luxury of my own self-delusions, won't you?"

"I'll try," I told him. I opened the bottle and smelled the contents. It smelled like Kool-Aid. "Is this what we're drinking with dinner?"

"Absolutely not. I actually bought you a nice bottle of Chianti." He pointed his spatula at me. "Don't even mention fava beans, or I guarantee you'll be sleeping on the porch."

"I don't mind," I told him, "as long you're sleeping there with me."

He turned his back to me, but not before I saw that he was pleased.

Date: Sept 16

From: Cole

To: Jared

I have to say, Sweets, the constant nagging for information is getting awfully tiresome. I haven't been telling you anything because there really is nothing to tell. Yes, you're correct in saying that we seem to be spending a great deal of time together. But your assumption that our relationship is becoming serious could not be further from the truth. This is a casual arrangement—nothing more—much like the one you and I enjoyed for so many years. I'm getting used to Jonathan being so ridiculously uptight, and I dare say he's getting used to me being... the way I am. In another month or two, I'll be heading back to Paris for the holidays. I'll probably come home to find him shacked up with some big angry cop. Now why does that story sound familiar?

Take care, Sweets, and say hello to your big angry cop for me. Let me know if steam actually emerges from his ears when you do.

HE SPENT Sunday and Monday night with me at my house. Tuesday morning, he lay in bed, talking nonstop as he watched me dress. He talked about needing a haircut and what we should have for dinner and made what I thought was an off-hand comment about not having been to Mazatlan since college. By the time I got home from work that afternoon, he was already on the beach. He called to tell me he would be gone at least a week. I could only marvel at how he seemed to flutter wherever the wind might carry him. I didn't hear from him the rest of the time he was gone, but two Fridays later, I came home to find him barefoot in my kitchen.

The next morning, I got up and went for my usual morning run and then showered. He was still sleeping when I came out of the bathroom. The sheets covered him to his waist. He was facing away from me. I could see only cinnamon-colored hair, a bare back, and narrow shoulders. His caramel skin looked even darker than usual against the clean white sheets.

I was surprised at how my desire for him only seemed to grow. With other partners, the excitement often waned. But not with him. Not yet, at any rate. I dropped my towel and climbed naked onto the bed behind him. I pushed up against him. As always, his hair smelled like strawberries. I kissed the back of his neck and ran my hand down his soft stomach.

"Mmm..." he mumbled sleepily. "If it's before six, I'll never forgive you."

"It's almost seven."

He stretched, leaning back against me. "Mmm..." he said again, but this time it sounded less like sleepiness and more like arousal. "In that case...."

I moved the sheet out of the way so I could press my growing erection against him, and he moaned. He let me push him on to his stomach and spread his legs so that I could wedge myself between them. I loved the way he felt when he was flat underneath me like this. His body was thin and seemed delicate, and yet I knew from experience that he was not the least bit fragile or timid when it came to sex. I kissed the back of his neck, flicking my tongue over that butterfly mark that always seemed to call to me. "I love the way your hair smells," I told him, and he laughed breathlessly.

I slid my hand underneath him, down to his erection. He arched his back, pushing his hips back against me. I had really only meant to tease him a little, but the pressure on my groin made me suddenly want to do more—and quickly. I wrapped my hand around his shaft and started to stroke him.

"More," he whispered.

"Tell me what you want," I said, keeping my strokes light and slow.

"What I always want," he said. He thrust his hips back against me again, causing my breath to catch in my throat in anticipation. "Hurry."

I was glad to hear that I wasn't the only one feeling a sense of urgency. I reached for the drawer next to the bed where the condoms and lube were, and—

My doorbell rang.

"You have *got* to be kidding," he said with obvious frustration, and I laughed. "Who on earth would be ringing your doorbell this time of the morning?"

"I don't know," I admitted. "Probably Julia."

"What a shame," he moaned. "I rather thought I liked her, too."

I was debating ignoring the doorbell, but he abruptly pushed me off of him, rolling away and causing me to fall off the bed. I landed in an inelegant pile on the floor. He didn't even look back. "You can make it up to me after breakfast," he said as he headed for the bathroom.

So much for ignoring the doorbell.

I dressed quickly and opened the door, hoping Julia wouldn't notice the telltale bulge in my pants that wasn't quite covered by my shirt. But it wasn't Julia on my porch. It was my father.

On the bright side, my erection went away in a hurry.

"Dad!" I said in alarm. "What are you doing here?"

He held up a bag from the local donut shop. "I was in the area and thought I'd stop by for breakfast."

"Oh," I said stupidly, because I wasn't sure what else to say. I was wondering if there was any chance of getting rid of him before Cole came out of the bedroom or of convincing Cole to stay in the bedroom until my dad left. It wasn't as if my dad didn't know that I was gay, but he rarely had to face it so head-on, and it always made him uncomfortable.

"I didn't wake you up, did I?" he asked. "You're usually up early."

"No, I was awake."

"Good." We stood there for a moment staring awkwardly at one another, and he finally said, "Jon, are you going to let me in?"

Shit! Why was my brain suddenly short-circuiting? "Of course," I said, and moved aside for him.

He looked at me suspiciously as he came in and headed for the dining room table. "Do you have any coffee?" he asked.

"I was just about to make some."

"Is something wrong, Jon?" he asked. "Did I interrupt something?"

I was debating coming clean and telling him there was a naked man in my bed, but Cole put my out of my misery by choosing that very moment to come walking out of my bedroom. He had his pants on, although they weren't buttoned, and he was just pulling his shirt on over his head. My dad's jaw dropped, and I felt my cheeks turning bright red.

"Oh shit," I said.

"Oh my God," my dad said.

"Oh hello there!" Cole said, advancing on my dad with a perfectly benign, open smile. "I'm Cole." He stopped in front of my dad with his hand out. My dad just stood there with his mouth open, staring dumbly at him.

"Cole, this is my father, George."

"Hello, George," Cole said. "It's nice to meet you." He still had his hand out, and my father was staring at it like he wasn't quite sure what to do with it. I could see the look in Cole's eyes slowly changing from his usual mocking humor to something much more guarded. He slowly pulled his hand back. He put it on his hip, and cocked his other hip out. He flipped his hair back out of his eyes. I could almost see him putting on each little piece of his affectation like some kind of suit. "Well, lovey," he said to me, although he was still looking at my dad. "I wish you had told me you were still in the closet."

"I'm not," I said. I grabbed the closest thing I could find, which happened to be that morning's folded up newspaper, and threw it across the table at my father. "Dad!"

It smacked into the back of his head, and he jumped about a foot. But it did the trick. "I'm sorry," he blurted out. "I'm George Kechter." He held out his hand, rather belatedly. Cole stood there eyeing him suspiciously for a moment, but then shook his hand.

"Nice to meet you, George," he repeated. He eyed the bag of donuts on the table with obvious distaste before turning to me. "I was going to make breakfast, but I think it might be best if I was on my way."

"Cole, I'm sorry—" I started to say, but he smiled at me.

"No worries, lovey. Give me a minute."

My father and I sat down on opposite sides of the table, not looking at each other. He was staring resolutely at the tabletop. I watched Cole as he went into the bedroom, came back out, found his shoes and his keys. All I could think about was how much I wished my father had waited another ten or fifteen minutes before ringing my doorbell. I was fairly certain, given the amount of urgency Cole and I had both been feeling, that would have been enough time.

He stopped at the door and held his hand up to his ear, thumb and little finger extended, in the universal sign for "call me." Or knowing him, it meant, "I'll call." I nodded, and then he was gone.

Once the front door closed, my father finally looked up at me, his cheeks red with embarrassment.

"What was he doing here?"

I couldn't help but grin at him. "Do you really want the details, Dad?"

His blush deepened and he looked away. "No!"

"I'm sorry if we made you uncomfortable."

"I didn't expect you to have company."

"I didn't expect you to show up on my porch unannounced at seven o'clock on a Saturday morning."

He was quiet for a minute, fidgeting with the donut bag. I knew he wanted to say something, and I waited. Finally he sighed. "He's not really your type, is he, Jon?"

"What do you mean?" I asked, challenging him. Of course I knew exactly what he meant, but I had no intention of making this easy for him.

"Well," he said defensively, "he's a little…."

He let his sentence trail away. "*Yes?*" I prompted. "A little *what?*"

"A little… fruity." I felt myself bristle at that, but said nothing. "Is he your boyfriend?"

I debated how to answer that. "Not exactly."

"So it was a one night stand?" he asked, and there was no mistaking the disgust in his voice.

"Which would offend you least, Dad?" I asked, fighting to keep my irritation in check. "Hearing that he was a one-night hook-up or hearing that I was in a relationship with him?"

He looked down at the table, and I could see the shame on his face. He wasn't ashamed of me. He was ashamed of himself. He tried very hard to be understanding of my homosexuality. Sometimes he succeeded. "I'm not sure," he admitted. He looked back up at me. "Why don't you just tell me the truth?"

"The truth," I told him, "is somewhere in between."

He sighed. "I suppose it usually is." He didn't seem to have anything else to say, so I went in the kitchen and started the coffee brewing, then came back out with napkins. He took a donut out and handed the bag to me across the table. "Are you seeing anybody else?" he asked. He was once again avoiding my gaze, looking only at the tabletop.

"No. There's only him right now."

"Jon, I know you're an adult—"

"I'm glad you noticed."

"—and it's none of my business—"

"You're right about that."

"—but I just hope you're being careful."

That wasn't what I was expecting, and it quelled my anger in a hurry. It took me a moment to respond. "Don't worry, Dad," I finally said, and he smiled.

"Okay," he said with obvious relief. "So, how about that coffee?"

THE following Friday I was working at the office when I received a message that Marcus needed to talk to me. I found him in his office, finishing off a greasy hamburger and fries. "Marcus? You wanted to see me?"

"I did! Come in, Jon. Close the door." I sat across from him and waited for him to throw away the remains of his lunch. It still smelled like fast food in his office. "Jon," he finally said, "I wanted to talk to you about the restructuring."

"Restructuring?" I asked stupidly. Of course, Marcus had told me back in May that our CEO was considering something like that, but after five months with no further mention of it, I had assumed that it wasn't going to happen. Now that it was coming up again, I found myself dreading the idea.

"Monty wants to go through with it. It won't actually go into effect for a few more months. There are other things that need to be put into place first. But I wanted you to know that it's definitely coming down the line."

"Meaning that I'll have to relocate?"

"Probably. I'm not sure yet how we'll decide who gets which territory, but I wanted to meet with each of you and find out if you have a preference."

"What were they again?"

"Arizona. San Diego, LA, San Francisco. Vegas, Colorado, and Utah."

"Well, obviously my first choice is Arizona." But I also had to assume that was everybody's first choice.

"What about the rest?"

What about the rest? Anywhere in California was acceptable to me. I knew my way around Vegas, but I wasn't sure I wanted to live there. The idea of Utah scared me. And Colorado? Well, Colorado was a whole different issue.

Colorado was where I had gone to college. Colorado was where I had met Zach and spent three years loving him. Colorado was where I left him and spent another year of my life waiting for him to come back to me. And Colorado was where he still lived to this day, with his new partner—the partner he loved more than he had ever loved me.

I knew it was foolish, but the thought of going back was unbearable. Yes, it was a big state. If I moved there for work, I would undoubtedly be living in Denver. Zach and Angelo lived in the mountains now. Chances of me seeing them at all were almost non-existent. On the other hand, chances of me running into them while in Vegas were probably equally slim, and yet, it had still happened.

The fact remained that, right or wrong, logical or not, moving back to Colorado would feel like a step in the wrong direction. It was linked in my mind in every way possible to my life with Zach, and it was a life I was never getting back. Somehow, being in a different state, I could accept that he had moved on. But if I were there, knowing that he was only an hour away, I wasn't sure I would be able to keep my mind off of him. I wasn't sure that I would be able to stop myself from seeking him out. It would be selfish and self-deluding. Zach had made it quite clear that he wanted nothing more to do with me. And Angelo would kick my ass as soon as look at me, with Matt to back him up just for good measure. And Jared would simply smile and ask about Cole. And Cole….

Well, there was also Cole. But I knew that I was nothing more to him than a convenient bed buddy, so I couldn't allow him to be a factor in my decision. And of course there was my dad to consider too.

"Jon?" Marcus asked, pulling me abruptly from my thoughts. "What do you think?"

"Not Colorado," I said to him. "Anywhere but Colorado."

He nodded. "As I said before, I don't know yet how we'll decide, but I'll keep your request in mind."

"Thank you."

"I'll let you know as soon as I know more. But nothing in this place happens quickly, Jon. For now at least, it's business as usual."

Date: October 10

From: Cole

To: Jared

I'm making cioppino tonight, which really should go with Tempranillo. Of course I'll have to buy the Barbera instead, because every time I buy a Spanish red, Jonathan starts to sulk. It's not that I'm jealous of Zach for being Jonathan's ex. I just wish his memory didn't have to join us for dinner quite so often. I hate having to compete with nostalgia.

I CAME home that afternoon to a house that smelled like seafood and Cole barefoot in my kitchen.

"Are you busy tomorrow night?" I asked him.

He glanced slyly at me. "I don't know, love. What are you offering?"

"I have tickets to see *Wicked*." It was the first time in months that I would actually be in town to use my own seats at the show, and I was looking forward to it.

"Two gay men going to the theater?" he teased. "Such a stereotype, isn't it?"

"You know, I've never understood that," I answered as I opened the wine that was sitting on the counter. "I go to the theater every chance I get, and I can tell you, the vast majority of the men there are straight. Believe me," I said, smiling at him, "I look!"

"I'm sure you do," he laughed. "It doesn't matter to me. I'd love to go."

"Good. How long until dinner's ready?"

"Long enough for you to shower, if that's what you were going to ask."

I emerged from the bathroom ten minutes later to find him sitting on the bed, grinning at me. He was giving me that look through his hair that told me he was laughing at me for something. "Hey, sweetie," he said. "Did you forget something?"

"I don't think so. Why?"

"Your phone rang while you were in the shower." I picked my cell phone up off of the dresser to check it, but he said, "Not that one. Your landline. I hope it wasn't terribly inappropriate of me to answer for you."

"That's fine. Who was it?"

"Your father."

"My father?" And then I realized why he was laughing at me. I was supposed to have dinner with my father tonight. "Shit! It's his birthday!" I checked my watch. I was already ten minutes late. If I hurried, I could make it to the restaurant in another twenty, but I also knew that Cole had dinner halfway ready. "Cole, I—"

"Relax," he said in that mocking tone. "We realized you must have had your days mixed up, so—"

"Was he angry?"

"I don't think so, but I dare say I don't know your father—"

"I should call him back."

"Honey, just wait and talk to him in person. He'll be here in five minutes."

"*What?*"

Now he looked even more amused. I wouldn't have thought it was possible if I hadn't seen it myself. "I've been trying to tell you, sweetie, but you won't keep quiet long enough listen to me. He was already on this end of town, and he obviously wanted to see you, and there's plenty of cioppino—"

"You invited him over?"

"Is that not what I've just been saying?"

I was trying to imagine the conversation between the two of them—Cole talking non-stop, calling my father "darling," and my dad trying to keep up. "And he said yes?"

"Of course." I had a feeling he just hadn't been able to come up with an excuse quickly enough to get out of it. "It's not a problem, is it?"

"I'm not sure it's a great idea, that's all. My dad isn't very comfortable with my sexuality, and—" Right then, the doorbell rang. I definitely would have preferred to answer it myself, but I realized I was still standing there wearing nothing but a towel. Cole smiled at me again.

"Don't worry, sweetie. I'll get it."

I got dressed quickly, telling myself the entire time that it would be fine. There was no reason to assume that dinner would be a disaster.

When I came out of the bedroom, I found that Cole had managed to shepherd my father straight into the dining room, where he had already set the table. Cole was talking a mile a minute. And my father? My father had a look on his face that was part shock and part horror. It would have been comical if it didn't confirm what I had already suspected. This was not going to be fun.

"George, I'm so sorry to have stolen your son away on your birthday," Cole was saying to him. "I never would have hijacked him like I did if I had known. But this is nicer, anyway. Restaurants can be so noisy and impersonal. This will be much more intimate, don't you think? We're having cioppino, but I think I told you that already. It makes the whole house smell like fish for a week, but it's so good, I make it anyway. I sure hope you don't have a shellfish allergy, honey. That would put a real damper on the evening, wouldn't it? I have no idea what we would do if you went into anaphylactic shock. I must admit, that CPR class I took in high school isn't going to do *anybody* any good *at all*! Even if I had paid attention back then, which I didn't, I dare say I would have forgotten it by now anyway. Here, let me get you some wine."

Listening to him, even my head was starting to spin, and my father looked like he had no idea what language Cole was even speaking. Cole, however, seemed oblivious. He went in the kitchen and came back with three glasses and an open bottle of wine, hardly breaking his running monologue in the process.

"Of course I didn't pay attention in that class to begin with. I tried. Really I did, George. But there we all were on our knees, with those horrible dummies in front of us. And Tommy Nelson was in front of me. That boy was on the wrestling team and had a body to kill for. And I have to say, every time he bent over to blow—"

"Cole!" I snapped, horrified, and he spun around to look at me.

"What is it, love? You don't want me to talk about Tommy Nelson?" He turned back to my dad and winked at him, and my dad's cheeks started to turn a little bit red. "I never realized Jonny was the jealous type."

It was strange to hear my name on his lips. I wasn't sure I had ever heard him say it before, and I wasn't surprised that he would choose the derivative of it that I hated the most. "He doesn't like to be called Jonny," my dad said suddenly, and Cole smiled at him.

"I *know*, honey. Why do you think I do it?" He slid a glass over to my dad and started to pour the wine. It was a red.

"He doesn't like red," I said. "Maybe we can open one of the Rieslings."

"Oh sweetie, you know we can't drink Riesling with cioppino." He shuddered dramatically. "That just wouldn't do at all. We could have gone with a Tempranillo, but I know how broody you get whenever I buy Spanish reds." I felt myself bristle a little at that. It wasn't my fault they reminded me of Zach. "So I bought the Barbera. It will be a nice pairing with the—"

"But my dad—"

"It's fine, Jon," my dad said, and I could tell he was trying to smile, although it came out more of a grimace.

Cole went into the kitchen, and my father and I sat there silently until he came back out with the food. My dad may have been looking at Cole like he was some kind of sideshow entertainment, but once he started to eat, I could tell he was impressed. "You cooked this?" he asked.

Cole actually batted his eyes at him, just a little. Was he actually flirting with my father? "Impressive, isn't it?"

"I've never known a man who could cook," my dad said, much to my horror.

"Dad!" I snapped. He looked over at me, confused for a moment, but then I saw a blush start to creep up his cheeks. He turned to Cole. "I didn't mean—"

"Honey, don't apologize," Cole said. "Listen, if it will make you feel better about it, I'll wear a dress next time. How about that?"

"Cole!" I said, but he ignored me.

"It's not something I normally do, but all modesty aside, George, I really do have fabulous legs."

Oh my God, this was worse than I had ever imagined. I had rarely seen Cole act so over-the-top, and I was starting to be embarrassed as well as uncomfortable. I could tell my dad was tempted to laugh at Cole, and I didn't want that to happen either. I wanted him to take Cole seriously. I wanted them to respect each other.

"Stop!" I snapped, and they both turned to look at me. My dad looked nervous and apologetic. Cole looked baffled and a little bit annoyed. "Can we just eat, please?" I asked, knowing even as I said that it sounded childish.

"Anything you want, love," Cole said with obvious amusement, and the rest of the meal was passed in awkward silence. But the reprieve was brief. Before long we had finished eating. The empty table seemed way too big once I had taken the dirty dishes back into the kitchen.

Despite my assertion that my dad hated red, we had finished the first bottle of wine, and Cole came out with a second bottle. "That was fantastic," my dad said to him as he refilled his glass, and Cole beamed at him. "What's for dessert?"

He was partially joking, but it annoyed me that he would assume Cole had made dessert too, and I snapped, "Dad!"

"No dessert, I'm afraid," Cole said. "I cook, but I don't bake."

"Is there a difference?"

"Honey, they're like night and day. Cooking is an art—you can substitute, improvise, experiment. But baking is a science. Everything has to be exactly right or it all falls apart. So many rules. It's terribly boring." I was thinking how that statement illustrated a great deal about Cole's character when he turned to me. "You should try it, sweetie," he said, with a hint of venom in his voice. It was subtle enough that my dad probably couldn't hear it, but I could.

"Me?" I asked, wondering what I had done to irritate him.

"Yes. It seems like a perfect hobby for an uptight accountant." I tried not to be offended at that character analysis.

"What do you do?" my dad asked Cole, and I managed not to groan audibly.

Cole got that mocking, amused look on his face that I sometimes found cute, but tonight only found annoying. "Exactly like Jonny, aren't you? What do you think I do?"

"Are you a chef?"

Cole smiled. "Yes. I'm a chef."

"Cole!"

"That explains the cooking then," my dad said, and I wondered if he meant a man would only bother to learn to cook if it was for in exchange for money.

"Dad, he's just being elusive. He's not a chef."

"What?" my dad asked, confused, and Cole rolled his eyes at me.

"Good lord, love. I *like* to cook. I'm good at it. Does that not make me a chef? It's not as if I'm lying."

"But you're implying—"

"I'm not implying anything, except that I cook—"

"Forget I asked," my dad said, but I wasn't listening.

"I don't know why you can't just be honest."

"I'm being honest. I *do* cook. You're the one who assumes that the question 'what do you do?' can only refer to a career—"

"That's not just *my* assumption, Cole! That's everybody's assumption!"

"It doesn't matter," my dad said, louder this time. "I was only trying to—"

"George," Cole said suddenly, turning to my father, "the truth is, I'm unemployed."

There was a moment of silence, and I wished I could kick Cole under the table, but he was sitting next to me, and it would have been anything but subtle. "Oh," my father said with obvious embarrassment. "I'm sorry to hear that."

"Don't be!" Cole said, smiling, and I could see that my dad was more confused than ever.

"Let's talk about something else, shall we?"

But I wasn't ready to let it go. I didn't want my dad thinking that Cole was a bum, or that he was somehow living off of me. "He's rich," I blurted out.

They both turned to look at me again. This time, the annoyance on Cole's face was obvious. Even my father must have seen it, because he asked suddenly, as if coming to my rescue, "Cole, are you from Phoenix originally?"

Cole kept his withering gaze on me for another fraction of a second before turning back to my dad. By the time his eyes landed on my father, the anger was gone from his face, and he was smiling again.

"No, although it's hard to say exactly where I *am* from, to tell you the truth. We spent a few months each year at my father's house in Orange County—"

"You have a house in Orange County, too?" I asked in surprise.

He cut me a quick sideways look. "Not anymore." Then back to my father: "When I was very young, my family spent a great deal of time in New York, because it was the house my mother liked best. But by the time I was eight or so, she and my father had split, and my father didn't like to go there. So we went to Paris instead. We were usually there at least six months out of the year. My father had extended family in the area. They're still there, I suppose, although I haven't heard from any of them since he died."

"I'm sorry—" my dad started to say, but Cole waved him off before he even finished the words.

"It's nothing, honey. It was twenty years ago."

"That's why you like to travel so much," I said with sudden understanding, and he shrugged.

"Traveling's not something I *like* to do so much as something I'm *compelled* to do. I've tried staying put, love, but it never works out. It makes me restless and cranky and terribly unpleasant."

"You must have been pretty young when your dad died," my dad said.

"Dad," I said, "I'm sure he doesn't want to talk about that." But Cole ignored me and answered.

"I was fifteen. My mother is still alive, so technically she had custody until I was eighteen, even though I never saw her. It's as predictable as the movie of the week, really. A couple of housekeepers kept me in line until I went off to college." He smiled, in an obvious attempt to lighten the mood. "My mother's single too, love, and lord knows she spends enough money on surgery, I imagine she's still gorgeous to boot. Maybe I should set you up sometime."

My dad looked a little alarmed. "Cole," I said, "no."

He rolled his eyes at me. "Honey, lighten up. It was a joke."

My mother was dead, and he was joking about setting my dad up on a blind date? "It's inappropriate."

"Jon," my dad said, "it's fine."

"See?" Cole said to me. "It's fine."

"It's not fine," I said. "He doesn't want to date anyone!"

"How do you know, love? Have you ever asked him? George, are you dating anyone?"

"Cole!"

"*What,* love? It was a simple question."

"My mother is *dead*!"

"Good lord, honey, I know! But it didn't happen yesterday, did it? Am I supposed to assume he's going to live a life of chastity for the rest of his days?"

"Boys—" my dad started to say, but Cole cut him off.

"George, I'm so sorry if I offended you. Truly. That was never my intent."

"You didn't—"

"That's not the point!" I said.

"Jon," my dad said, "the truth is, I've been thinking about trying one of those dating services—"

"Oh my God! Can we talk about something else please?" I snapped.

Cole gave me a venomous glare, and my dad sighed heavily before coming to my rescue yet again by asking, "So, how did the two of you meet?"

Cole and I eyed each other for a second. There was a challenge blazing in his hazel eyes. He was definitely not happy with me. I turned back to my father. "We were set up by a mutual friend."

"Yes," Cole said sarcastically. "Lord knows *what* Jared was thinking."

"Nobody's making you stay," I snapped in irritation.

He smiled at me. "Good point, lovey." He turned to my father. "It was lovely seeing you again, George, and I hope you had a wonderful birthday. I know it's terribly improper to rush out like this, but I'm sure you and Jonny would like some time alone anyway." He stood up from the table without even looking at me.

"You're leaving?" I asked in surprise. I hadn't really meant for him to go.

"As a matter of fact, I am."

My dad once again looked uncomfortable, and I was trying not to be pissed. I followed him into the living room where he put on his shoes and grabbed his keys. "I can't believe you're just walking out on dinner," I hissed at him, hoping my father couldn't hear. "It's rude."

"You're the one who's rude," he said, turning on me. "You're so busy treating us like children you don't notice when you're not needed!"

"What the hell's that supposed to mean?"

"Nothing at all," he said, and slammed the door behind him.

I stood there in the living room, trying to compose myself before going back to my dad. I counted to five. Or maybe it was twenty-five. Once I had quit seeing red, I went back in the dining room to find that my dad wasn't there. I found him in the kitchen, using a piece of bread to mop the cioppino pot clean.

"That boy may be a fruitcake," he said, "but he sure can cook!"

I DIDN'T hear from Cole the next day, and I was annoyed enough at him that I would have been perfectly happy to leave it that way for a few days, but that was the night we were supposed to go to the theater. I broke down and called him at four to confirm that we were still on. Normally, we probably would have gone to dinner first, but we both seemed to feel it was best to skip it tonight. He agreed to meet me at my house, and we would ride together from there.

I really was looking forward to the show. My love of the theater had come from my mother. She went as often as possible. My dad hated it, and so, starting when I was about ten, my mother took me instead. I loved the music and the stories, but more than anything, I liked going simply because it reminded me of her. I treated the theater with a reverence most people reserved for church. Despite being annoyed at Cole, I was happy to be able to use my tickets for once. It had been far too long.

Unfortunately, I could tell from the minute he walked into my house that Cole and I were going to clash that evening. He was dressed as he always was—thin dark pants with a light sweater and a scarf. He had a jacket, but it wasn't a suit jacket. It was white and trendier than anything I had ever owned, and I would have bet a month's pay he had bought it in Paris. I knew nothing about fashion, but it definitely looked like something right off of a fashion-show runway. It was cut long in a way that almost seemed military and yet still oddly ostentatious. "Is that what you're wearing?" I asked, before I could help myself.

"No, love," he said. "I have an Armani hidden underneath this. I was planning a Superman-style change of wardrobe in the car."

Maybe I deserved that, but I wasn't going to apologize. "I thought you would wear a suit," I said.

"Not even if this were my own funeral."

"Fine."

We hardly spoke in my car, and as soon as we entered the theater, he headed for the bar, with me tagging along behind. I was reminded immediately of the night in Vegas when we had gone to the restaurant. At home, when it was only the two of us, his flamboyance seemed to fade. In public, it always came back to some degree. I thought I had grown used to it over the last few months, but tonight it seemed worse than ever. His walk was too swishy, his gestures too broad, his voice too lilting. I didn't normally feel that I had to hide my sexuality, but I didn't feel compelled to broadcast it, either. Being with Cole, I may as well have been carrying a neon sign that said, "I'm gay!" He made me self-conscious of my own mannerisms, and I found myself making an effort to look as *straight* as possible, something I hadn't thought about in years.

We got in line at the bar. For once, he wasn't talking a mile a minute. At first I was simply happy to not have to listen to him. I reminded myself that this was supposed to be fun. Then I looked at the bar, and my anger returned, stronger than ever. The bartender was young, cute, and as blatantly queer as Cole. He was busy helping the customers in front of him, but his glance kept returning to Cole, and they would smile at each other every time.

"Did you pick this line on purpose?" I snapped.

"What if I did?" he snapped back. He eyed me up and down before turning his back on me. "Your condescension is getting a little old, darling."

I bit back my response, and then it was our turn. The bartender—his name tag said Trey—leaned forward so he was a few inches closer to Cole. "What would you like, sir?" he asked in a tone that was rife with suggestion, and Cole grinned wickedly at him.

"How long has that Pinot Noir been open, sweetie?"

"That one? Since last night. But I'll open a fresh one for you if you like."

Cole gave him a look that was so flirtatious I wondered that the people standing next to us couldn't feel the vibes coming off of him. "I would appreciate that very much. I'll have a glass of that and a glass of Chianti too."

"Would you like me to open a fresh one of that as well?"

"No, sweetie," Cole said, cutting me a sideways glance. "Don't bother."

"Would you like to place an order for intermission? You can pay now, and the drinks will be waiting for you at the end of the bar."

"That sounds perfect."

Trey poured my drink first, and Cole handed it back to me. Trey eyed me with obvious curiosity, and I did my best to incinerate him with my eyes. I failed, unfortunately. He turned away to open Cole's wine and pour it. I couldn't quite see what he was doing, but when he turned back around, he placed the glass in front of Cole on a cocktail napkin. I had a mere second to see that there was a phone number written on it before Cole picked it up and put it in his pocket. "Thanks, sweetie," he said, winking at him and handing him two twenty dollar bills. "Keep the change."

"You are unbelievable," I hissed at him as we walked away.

"Good lord, love. *What* is your problem? Did you see me ask for his number? No. And even if I had, it's not exactly your business anyway, is it?"

"It's not the number! It's—" I stopped short, because the truth was, I wasn't sure exactly what to say. Yes, the phone number had bothered me, as had the obviously giant tip he had given in exchange. But it was his blatant dismissal of me that pissed me off more. On the other hand, I was being honest enough with myself to accept that almost everything he did was rubbing me the wrong way tonight. It was unfair to attack him for it. I made myself stop and count to five. I drank my wine, and we pointedly ignored each other until it was time to find our seats.

Intermission passed much the same way, and although Trey was busy pouring drinks, I saw the looks they gave each other when we picked up the wine Cole had ordered ahead of time.

"So," Cole said in an obvious effort to cut the tension between us, "have you seen this play before?"

"No. But it's very popular."

"The costumes are absolutely amazing, aren't they?"

"I suppose." I hadn't really noticed the costumes, and the fact that he *would* notice annoyed me for no good reason. It seemed to underline my conviction that we had nothing in common. "What do you think so far?" I asked, and I couldn't make my voice sound friendly.

He eyed me warily before saying drolly, "I think you and Elphaba have a great deal in common."

"I'm not green."

"Of course not, love. It's more the attitude. Uptight and with absolutely no sense of humor."

"I suppose we should all be more flighty, like Galinda?" I asked, and I saw by the way his eyes narrowed that he did not miss my meaning. He turned away from me and drained his glass of wine, then walked back into the theater without me.

I didn't care if he was angry. I didn't care if I had hurt him. I stood there cursing myself for everything I could think of, from first agreeing to meet him for dinner so many months ago to asking him out tonight. I finished my wine and went back in, taking my seat next to him without saying a word.

After the play, I wanted only to get out of there as quickly as possible. What was normally a pleasant experience for me had been ruined, and I wanted nothing more than to be away from him. The lobby was packed with people shopping at the merchandise booths and buying more drinks, and some like us, who were simply trying to get to the door.

We were almost there when a familiar voice said, "Jonathan!" I turned in the crush of people to find Marcus next to me. "It's good to see you don't work all the time!" he said cheerfully. "Let me buy you a drink."

Shit. There was no way I wanted to tell Marcus no. On the other hand....

"Come on," he said, sensing my hesitation. "My wife is over there," he waved vaguely in the direction of the bathroom, "talking to her sister. I'll be here at least another hour."

"Well, sir—"

"We would love to join you," Cole suddenly said from just behind my right elbow, and Marcus looked at him in surprise. I felt dread forming in the pit of my stomach. Cole held his hand out to Marcus. "I'm Cole. And you are?"

"Marcus Barry," Marcus said uneasily, shaking Cole's hand.

"He's my boss," I said to Cole, hoping he would realize that I was pleading with him not to embarrass me.

"Marcus! Of course. It's nice to finally meet you. I've heard all about you, of course."

Marcus was looking back and forth between us, his cheeks slowly turning red. "I'm sorry," he said, obviously flustered. "You're a friend of Jonathan's?"

Oh God. I wished there was a nearby hole I could climb into to hide. It wasn't that I hid my homosexuality at work. It was simply that it had never come up. I didn't go to the company Christmas parties, and I didn't go out for beers with the guys. I did my work and I kept to myself. It was my own self-imposed version of "Don't ask, don't tell." And although I knew some of my co-workers had their suspicions, nobody had ever had the nerve to question me.

Cole was looking at me for help, and I was standing there like an idiot, trying to figure out what to say. Saying he was just a friend seemed like an insult. Saying he was my partner was vastly untrue. Saying he was my lover would certainly embarrass Marcus.

Cole finally gave up on me and turned back to Marcus. "What Jonny seems unable to say is that I am his date."

"Oh," Marcus stammered, as his face turned even more red. "So the two of you are, ummm… a couple?"

Cole smiled at him, actually batted his eyes a little, and I worried that Marcus's imminent heart attack might be even closer than I had anticipated. "I guess you could call us friends with benefits," Cole said.

"Oh," Marcus said again. He was starting to sweat a little, and I could see him frantically scanning the crowd. I assumed he was looking for his wife to come and rescue him.

"Cole!" I said in alarm.

"Do you object to that definition, love? How exactly would *you* classify our relationship?"

"Marcus, thanks for the drink offer, but we really need to go—"

"Of course," Marcus said with obvious relief.

I grabbed Cole's arm and steered him toward the door. Once we were outside, he pulled away from me angrily. "Let go of me! I'm not a child!"

"Why in the world did you say that him?" I snapped.

"I waited for you to answer him, and you were just standing there with your mouth hanging open! I thought the man at least deserved a response."

"You couldn't have been a little less obvious?"

"Was I supposed to lie to him? You're the one that invited me out! You're the one that obviously has a problem with this. Maybe you'd like to make me a list of all the things I'm allowed to say when we run into people you know. Maybe you'd like to inform me of exactly how I *should* classify our relationship, in case we're ever asked again. Lord knows I wouldn't want to *embarrass* you."

He turned and walked toward the car, and I trailed along behind him, fuming the entire time. We drove back to my place in stony silence. I couldn't believe how angry I was. I fought back the urge to lash out at him. I knew it would only make matters worse. The best thing would be to get back to my house, where his car was parked, and go our separate ways, at least for a few days. At least until I could look at him without feeling rage welling up inside of me.

We got to my house, and I expected him to head straight for his car. Instead, he followed me to the door, and I realized that he had probably left his keys inside, on the table by the door. I opened the door and we went in. He didn't pick up his keys and leave, but I knew he wasn't planning on staying by the fact that he didn't take off his shoes the minute we were in the door.

"Well," he said, crossing the room and turning to stare at me challengingly with one hand on his hip, "let's hear it, then."

"Hear *what*?" I asked through clenched teeth.

"Whatever it is that's got you in such a lather. You're obviously furious at me. You've been completely unbearable all night, and now you're practically foaming at the mouth. So quit stewing in your own juices, and let's just get this over with, shall we? What the hell is your problem?"

I wanted to tell him that it was nothing. I wanted to tell him to go home before I said something cruel. But his attitude only made me angrier. Every aspect of his flamboyance was worse now. Every layer of his affectation was accentuated: the cadence of his speech, the way he stood with his hand on his hip as he flipped his hair out of his eyes, and the way he managed to look down his nose at me, even though I was taller than him by at least two inches. "You really don't know?" I asked.

He turned away from me, flipping his hair in theatrical dismissal. "I have my suspicions, but we may as well work with the cold, hard facts, don't you think, love?"

"Fine!" I said, fighting to keep from yelling. "You want to know what's bothering me? *You're* bothering me! I can't believe the way you acted tonight. With my *boss*! And last night, with my father! It's embarrassing—"

"Last night was your fault, not mine—"

"*What*?"

"—and it's not my problem if you're embarrassed by your sexuality."

"I'm not embarrassed about being gay! I'm embarrassed by *you*! Why do you have to act so goddamn flamboyant?"

He froze. For just a moment, he was deathly still. And then he turned, very slowly, to look at me. "What did you just say to me?" There was an angry warning in his eyes, but I ignored it.

"You heard me."

"Of course I heard you," he said icily. "I thought I would allow you the luxury of taking it back. Rather diplomatic of me, don't you think?"

"I don't need to take it back!"

"Are you *quite* sure about that, darling?" He turned away from me with a perfectly orchestrated toss of his head.

He was giving me a chance to get out of this before I pushed it too far, but I wasn't about to take it. All I could think about was the way he had acted with my father and the embarrassment on Marcus's face, and it made me furious. "I don't *want* to take it back, Cole! I want you to answer me! Why do you have to act like such a, a, a—" I stumbled, stopped short, not really wanting to say any of the words that had popped into my head. But it was too late.

He turned and pinned me with a piercing stare. "A *what*?" he asked, advancing on me. "Which term will you throw at me, lovey? Do you think I haven't heard them all? Queen, fag, fairy, flamer—"

Those were the terms that had come to mind, but they sounded even worse out loud than they had in my head. It should have made me ashamed, but instead it only made me angrier at him for throwing them back in my face. "Jesus Christ, Cole, I wasn't going to say *any* of those things!"

"Don't kid yourself, darling. It was all over your face." He put one hand on his hip, cocked his other hip out, and tossed his head back. He was amping it up, turning it into a performance just for my benefit. He batted his eyelashes at me. "Does it offend you *so much*, darling? You never seem to mind when we're in the bedroom."

"Goddamn it, Cole, I'm not talking about *in the bedroom*! I'm talking about when we're out *in public*! Why do you have to act like every bad stereotype Hollywood has ever dreamed up for us?"

"Why do you have to act like such an arrogant, uptight prick?"

"So we're going to resort to name calling, rather than discussing this rationally?"

"Oh, I'm sorry. Are we actually *discussing* something? You'll have to forgive my confusion. I thought you were simply attacking me for not being a perfect carbon copy of every *straight* man you've ever wished you could fuck!"

That word, coming from him, sounded more obscene than normal. I realized I had never actually heard him swear before. "Cole, *stop*! I'm not attacking you."

"It certainly feels like you are. My mistake, darling."

"My name is *not* 'darling'. It's *Jonathan*. And if that's too hard for you to remember, you can just call me Jon."

"I can think of plenty of other things I would *rather* call you right at this particular moment."

"That was my *boss*, for God's sake. I have to work with him! I need him to respect me! Would it kill you tone it down a bit?"

His eyes flashed, and to my surprise, in the blink of an eye, he cut the act. It was like a curtain came down, and suddenly he there in front of me—no affectation at all. And he was livid. "Do you think you're the first man to be embarrassed by me, Jonny-boy? Do you think you're the first man who's ever asked me to 'tone it down'? Because you're not! Better men than you have asked me to change, and I'll tell you what I told them: go to hell!"

He turned and headed for the door, grabbing his keys off of the table as he went.

"Damn it, Cole! Wait!"

But he didn't stop. He slammed my front door so hard that my windows rattled. I didn't go after him.

Date: October 12

From: Cole

To: Jared

Good lord Sweets, if you never set me up again, it will be too soon! I honestly have no idea what you were thinking.

I THOUGHT at first that he would call. He didn't. I thought that when I got home from work the next night, he would be there waiting for me like always. He wasn't.

I realized then that it was up to me.

I was torn. Part of me was still angry. I didn't believe that I had done anything wrong. I had seen him turn the levels of his flamboyance up and down like the volume on the TV. I knew he could do it. I just didn't understand why he was unwilling to do it when it mattered the most to me. But I also knew that I didn't want things to end between us. I especially didn't want them to end on such unfriendly terms. I felt certain that if I could just talk to him about it reasonably, without it turning into a shouting match, we could reach some sort of understanding.

I finally broke down and called him three days later. He picked up on the fourth ring, right before it would have gone to his voice mail.

"What?" he snapped, in lieu of saying hello. Any doubts I might have had that he was still angry went right out the window.

"It's me."

"I know."

Not a good start to the conversation. I made myself count to five, then said, "I'm sorry."

"Sorry for what *exactly*, darling?"

"I'm sorry for—" I stumbled, trying to figure out what I was supposed to say. "For making you angry."

There was a stony silence on the other end of the line, and then he asked, "Are you *really* sorry, or is it only that your bed felt awfully empty these last few nights?"

"Jesus, Cole," I said, fighting back my anger. "Do you have to make this so hard? I'm trying to apologize—"

"Listen, honey," he interrupted me, "here's the thing: I leave for Hawaii at the crack of dawn, so—"

"What?"

"—I really don't have the time to wait for you to pull your head out of your ass."

"You're *leaving*?"

"Did I not just say that?"

"We have *one* fight, and you're just going to fly off to Hawaii?"

"As a matter of fact, I am. I dare say you'd leave yourself too, darling, if only you could." There was an almost inaudible click, and he was gone.

The entire thing made me furious. I couldn't decide which one of us I was annoyed at more—him for being so arrogant or myself for even trying to apologize. I spent the evening getting gloriously drunk, and the entire next day at work regretting it. By five o'clock the nausea and headache had passed, but I still felt like I had been run over by a freight train. I managed to leave the office a few minutes early and drove home. My plan was a frozen pizza with an Alka-Seltzer chaser followed by a shower and then straight to bed.

It wasn't until after my shower that I noticed the light on my answering machine blinking at me. Every person I knew had my cell phone number. I rarely even paid attention to my land line. I hit play, and Cole's voice filled the room, light and feminine and mocking. But there was a bitter edge to it this time too. There was not a doubt in my mind that he had intentionally called my home number while I was at work in order to avoid having to actually talk to me.

"Here's what it boils down to: I don't want things to end between us. Not really. And especially not like this. Even if you are an uptight prick, you're still my favorite person in all of Phoenix. But there are three things you need to know, and you better believe me when I tell you that these three things are one hundred percent non-negotiable. I won't change who I am. I won't spend all of our time together holed up in your bedroom just to keep from embarrassing you. And I won't *ever* talk to you about this again." There was a pause, and I wondered if he had stopped to count to five. "I'll be home in exactly two weeks, Jonny-Boy. Ball's in your court now."

I SPENT the next few days telling myself that I didn't need him. It wasn't as if I loved him. It wasn't as if we had any kind of real relationship at all. We were fuck buddies, plain and simple. It was better to just forget him and move on.

The problem was I couldn't quite convince myself that it was true. Although I wouldn't have called it love, the fact was I had grown used to having him around. I could not deny that I was fond of him, and more than that, I missed him. When I was being honest with myself, which was only about half of the time, I knew that I didn't want things to end between us any more than he did. But despite all that, I still felt that he should have been willing to take my feelings into account too.

I had lunch with my dad the following week. I tried to act like everything was normal, but I failed miserably. I knew I was being surly and short-tempered, but I couldn't seem to do anything to stop. Finally, as we were finishing our meal, he asked in exasperation, "What's wrong, Jon?"

"Nothing!" I snapped.

"Uh-*huh*," he said, smiling. It annoyed me, because it meant he thought my bad mood was funny, more than anything. "Is this about the fruitcake?"

I bristled at that, and then was even more annoyed at myself for the fact my dad was right. It was Cole's "fruitiness," as my dad called it, that had caused this entire predicament.

"Yes," I admitted. "It's Cole."

He eyed me with wary curiosity for a moment. "The two of you have a fight?"

"I guess you could say that."

"Did you break up?"

I sighed. "I don't know, Dad. I'm not really sure we were ever together to begin with."

"Was it because of what happened at dinner?"

I hesitated, not wanting to talk about it. But I knew my dad. If I didn't start talking, he would. He'd sit there speculating and giving me his opinion, whether I cooperated or not. "That was part of it. But the next night, we went to theater, and it didn't exactly go the way I planned."

"Uh-*huh*," he said again, looking amused.

"What?" I asked defensively.

"What exactly did you say to him?"

"I told him he was too flamboyant. And I asked him to tone it down."

"And did he tell you to kiss his lily-white ass?"

I had to fight back a smile. Partly because he was right, but also because my first instinct was to tell him that Cole's ass was in fact *not* lily white. But I was pretty sure he would rather not know that. "Not in those exact words, but yes. That's basically what he told me."

"Uh-*huh*," he said yet again in that annoyingly amused tone.

"*What?*"

He shook his head. "Nothing really. It just got me thinking. That's all."

He let that hang there, and I finally gave in and said, "About what?"

"Do you remember David's wedding?" I closed my eyes, seeing exactly where he was headed, but unable to stop him. "Do you remember what happened at the reception?"

Of course I remembered. David was my cousin. He married when I was in college, only a few months after I had come out to my family. I took a date to David's reception—Zach. It was the first time I had ever shown up at a family function of any type with another man. "Yes," I finally said, "I remember."

"You and Zach were so nervous, weren't you? I mean, I didn't know it at the time. I was too busy being disgusted and trying hard to *not* be disgusted. But I realize now. You were both being so careful not to sit too close, not to touch each other. But the fact was anybody who looked at the two of you could see it. You were both grinning like fools, and you couldn't keep your eyes off of each other."

He was right. I remembered with perfect clarity how Zach and I had been—trying to act casual when we both knew we were going to tear each other's clothes off the first chance we got. We didn't even make it out of the parking lot. I felt myself blushing as I remembered groping hands and the wonderful urgency that had overtaken us in his car after the reception.

"So there you two were," Dad went on, "trying not to touch each other. And there I was, trying not to *think* about the two of you touching each other. And in the end, I had a few too many drinks, and I pulled the two of you aside—"

"Yes."

"—and I told you to stop being so obvious."

"I remember."

"And do you remember what you told me?"

"I told you that you better get used to having a fucking faggot for a son."

He nodded. "Exactly. And then you told me that if I really loved you, I wouldn't ask you to change. I would learn to accept you exactly the way you were."

"What's your point, Dad?" I asked, although I thought I knew.

"My point is you were right." He picked up his menu and held it up so I couldn't see his face. But I could still hear him, for better or worse. "Let's face it, Jon: that doesn't happen very damn often, does it?"

EVEN after I knew he was home, it took me three days and half a bottle of wine to get up enough nerve to call him.

"Hello?"

"It's Jonathan."

There was a pause, and then, "I know."

"I'm sorry, Cole. I really am."

"Sorry for what?"

"For being embarrassed. For being so mad. For all the things I said, and even for the things I thought but didn't say."

"You're on a roll, darling. Keep going."

"I'm sorry for wanting you to change. And I'm sorry for being an uptight prick."

"Is that all?"

"Did I miss something?"

"I suppose you covered the major points."

"I missed you."

"That's excellent. You're really getting the hang of it now."

"I don't want it to be over."

I thought he was going to make another smart-ass reply, but instead he said softly, "I don't either, Jonny." And I knew that the derivative of my name, even said in mockery, was a peace offering of sorts.

"Can I see you tonight?"

"Tonight? I don't know, darling. I'm terribly busy."

"Then when?"

"I'll have to check my calendar and get back to you."

"Really?"

"You don't believe me?"

"I think maybe you're just trying to punish me."

"Don't be silly, darling. *Of course* I'm trying to punish you. Bye now!"

"Cole?" I said, but the line was already dead. "*Shit!*" I yelled, flinging my phone across the room. It hit the wall with a clatter. The batteries came flying out, and there was an undeniable dent in my drywall now. Good thing it was my home phone and not my cell phone that was now lying in pieces on the floor.

Why the hell had I ever decided to call?

I drank some more wine. I flipped endlessly through the channels of crap on TV. Eventually, I went in the kitchen and raided my cabinets. Cole's time cooking in my house had added a lot to my pantry, but it was nothing I could use. Lots of spices and oils, but nothing I could actually eat. I finally found a TV dinner in the back of the freezer. I put it in the microwave, but before I could turn it on, the doorbell rang.

I crossed over to the door, kicking what remained of my phone across the room as I passed, just for good measure. I stopped with my hand on the knob to compose myself. I counted to five. I counted to five again. Then I opened it.

It was Cole. He looked more unsure of himself than I had ever seen him. His cheeks were red with embarrassment, and he looked up at me through his bangs. "I think I'm done punishing you now," he said. And the next thing I knew, he was all over me.

He was breathless, his hands tearing at my clothes. He even let me kiss him, which he didn't do often. He tasted like something sweet and fruity. His lips were soft and warm, the sweet smell of his hair so familiar, and whatever had happened, it was all forgotten in a moment. I couldn't wait to get his clothes off of him.

I pulled him over to the couch, and he pushed me backward so that I sat down on it. He got on his knees in front of me and started to undo my pants. It was exactly like him to go straight for what he wanted, but for the first time ever with him, I found myself wanting to slow things down. I wanted to pull him into my lap and kiss him more. I wanted to keep smelling that ridiculous shampoo. But as quickly as he could, he pulled my pants out of the way, and before I could object, his mouth was on me.

It may not have been the best blowjob he had ever given me, but it was certainly the most enthusiastic. He had one hand around the base of my shaft, and the fingers of his other hand were digging into my thigh, painful yet undeniably erotic. His hair was silky-soft in my hands, his mouth was unbelievably warm, and the sounds he was making were enough to drive me wild. He was moving fast, moaning, almost whimpering, and I could tell he was so turned on I might not need to touch him at all.

It had been nearly three weeks since I'd had anybody's hands on me but my own, and needless to say, his mouth was infinitely better. It didn't take me long at all, and my moans seemed to make him even more desperate. As soon as I was done, he stood up, fumbling at the buttons of his own pants. I knew if I had lasted only a little longer, he probably wouldn't have made it even this far. I pushed his hands out of the way, tore them open, and pulled his erection free. I put only the tip in my mouth, thinking I would tease him for a moment, but he grabbed me by the back of the head and pushed himself deep into my mouth. Just one thrust, and he was already crying out with the force of his orgasm.

He usually pulled away quickly. He usually had an off-hand comment to make as he disengaged himself from me. He would go into the bathroom, and when he came back out, we would be companions still but not lovers. This time was different. He had barely even finished when he pushed me back on the couch. Before I knew what was happening, he was in my lap and his arms were tight around my neck.

I hadn't thought before that I missed the intimacy of cuddling after sex, but I realized at that moment how good it felt. It felt right. I wrapped my arms around him and held him against me. I turned my head toward him so I could smell his hair, and whispered, "What's wrong?"

"Three days," he said, his voice a shaky whisper in my ear. "Three days you made me wait. Why?"

"I don't know," I told him honestly. "I guess I was scared."

"I was so horribly afraid that you were never going to call at all."

I held him tighter, felt him trembling in my arms. I kissed the side of his head. "I was afraid of that too."

"I can't change what I am."

"I know," I told him. "I don't know why I ever thought you could."

I HAD a lunch date with my dad the next day. I invited Cole to join us, because it seemed like the polite thing to do, but I was a little bit relieved when he declined. I wasn't sure I was ready to rock the boat between us again so soon.

"So," my dad said to me with a sly grin as I sat down across from him at our usual restaurant, "I take it the two of you made up."

"How do you know that?" I asked.

"Because you're smiling."

"Oh." It made me feel ridiculous, knowing that I was so transparent. I hid behind my menu.

"It seems like your relationship with him is becoming more serious after all?"

I peeked at him over the top of my menu. He wasn't looking at me. He was fiddling with his salad fork. I put my menu down again. "I think it might be." He sighed, and now it was his turn to pick up his menu and hide behind it. "Does that bother you?" I asked.

"Of course not," he said, although I could hear the lie in his voice. "It's none of my business."

"You're right," I said evenly. "It doesn't concern you in the least."

We sat there for a minute, both of us pretending to read the menu again. Finally he put his down. "I don't understand, Jon. You know I've never really understood that you liked men. And now, you find one that's—"

"Don't you dare say it!"

He stopped short, seemed to reconsider his words, and then said, "He's not exactly masculine."

"And if he's not your idea of what a man is, then I might as well be with a woman. Is that it?" I asked, doing my best to keep my voice low in the restaurant, despite the fact that I was so angry I could have punched him.

Luckily for him or maybe for both of us, the waiter showed up then and took our order. Once we were along again, Dad held up his hands in surrender. "Forget I said anything, Jon. Let's change the subject."

"Fine."

"Tell me about work."

"What about it?" I asked, although I knew I was only being difficult because I was still annoyed at him.

"Do you know any more about this restructuring? Where you'll be going, or when it will happen?"

"No." The truth was, I had been doing my absolute best to not think of it at all. "I still don't know anything."

"At the rate they're moving, you'll be able to retire before they can ask you to relocate."

"I couldn't be that lucky."

Date:	November 8
From:	Cole
To:	Jared

Fine! I admit it: we made up! Are you happy now? Jonathan realized the error of his ways and begged for my forgiveness. And if that's not exactly the way it happened, then it's really no business of yours anyway, is it? Now, for heaven's sake, please stop gloating. I've always thought your humility was one of your better qualities. No reason to go and ruin that now.

Of course now I'm busy thinking about some of your other better qualities. I won't elaborate, though, just in case that big bad boyfriend of yours is reading over your shoulder. I'd hate for him to have a coronary on my account.

WE SPENT the next few days in a blissful, honeymoon-type state that was a little bit ridiculous, but fun, too. I was worried, though. November twelfth was my birthday. I had plans to have dinner with my father that evening. I was afraid of hurting Cole's feelings by excluding him but equally afraid of asking him to join us. I didn't even tell him about it until the night of the tenth. "You could come with us if you want," I said guiltily, but he just smiled.

"I don't want you to spend your birthday worrying," he said.

Right or wrong, I was relieved. Although I doubted it would end as badly as it had the time before, I was happy to know it would not be an issue. He spent the night with me on the eleventh and made breakfast for me the next morning. Unfortunately, I was running late, and knew I was going to have to eat fast.

"What took you so long?" he asked when I finally emerged from the bedroom in my suit.

"I'm running out of shirts," I said as I sat down to eat. "I hate shopping." I hated it so much that once I found something I liked, I bought ten of them to avoid having to shop again anytime soon. The problem was, buying everything at the same time meant they all wore out at the same time too. "Are you sure you don't mind that I'm having dinner with my dad?" I asked for at least the fourth time in two days.

"I'm sure."

"Will I see you tonight?"

"I don't know, love. I might be busy."

"Okay," I said, smiling. I knew he would be waiting for me when I got home.

My day at the office was long and tedious, and I didn't have time to go home before meeting my dad for dinner. It was traditional for my father to buy my dinner on my birthday in lieu of a gift, so I was surprised when he showed up with a box. It wasn't wrapped. It was metal, green with flowers on it—not exactly my style—and looked vaguely familiar.

He set it down in front of me without much fanfare. "Is this for me?" I asked.

"It's for your friend."

"My friend?" I asked, surprised.

"It was your mother's. It's been in the kitchen cabinet all these years." He shrugged. "I never knew what to do with it. It seemed wrong to throw it out, but I don't cook, and neither do you." That explained why it looked familiar. It had sat on our kitchen countertop for most of my childhood. It was my mother's recipe box. "I thought the fruitcake might want it."

"His name is *Cole*," I said sternly. He shrugged again, as if Cole's name was inconsequential. And yet he was giving him something that had belonged to my mother, which meant that he respected my decision to be with him—to some extent at least. "You want me to give this to him?"

"Isn't that what I just said?" he asked, and I almost laughed, because he sounded so much like Cole.

"I'm not sure Mom's tater-tot casserole is exactly his style," I said.

I regretted having said it immediately. All at once, his ghosts were upon him again, and he looked down at the table in front of him. "Jon," he said quietly, "I can't hang on to these things forever. He's the only person I know who might want it."

I suspected Cole would laugh when I gave it to him, but my dad didn't have to know that. "Okay, Dad," I said. "I'll give it to him."

We ended up having a good time. He wanted to take me to a game, and he hounded me the entire time to choose between the Suns and the Cardinals, and when I finally chose the Cardinals he asked if he should buy three tickets. I couldn't imagine Cole going to a football game and told him no.

I got home around eight and found Cole reading on my couch, exactly as I had anticipated. "How was dinner?" he asked as he set his book aside.

"Good."

"What did your father give you?" he asked, holding his hand out for the box I was carrying.

"This isn't for me," I said. "It's for you. My dad asked me to give it to you."

"To *me*?" he asked, his eyes wide with astonishment.

"It's silly, I know," I said as he took the box and opened it, "but he wanted you to have it."

He pulled out the first card and looked at it. And then he went very, very still. "Where did this come from?"

"It was my mother's."

"Really?" he asked, turning to me, and the light in his eyes was at once beautiful and painful to see. There was something like hope there, and he might even have been close to tears. It surprised me. Not only did he not think it was silly, but he seemed to be truly touched. How could that little box mean so much to him?

"I doubt there's anything there you want," I said skeptically.

He put the box down on the table and came over to me. He took my head in his hands and stood on his toes a little so he could look in my eyes. "Sometimes you're such a fool," he said. But he said it lightly. He kissed me on the cheek. "Thank you."

"It's from my father," I said, still unsure why it mattered.

"I'll be sure to thank him, too," he said, letting go of me.

He followed me into the bedroom—I couldn't wait to get out of my suit—and I was surprised to find two large shopping bags on my bed. "What are these?" I asked as I hung up my suit jacket.

"You said you needed shirts."

"Well, yeah. But I didn't mean for *you* to buy them!"

"You hate shopping. I don't. I have time. You don't. It seemed like the obvious solution. It's not a big deal, love."

I started looking through the bags. There were at least a dozen shirts. Only three of them were white, which was what I normally wore. And there were five ties in colors that were all well outside my comfort zone. "I'm not sure I can wear these."

"Oh honey, just once in a while, can't you loosen up? Try something new? Maybe live a little?"

A dozen shirts, five ties, and all from a store I knew to be fairly expensive. "This is too much for a birthday gift."

"They're not for your birthday." He pulled a receipt out of his pocket and handed it to me. "I knew you would make a fuss about it, so I'll let you pay me back."

The total on the receipt was high, but not outlandish for what he had bought. And it would save me the trouble of shopping for myself.

"Thank you," I said, "for the clothes *and* for not arguing with me about the money."

"You're welcome, love." He took another envelope off of the dresser and handed it to me. "*This* is your gift. And don't you dare ask to reimburse me for this, too."

"I won't," I said, but I hoped he hadn't gone too overboard. I opened the envelope and pulled out a card. And a gift certificate. "*Skydiving?*" I asked in bewilderment.

"Yes," he said, smiling at me. "I thought you might enjoy it."

Just the thought of it was enough to make my stomach turn somersaults. The idea was horrifying. "Are you kidding?" I asked.

"Not at all," he said, obviously amused.

"Are you coming with me?"

He shuddered dramatically. "Honey, please! Can you even *imagine* me jumping out of a perfectly good airplane?" He shook his head at me as he started to undo the buttons on my shirt. "Sometimes I think you don't know me at all," he teased.

That seemed like the pot calling the kettle black. "What makes you think *I* want to jump out of a perfectly good airplane?"

He stopped and seemed to think about it for a moment. When he looked up at me, his eyes weren't laughing at all. "You're so serious all the time, love. You're the most down-to-earth person I know." He shrugged. "I thought you might long to fly."

Date: December 4

From: Cole

To: Jared

I'm in Paris now for the holidays. Don't act so surprised. I know you think I live only for Jonathan these days, but I assure you, that is not the case. I find it amusing that your sense of romanticism is so heightened now that you have that big mean cop in your life. It's adorable, really.

I came to Paris like I always do for Christmas. I must admit that it's dreadfully dull. I find the company of my usual friends here rather tedious, and I'm just not inclined to hunt down anyone new. I suppose I'm also a little put out because I was supposed to meet my dear mother here, and she of course made an excuse at the last minute, as she always does. I expected it, although I must say, it still annoys me more than it should. At least I no longer have to feel guilty for not having put much thought into her gift.

Speaking of gifts, I have absolutely no idea what to get Jonathan. And lord knows I can't spend too much money on him. Everything about that man is a struggle.

COLE'S announcement shortly before Thanksgiving that he was leaving the country for the holidays took me completely by surprise. When we had first started seeing each other, he had been away as much as he was home. Coupled with my own frequent traveling for work, we had only been able to see each other erratically. I realized now that over the last few months, he had been in town more often than not. And nearly any night that I was in Phoenix, we spent together. I was surprised at how much I missed him.

For better or worse, I was away myself for the better part of the first three weeks of December. Half of that time was spent in Vegas and half in LA. I arrived back in Phoenix on December twenty-second. The good news was there were no plans to send me back out of town for at least a month. I breathed a mental sigh of relief over that.

I spent Christmas Eve with my dad like always. We exchanged gifts and went out to dinner, then attended a midnight mass. I was one of those people who never stepped foot in a church except for on Christmas Eve night, and then only because I couldn't imagine making my dad go alone. Christmas was a time when the ghosts of my mother and sister seemed to haunt him the most. This year seemed worse. I knew he was lonely, but I had no idea how to help. He said goodbye with a voice that was thick with tears. I drove home and went to bed feeling lonely and depressed.

My phone was ringing at six o'clock on Christmas morning, and I dragged myself out of bed, cursing whoever it was until I looked at the display and saw Cole's name. Then I found myself smiling.

"Hello?"

"I know it's terribly early there, honey, but it's four in the afternoon here, and I got tired of waiting."

I couldn't believe how happy it made me just hearing his voice. "I think I forgive you."

"I don't miss you at all."

"I don't miss you either. Please tell me you're coming home."

"Ten more days. Did you have a good Christmas Eve?"

"It was fine," I lied, because I didn't want to tell him how depressing it had actually been. "How about you?"

"I went to the market at the Avenue des Champs-Elysées. I spent the entire time trying to find you the perfect present, and I failed miserably."

"Don't buy me anything," I begged. "Just come home and make me dinner."

"Is that how it is?" he asked jokingly. "You don't miss *me*, but you do miss my cooking?"

"I've been eating frozen pizzas almost every night."

"Honey, I don't know how you ever survived without me," he said, and I laughed.

"I'm not sure either."

We talked for over an hour, and at the end, I couldn't believe how hard it was to hang up the phone. I told myself it was only because it was Christmas Day and I was completely alone. I mostly believed it.

I DIDN'T hear from him again until the first Thursday in January. It was past ten, and I was getting ready to go to bed.

"Hey, sweetie. I just got in."

"It's about time," I said, smiling.

"Did you miss me?"

"Not at all," I told him. "Not even a little bit. Certainly not every single day."

"Since we haven't missed each other these last few weeks, I suppose there's no point in asking you to come and spend the weekend with me."

"I'll be there in time for dinner."

"Is that the best you can do?"

It made me smile, knowing that he wanted to see me as much as I wanted to see him. "I might be able to sneak out a couple of hours early."

"Only if you want to," he said, but I could tell by his voice that he was pleased.

I wasn't able to leave quite as early as I had hoped, but I still made it to his house shortly before five. I knocked on the door, but didn't bother waiting for him to answer. I dropped my bag inside the door, but kept his wrapped present with me. I hadn't seen him in nearly six weeks, and I was actually surprised at how nervous I was. I assumed he would be cooking, but the kitchen was empty. Not only that, there didn't seem to be anything on the stove or in the oven. No tantalizing aromas filled the room.

I found him in the living room, sound asleep. He was wrapped in a blanket, curled into a corner of his couch. His hair had been cut since I had seen him last, and I thought of the butterfly on the back of his neck, which would be completely accessible now. I couldn't wait to put my lips on it. I crept silently up next to him. He never allowed me any intimacy that was not a part of sex, but I hoped he would be too tired to push me away this time.

I leaned close, my nose almost in his hair, and breathed in his sweet scent. I moved the blanket off of his neck, and just barely, put my lips against his skin—

And was immediately slammed in the nose by the side of his head as he startled awake, shoving me away in surprise.

"Ow!" I said, clutching my nose.

"Good lord, Jonny! You about gave me a heart attack!"

My eyes were watering, but I was still pleased that I had shocked him enough to make him say some version of my name. "I didn't mean to startle you," I said around my hand, "but I can't tell you how glad I am that you're home."

"Even though you didn't miss me at all?" he teased.

"Even though."

There were tissues on the table next to him, and he handed me one. "Did I hurt you?"

"Only a little," I said as I dried my eyes. "I suppose it serves me right for sneaking up on you."

"You really did deserve it," he said.

I reached behind me for his gift and presented it to him. It was a bottle of wine, wrapped in silver foil. "Merry Christmas."

"I didn't get you anything," he said as he started to unwrap it.

"I don't mind." His cheeks turned bright red when he saw the label, but he smiled. It was a bottle of Arbor Mist Blackberry Merlot. "You'll never let me live this down, will you?"

"Most definitely not," I teased. "I hope it goes with dinner."

Suddenly the smile disappeared from his face. "Dinner! What time is it?"

"About five," I said, trying to pull him close so I could kiss his neck again.

"I have to make dinner!" he said, trying to push me away, but I had managed to get his arms pinned between us so he didn't have a lot of leverage.

"No, you don't."

"I shouldn't have fallen asleep," he said. He was still pushing against me, but not too hard. I kissed his neck, although I had to fight him a little to do it. "I was just so tired. I usually spend a day or two adjusting to the time, but I wanted so much to see you—" His sudden admission that he wanted to see me was completely uncharacteristic for him, and it surprised me enough that I quit fighting him for a moment.

"Really?" I asked, but he didn't answer me. He pushed me away and stood up, much to my dismay. "Where are you going?" I asked.

"Honey, have you been listening at all? I need to start cooking—"

"No you don't," I said. I stood up and took his hand. "Just sit with me for a minute."

"There's not time—"

I tried to pull him back over to me, but he resisted. "A few more minutes won't hurt." He looked skeptical, and I couldn't help but roll my eyes at him. "Come here," I said, half-teasing but half-frustrated as I tried again to pull him toward me.

"If I don't start dinner now, we'll be eating at a ridiculously late hour."

"I don't care," I told him, and he stopped trying to pull away and looked at me in surprise.

"You don't want me to cook?" he asked, and he sounded hurt.

"It's not that I don't want you to cook," I assured him. "But there's something else I want more."

His hurt look evaporated into a teasing grin. "And you can't wait?" he asked. I could tell he was giving in.

"No," I said. "And you *do* owe me a Christmas present."

"Hmmm…" he said as he stepped closer to me. "I love that you're so impatient, sugar." His hands moved to the buttons on my jeans, but didn't open them. "What would you like?" he asked, giving me that flirtatious look through his bangs.

I pushed his hands away from my groin. "I just want to kiss you," I told him. His reaction was far from what I had hoped for. He looked a little dismayed, and he started to step away, but I put my arms around him and pulled him closer. "Let me kiss you once, and then I'll let you go cook dinner."

He looked reluctant, but he relaxed against me. "Whatever you want, sugar."

I took his face in my hands, my palms against his cheekbones, and my fingers in his silky hair. I tilted his head back and let my mouth find his. I kept my touch light and my lips mostly closed. I had learned early on that he did not like to have my tongue deep in his mouth, so I used only my lips. He wasn't uncooperative, but he wasn't exactly enthusiastic either. His lips barely parted for me.

That was fine. I could be patient.

It wasn't as if I had never kissed him before, but it had mostly been during sex, and even then I could sense that it wasn't something he enjoyed much. He had never allowed me to kiss him like this, as a sensual act unrelated to something more explicit, and I found it unbelievably arousing in a way it hadn't been ever before. I wanted only to keep kissing him and touching him but nothing more. It wasn't that the desire for sex wasn't there—it definitely was. I felt as if I was thrumming with it, every nerve of my body straining for him. And yet, even though it had been nearly six weeks, the idea of sex was still somehow secondary. What I really wanted was simply to feel him, and more than that, to please him. It was something I had felt before with other lovers, but not often and not for a very long time.

I finally felt him relax a little. I moved slow, keeping my touch gentle. I opened my lips a little and lightly brushed my tongue over his lip. His breath caught in his throat. He went a little bit rigid, but only for a second. Then he leaned into me, and I felt his arms go around my waist. He parted his lips a bit more and I allowed my tongue to caress his upper lip as I kissed him. The sensation made him whimper a little, and I heard myself moan in response. I had to restrain myself from pushing further.

I stopped long enough to pull his shirt off of him, and then my own, dropping them on the floor. I wanted to feel his smooth skin against mine, but he took my break as a sign that I was ready to move on, and he started to unbutton my pants. It wasn't his way to waste time with foreplay. He knew what he wanted, and he always went for it without hesitation. But I wasn't about to let this moment go yet.

I grabbed his thin wrists, and he looked up at me in surprise. "Not yet," I whispered.

I kissed him again, lightly touching my lips to his. I brushed the tip of my tongue over his top lip and felt him shiver. I was still holding his wrists, and his hands started to move again toward my groin. His impatience frustrated me. I wanted him to slow down. I wanted to savor what he was giving me. It bothered me that he would not allow me this *one* thing. His fingers fumbled at my buttons again, and I let anger take over for only a moment. I used my grip on his wrists to force his hands away, pushing them hard behind his back and gripping his wrists tight in my hands. I was rougher than I meant to be, but his reaction was immediate and completely unmistakable. His eyes closed and he made a quiet whimpering sound, and he went a little bit limp in my arms, as if his knees couldn't quite hold him up any more. I pulled back a little in surprise so that I could see his face better. I gripped his wrists tighter and pulled him hard against me so that he was trapped in my arms. He practically melted against me with a soft moan that went straight to my groin.

It had never occurred to me before to try to restrain him, but suddenly I saw the path open up before me—the perfect way to get the time I wanted to kiss him and touch him while still pleasing him. It was so simple and so incredibly erotic that it took my breath away.

I pushed him down onto the floor, and he went willingly. I let go of his wrists, pushing him onto his back. I unbuttoned his pants. I still wasn't moving on to sex, but I wanted to be able to feel that part of him against me too. He watched me silently as I did it. I could see the arousal in his eyes, but there was something else there too. Something a little bit like fear but with a great deal of anticipation as well. I pulled his pants off of him, but left my own on.

I took a moment to look at him. I had always been attracted to bigger men, more masculine men. Yet now, at this moment, I had no idea why. His body seemed absolutely perfect. He was so thin. At one point, ten years before we ever met, I imagined I might have counted his ribs with ease. We were both well past that age now, but where the thirties had given so many men extra weight, it had only given him softness. His stomach was still flat, his waist narrow, his legs still slender. His groin was shaved perfectly clean, the skin there soft and smooth. I found myself thinking that even his dick was beautiful— slender and with a pronounced curve toward his stomach when it was hard, as it was now.

I ran my hands up his thighs, over his hips, past his erection, and heard his breathing speed up in response. I slowly moved on top of him so that I could look down at his face. His eyes were wide and apprehensive, but burning, too, with unmistakable need. And his lips— God, I loved his lips. They were perfectly shaped, full and soft. I had never realized how attractive somebody's mouth could be. I leaned down to kiss him again. I wanted to taste every part of his lips. I started at the corner of his mouth, brushing his top lip with the tip of my tongue, softly sucking, moving toward the center. He moaned again, and his hands moved toward my groin.

"No," I hissed at him. I grabbed his wrists again and pushed his hands above his head, holding him down. His reaction was even stronger than before. He moaned and arched against me, grinding his erection into me. He wasn't trying to break free, but it seemed he wanted to bring as much of himself in contact with me as he could. He whimpered again, and I held him there, my weight on his wrists, until he stopped straining and fell back to the floor, panting. I kept my hands on his wrists. I moved back to his lips. I finished tracing the full length of the top one, then began to tease the bottom one. It was full and soft, almost a natural pout, and I sucked it into my mouth, biting gently. He whimpered again, and this time he did strain against my hands, but he wasn't very strong. It was easy for me to keep him pinned to the floor.

I shifted both of his wrists to one hand so my other hand was free to roam down his arms, over his shoulder. I teased one of his nipples with my thumb, and he moaned but didn't try to pull away. My hand moved down his side, over his hip, then underneath him. I cupped one soft buttock in my hand and pulled him tighter against me. I moved away from his lips then. They were red and slightly swollen, and just looking at them made my own arousal burn hotter than before.

I kissed his eyes, then his cheekbone, and then my tongue found the soft shell of his ear and traced its way around the edge. He whimpered again and strained against my grip on his wrists—but only a little. I didn't think he really wanted to break free. He only wanted to reassure himself that I was still holding him captive. It was only enough to renew that feeling of being restrained, and then he relaxed again, although he was breathing hard. I sucked on his earlobe a little, then kissed his jaw.

I brought my free hand forward, over his hip, and although my body was pinning him down, I could feel him straining toward my hand, aching for some real contact. I moved back to his mouth, gently sucking on his lips as my fingertips inched closer to his erection, teasing the soft, naked skin where his patch of hair would have been. He was whimpering, panting, moaning. I let my fingertips lightly brush the base of his shaft, and then teased them up his length. His reaction was almost enough to make me come. He arched against me, his wrists strained against my grip. His breath hissed between his teeth. I pulled my fingers away from his groin, and he relaxed again, panting.

"Oh dear God," he breathed. "If you do that again, it will be all over."

"Oh?" I asked quietly. "Does that mean I should do it again or wait?"

He made a soft noise, almost a laugh. "*Yes!*" he hissed, and I smiled.

I went back to those perfect lips, sucking gently on his lower one, and then moving to truly kiss him. This time when my mouth met his, he actually opened up to me. His lips parted, and he moaned deep in his throat as my tongue touched his. I didn't push too far though. Not enough to make him regret having yielded to me. I pulled back and kissed him with only my lips until I felt the tip of his tongue hesitantly pushing past my own lips. When I allowed it to touch mine again, he moaned and tried to pull his hands free. He made more of an effort this time, and I had to put both hands on his wrists again for a moment. The force of it made him gasp, and he arched his body against mine.

"Please," he whimpered. I didn't answer. It was all I could do at that moment to hold my own arousal in check. I waited for him to relax again, to stop straining against me so that I could go back to holding him with only one hand. When he did, I used my free hand to release my own erection from my pants. I pushed against him, allowing our shafts to rub together. He whimpered again, pulled against my hand but not too hard.

I kissed him, savoring the taste of him as his tongue followed mine, brushing my lips as I had done to him. I wrapped my hand around both of our shafts. He moaned as my fist closed around us. I started stroking us both, slow but not gentle. My grip was tight, but I kept my kiss as soft as I could.

"Oh God," he moaned against my lips, and I knew from the tone of his voice that he was going to come. As my fist reached our heads, rubbing them against each other, he cried out with gut-wrenching relief. He arched against me, and I felt him pulsing in my hand as he came, his cries loud and hoarse in my ear. It was all too much: the sounds he made and the feel of his thin body straining against me and the sensation of my fist, slick from his come, stroking my own erection—I finally let go. I buried my face in his strawberry-scented hair and let my orgasm wash over me while he trembled beneath me. I must have let go of his wrists because I was vaguely aware of him wrapping one arm around my neck and his other hand between us, soft on my own as I finished stroking. When it was over, I put my arms around him, and for some indefinable length of time—maybe only a second or maybe a year—we just lay there on the floor together, shaking.

I kept my face in his silky hair and kissed the side of his head. "See?" I whispered. "Was that so bad?" He laughed out loud, and it seemed like the most beautiful sound in the world.

"To think I spent all that time scouring the market in Paris for your present."

"You'll know better next time."

Once we were both breathing normally again, I sat up. I found my shirt on the floor next to us and used it to wipe myself off, and then him. He watched me silently as I did it. I stood up and held my hand down to help him up off of the floor. He didn't look at me as he found his pants and shirt and put them back on. He was so quiet, I started to worry that I had somehow offended him, but when he was dressed again, he stepped up close to me and looked up into my eyes. His lips were still red and swollen, and I couldn't take my eyes off of them.

"I've never really liked being kissed before," he said quietly. "But nobody's ever done it the way you do."

"I'm glad you're changing your mind," I said as I brushed my thumb over his mouth, "because you have the most beautiful lips I've ever seen. I think I'm falling in love with them." He closed his eyes, and he smiled. A blush was creeping up his cheeks, but for once he didn't try to hide it from me. "Do you want me to take you out for dinner?" I asked.

He opened his eyes again and nodded. "Yes," he said. "I'll cook tomorrow."

"Okay."

"But first." He stood on his toes and wrapped his arms around my neck. "Kiss me just one more time."

I was happy to oblige.

WE HAD dinner at an Italian restaurant not far from his house. It was good, but his cooking was better. I told him that every time, and he always laughed. But I wasn't lying. We never argued about the check anymore. He always let me pay. I knew he didn't understand and found it vaguely amusing that it mattered to me at all. But he always bought the food when he cooked, and paying for our meals the few times we ate out was the least I could do.

That night we went to bed like always, with him on one side and me on the other. The room was dark. He was nothing more than a shadow on the other side of a bed that seemed impossibly big. I resisted the urge to try to touch him, but I listened to his breathing. I could tell he was still awake. I was just starting to drift off when he said suddenly, "I keep thinking about college."

It was a strange statement, and I wished that there was enough light in the room that I could see his face. I waited for him to go on, but he didn't until I asked, "What about it?"

"Do you realize we were there at the same time, right down the road from each other? You and Zach at CU. Jared and I at CSU." He stopped for a moment, and I wasn't sure what to say. It wasn't something I had ever really thought about before. "Tell me about Zach."

"What about him?"

"What was he like?"

"He was funny without really meaning to be. Easygoing. He never took anything seriously. He liked to cook, like you. He wasn't nearly as good at it." That wasn't just flattery. It was the truth. "But he enjoyed it the way you do."

"What happened?"

I had to think about it for a bit—about exactly how to explain what had gone wrong. For years after the split, I kept a rosy picture of our time together in my mind. I let myself believe that we really had been great together, and that our break-up had been the result of a tragic misunderstanding. Since running into him in Vegas, though, I had started to be a little more honest with myself about it.

"I always felt like Zach only needed a push, you know? Like he was drifting along with his eyes closed, and if I could just get him on the right track, he would be perfect." Of course I could see now how wrong that was—to love him, and yet expect him to be something other than what he was. "I pushed and pushed for him to do more with his life. I thought I was helping. All I was really doing was pushing him away." This was met with only silence, and I asked, "What about you?"

"What about me?"

"You told me your life isn't conducive to committed relationships."

"I'm pleased to hear that you were paying attention."

"Have you ever tried?"

"Why would I want to do that?" he asked. "My life is perfect the way it is." I knew he was trying to throw me off of the subject, but I wasn't going to let him.

"What about with Jared?"

"No. It was never like that between us. We were friends, that's all. If it happened that neither of us was seeing anyone else at the time, we would sleep together. But we both knew it wasn't ever going any further than that."

That sounded sad to me, for no reason I could identify, and I said, "I'm sorry."

"Whatever for, love? My friendship with Jared is probably the most perfect relationship I've ever been in. Absolutely no complications. No misunderstandings. No disappointment. I wouldn't change it for anything, and I'm sure he'd tell you the same."

"So there was never anybody else?" He didn't answer, and I wished now even more than before that there was enough light in the room for me to read his expression. Of course, if it had been light in the room, he never would have allowed the conversation to go this far to begin with. The darkness gave him cover. I reached across the bed and put my hand on his arm, hoping he would allow me at least that much intimacy. I should have known better. He pulled away, rolling onto his side, so that I lost contact with him, and I tried not to be disappointed.

"Goodnight, love," he said.

And that was the end of that.

I GOT up early the next morning and went for a jog. When I came back, he was just coming out of the shower with a towel around his waist and his hair damp.

"I'll make breakfast in a bit," he said.

"Only if you want to." I still felt the need to say that, even knowing that he never did *anything* that wasn't his own idea. If he thought I expected it, he would have refused to do it out of sheer stubbornness. "Otherwise, we can eat out or I can go get donuts."

That last was said as a joke more than anything. He was the only person I'd ever met who didn't like fried sugary things, and sure enough, he rolled his eyes at me. "Definitely not."

I stripped out of my jogging clothes, intending to take a shower, but before I could get into the bathroom he said, "Wait!"

"What?" I turned to find him sitting on the bed, still wearing only a towel. And the tent that was forming under it told me why he had stopped me, along with the lecherous grin on his face.

"No need to shower yet, love," he said. "Why don't you come over here for a bit?"

"I just ran four miles," I said, although I did cross over to where he was sitting on the bed. "Are you sure you don't want me to shower first?"

He kissed my stomach, and his soft fingers wrapped around my stiffening cock. "I'm sure," he said, looking up at me with a heat burning in his eyes that made me weak in the knees.

I pushed him back on the bed. I opened his towel, exposing his erection so I could stroke him while he stroked me. I kissed his neck. His hair was still wet from the shower. "But you're so clean," I said, rubbing against him. "Aren't you worried I'll get you all dirty?"

He laughed and wrapped his legs around me. "I'm looking forward to it, actually." He pushed my hand off of his erection, and I felt his shaft against mine. He wrapped his thin hand around us both and started to stroke. He put his other arm around my neck. "Kiss me again," he said quietly.

He didn't need to ask me twice. I gently bit at his lower lip, and he moaned in response. I loved the sounds he made—they started out soft but became louder and more urgent as he got closer to the end, and they always turned me on. Hearing his breathless cries was one of my favorite parts of sex with him. His soft hand was still moving on us, and I was debating if I wanted to stop him so that I could get a condom and lube or if I wanted to let him finish this way when my phone rang.

"Shit!" I said, as his hand came to a stop.

"You're not really going to answer that, are you?"

"I have to," I told him as I tried to disentangle myself from him. It wasn't working though, because he wasn't cooperating. His legs were still wrapped tight around my hips, and he didn't seem inclined to let go. "It's either a client or my boss," I said.

"Okay, love," he said, grinning wickedly up at me. But he didn't let go. I tried to stand up, and managed to drag him an inch or two. He reached over and grabbed the headboard, still grinning at me, which brought us both to a stop, and I quit pulling against him.

My phone rang again. "You have to let me go," I said, although I couldn't help but smile back at the mockery I saw in his eyes.

"Darling, you have *got* to learn to relax. What would be the harm in letting it go to voice mail? You can call them back in a few minutes—"

"It will be longer than a 'few minutes', and you know it," I teased, and he laughed. But his legs fell from around my hips, and I was able to stand up. I took the phone into the living room to answer, because seeing him lying there naked and waiting was too much of a distraction.

"This is Jonathan."

"Jonathan, it's Marcus."

My gut reaction was dread. Marcus never called me with good news. But I tried to keep my voice light. "Good morning, Marcus."

"Nguyen's mother-in-law died last night."

"I'm sorry to hear that," I said, although I hardly knew Nguyen at all. And even though I knew it was selfish, I couldn't help but wonder why the death of his wife's mother had anything to do with me.

"He was supposed to leave for San Diego on Monday, but now he has to fly to Miami with his wife. I'm going to need you to cover."

Shit. I closed my eyes. I counted to five. I started to count to five again.

"Jon?" he interrupted me. "Are you there?"

"Yes, sir. The thing is, this is supposed to be downtime for me. You told me before Christmas that I wouldn't have to travel until the end of the month, and I was really counting on having that time to—"

"Jonathan, I'm sorry if this is inconvenient, but I really need you to take care of this. I'll email you the account summary. You'll need to leave Monday."

"There's nobody else who can do it?"

"I want it to be you."

I sighed, not even caring if he heard me. "How long?" I asked.

"Two weeks, max. Maybe less."

Two weeks. I hadn't seen Cole since before Thanksgiving. Six weeks apart, and now we would have only one more night together before I had to leave again. But what could I do? "Yes, sir. I'll take care of it."

"Thanks, Jonathan. Enjoy the rest of your weekend."

I hung up with a heavy heart. I didn't want to go. More than ever, I wanted to stay home. With Cole. The remainder of my weekend looked darker knowing that I would be saying goodbye to him again the next day.

"So?" he asked mockingly when I came back into the bedroom ten minutes later. "I hope it was worth it."

"It definitely wasn't. One of the other accountants had a death in the family," I told him as I lay back down next to him. "I have to cover for him next week."

"What does that mean exactly, love?"

"It means I'll be leaving for San Diego on Monday."

"Honey, I just got home!"

"I know," I said. "I'm sorry." He had to hear how much I meant it, too.

He was quiet for a moment, and then suddenly he sat up. He sat across my hips, looking down at me. "Why you, love? Do all of the *Senior Liaison Account Directors*—" he always used that mocking tone when he mentioned my job—"get sent out of town at the drop of a hat?"

"Yes and no. It happens to all of us, but it probably happens to me more."

"And why is that?"

"Because most of the other guys are married and have families."

"So your free time has less value than theirs, simply because of your lifestyle?"

"Well, I…." I wasn't really sure what to say to that. I hadn't ever thought about it that way before.

"And this trip now—it's not even your client, right, love?"

"Right."

"And what would happen if you said no?"

"Are you telling me I should have?"

"Of course not. I'm just curious. Would you be fired?"

"No."

"Is there any benefit for you if you take it? Do you get paid more?"

"I'm on salary. I suppose it might be taken into account when it's time for bonuses, but other than that, no."

He shook his head at me. "I'm sure I'll never understand you." He trailed his slender fingers through the hair on my chest. It tapered to a point around my navel, then down from there, and his fingers followed it. "I don't think I should have to share you with your clients," he said.

I grabbed him and rolled, flipping him onto his back and landing on top of him so I could look down into his laughing eyes. "I don't think I should have to share you, either." Only it wasn't his job I had to share him with. It was his other lovers.

He smiled up at me. "Only when I leave town, love. When I'm in Phoenix, I'm all yours."

"Really?" I asked in surprise.

"Really. Now…." He wrapped his legs around my hips and pushed against me suggestively. "Where were we?"

Date:	January 18
From:	Cole
To:	Jared

Sweets, you don't have to tell me that ski season is already half over. I know! And I know I haven't been to Colorado even once. I would like to tell you that I'll be there eventually, but I'm just not sure it will happen this year. Well, what's the point when Coda's hottest bachelor is no longer eligible? That will teach you to enter monogamous relationships with angry cops! Anyway, I've barely seen Jonathan in weeks. He should be home any day now, and I'm so glad. I know you're going to try to read way too much into that. But trust me, Sweets. It's not what you think.

I WAS stuck in San Diego for nearly two weeks, and I found myself thinking of Cole the entire time. It had surprised me to learn that he was no longer seeing anybody else in Phoenix. I had assumed from day one that I was not the only man he saw when he was home. Of course, I hadn't ever known how many others there were or how often he saw them, and I had never wanted to ask, at first because it was none of my business and I didn't really care, and later because I was afraid of what the answer would be. I hadn't quite realized how much it bothered me until the moment when I found out I was wrong.

I also couldn't stop thinking about how it felt to hold him down while I kissed him. It turned me on every single time I thought about it, which wasn't necessarily good since I was on a business trip. I debated calling him and asking him to fly to San Diego to keep me company, but in the end, I didn't have the nerve. It wasn't his idea, and I was sure he would say no.

I got back into Phoenix early Friday afternoon. As soon as I was off the plane, I called Cole.

"Hey, sugar," he said when he answered. "Are you finally home?"

"I am. Why? Did you miss me?"

"Not even a little bit."

"Then you won't mind that I have to go to the office before I come home."

"Honey, you've been gone for twelve days! It really can't wait until tomorrow?"

"It can't. But it should be quick. I'll be home by five."

"Well," he said, "I'm awfully busy tonight anyway, sugar. Maybe I'll call you tomorrow."

"Okay," I said, smiling. I wasn't fooled.

I was still grinning like an idiot when I got to Marcus's office, and I had to make an effort to get my mind off of Cole and back to business.

"Come on in, Jon," Marcus said. "Close the door."

"Yes sir."

"Jon, we're getting close to having this 'restructuring' bullshit wrapped up," he told me, once I was sitting down. "We're letting the Senior Liaison Account Directors pick where they're going based on seniority. Jensen, MacDonald, Nguyen, and Simmons were ahead of you, so now it's your turn."

I hadn't really thought much about the restructuring since our last meeting, and I found that the misgivings I felt before were only amplified now. The thought of moving was completely unappealing, and I was being honest enough with myself at that moment to admit that it was largely because of Cole.

"What are my choices?" I asked.

"Utah, Vegas, or Colorado."

"Shit!" I said before I could stop myself. Luckily, Marcus wasn't the type to be offended. I put my head in my hands, closed my eyes, and counted to five. I counted to five again. Then I considered my options.

It figured that Arizona and the three California locations would have gone first. Of the three that were still available, I felt Colorado really was the best choice. If only I could convince myself that it would not be a step backward. Utah was a beautiful state, but seemed like a bad choice for anybody who wanted to live openly as a homosexual. Maybe that was a poor assumption on my part. Maybe I would find more acceptance there than I thought. But I wasn't sure I wanted to risk it.

Which left Sin City.

"You don't have to decide right now, Jon. Take the weekend to think about it. I'll need your decision by Monday," Marcus said. That came as a relief, although I doubted having two more days to mull it over would make my decision any less painful.

I drove home in a bit of a daze. I was trying to convince myself that the knot of trepidation in my stomach was unwarranted. Maybe Vegas wouldn't be so bad. I had spent a lot of time there over the past few years. I knew my way around, to some extent at least. I knew where to eat, but the restaurants were all overpriced, and I liked Cole's cooking better. I knew where to shop, even though I hated to do it. And I knew where to go when I wanted to get laid. Although right at that moment, I had absolutely no desire to go to any of those places ever again.

I didn't know what to tell Cole. And more importantly, I had no idea how he would react. He might be upset. He might offer to visit—it wasn't as if he couldn't afford it—and I would become nothing more than another "friend" in his travels. On the other hand, it was equally possible he would cut me loose and find somebody to take my place without a second thought. I wasn't sure how I would handle it if that were the case.

Despite his words on the phone, I wasn't surprised to find Cole's car in my driveway when I got home. I found him in the kitchen of course, chopping vegetables, barefoot like always. I had been thinking about him nonstop for days, yet my pleasure at seeing him was tainted by the dread I felt over having to leave Phoenix in the near future.

"Not so busy after all, I see," I said as I wrapped my arms around him from behind. He was stiff in my arms, but he didn't pull away.

"I decided I could squeeze you in."

I ran my hand down his stomach to his groin and kissed the butterfly on the back of his neck. "I sure hope there's some secondary meaning to those words," I said, and he laughed.

"It's possible." He finally pushed me away, like he always did. "After dinner."

I left him to cook while I showered and unpacked. There was a bottle of his strawberry shampoo in my shower, and it made me smile. I actually took the lid off and smelled it, just because it made me happy to do it. Then I remembered my conversation with Marcus, and my heart sank.

Coming out of the shower, I was met by the smell of what I suspected was étouffée. It was one of Cole's favorites, and I knew that meant a Rioja Crianza to drink. I followed my nose into the kitchen and discovered that I was right. The wine was already open. I resisted the urge to kiss him again as I passed. I poured a glass and took it with me back into the bedroom to finish unpacking.

I was halfway through the glass before it occurred to me that it was a Spanish red—Zach's favorite. I waited for the pain to come and the regret. I steeled myself for the melancholy that always followed. But this time….

It didn't.

It was a surprise to me to realize that the tiny sense of loss that had come with the thought of Zach for ten years now was gone at last. There was nothing but fond remembrance in its place. I had spent so many years of my life looking back at what might have been, but now I realized that I no longer cared. It was like an epiphany. A revelation. An overwhelming feeling of liberation that almost made me giddy.

I truly felt like I was home. And it felt so good, having Cole there with me. It felt *right*.

And then like a punch in the gut came the realization that it couldn't last. That sometime in the near future, I would be moving out of the state. What would happen then?

"Good lord," Cole called from the other room. "Are you coming out, or are you going to make me eat alone?"

He couldn't ever just tell me it was ready. He always had to turn it around and make it sounds as if I should have known, and I couldn't help but smile. "I'm a little busy," I teased.

"That's fine, love. More for me."

Of course I wasn't busy at all, and I went into the dining room to join him. The food was amazing, like it always was, and I thought about the first time he had made me étouffée at my condo in Vegas. It was a warm memory for me. But on its tail came the realization that I would be moving there for good, very soon.

And he wouldn't be there.

"Are you going to tell me what's wrong," he asked, startling me out of my thoughts, "or are you just going to sit there and stew all night?"

And even when he was scolding me like I was a petulant child, it made me smile. "Am I that transparent?" I asked.

"Like crystal."

I debated for a moment how to tell him, but in the end, there weren't that many options. The only thing to do was say it. "My company is being restructured, and they want me to relocate."

He didn't say anything. He barely reacted at all, except to go very, very still. "How long have you known this?" he finally asked.

"I've known for months that it was a possibility. But I didn't know for sure until today."

He seemed to think about that for a moment, and then suddenly that strange stillness was gone, and he was completely himself again. "Where will you go?"

"I have my choice of Colorado, Utah, or Vegas."

"I assume you'll choose Colorado, then."

"No."

"Why not?" he asked in surprise. "You lived there before. It seems like the obvious choice."

"It does, but...." I wasn't really sure what to tell him. I didn't want to talk about Zach. "It's part of my past, and I don't want to go back."

And I saw in his eyes that he understood. And more than that, it pleased him. He tried to hide it. He looked quickly down at his plate. But it was there, just the same.

"Vegas or Utah, then," he said. "Which will it be: Zion or Sin City?"

"I suppose it will be Vegas."

"It's a good choice, love," he said, keeping his head down so that his hair hid his expression from me. I realized it was something he had done frequently when we were first seeing each other. He did it less often with me now. "All-you-can-eat bacon really is preferable to eternal salvation, isn't it?"

We didn't talk about it for the rest of the evening. He kept up a constant stream of small talk, and I had a feeling he was deliberately not allowing me to revisit the subject. He fell asleep on the couch next to me, like he often did. I nudged him awake, and he followed me into the bedroom. He got in on his own side of the bed, which would have been normal if we had already had sex. But it was unusual for him to be uninterested on my first night back. I didn't push it. I got in on my side and turned out the light.

We lay in the silent darkness for a while, and I could tell by his breathing, and his stillness, that he wasn't asleep.

"Do you want to go?" he finally asked.

"No."

"But you will." It wasn't even a question.

"What else can I do?"

He was quiet for a moment. I wished I could see his face to get some idea of what he was thinking, but I knew he had waited until now to have this conversation specifically so he could keep me from seeing... something. "I don't know, love," he finally said. "You tell me: what else can you do?"

"Nothing."

"If you say no, you'll be let go?"

"No."

"No? They won't fire you? Then what's the problem? Why go if you don't have to?"

"It will mean accepting a demotion."

He was still for a moment, and then suddenly he sat up. He sat across my hips so that he could look down at me, although in the darkness, my expression had to be as hidden from him as his was from me. "Would you lose money? Is that what this is about? Can you not afford a pay cut?"

"No!" I hated when he talked about money. He was ridiculously wealthy, and his idea of how much money normal people had was somewhat skewed. Sometimes it seemed that in his mind, everyone who wasn't a millionaire was only pennies away from living on the street. "I have plenty of money," I said in irritation. "That has nothing to do with it."

"Then what, love? Make me understand. Why would you choose to do something you don't want to do simply because they ask it? Why would you *not* choose the option that makes you happy?"

"I haven't worked my ass off for this company for nine years just to accept a demotion!"

He sat there, perfectly still, looking down at me. And then suddenly he rolled away. He moved back to his side of the bed, and I could see just enough in the darkness to determine that his back was to me as he pulled the covers up to his chin.

"That's it?" I asked, annoyed. "You have nothing else to say?"

He sighed. "You accept that the shadows on the wall are real, love. I have no idea how to make you turn around and see the light."

"What the hell's that supposed to mean?"

"Nothing at all. Goodnight."

I hardly slept that night. I wanted to wake Cole up and make him talk to me. I wanted to make love to him. I wanted to hold him. But as always, I respected the walls he maintained, and I let him sleep. We passed our morning in stiff, awkward formality. It felt wrong, and it made me sad. It was as if the eight months we had been seeing each other had never been and we were little more than strangers.

After breakfast, he showered, and I sat on my bed watching him while he shaved and got dressed. He was silent the entire time, watching me with wary eyes, but finally he turned to me with a dramatic sigh. "Good lord, love. Stop sulking and say whatever it is you want to say."

His brusqueness made me smile. "Cole, I need to know...." I trailed off, not knowing how to ask the question that was in my heart. Not knowing if he would answer or if I would want to hear it if he did.

"You need to know *what*, love?"

I couldn't even look at him when I said it for fear that I would see only mockery in his eyes. I looked down at the floor between my feet instead. "I need to know what will happen to us if I move."

He didn't answer at first. We were frozen there, unmoving, for what felt like a painfully long time. I couldn't meet his eyes. I watched his bare feet instead. It was completely quiet in the room, and the silence seemed to stretch on forever. I started to debate telling him to forget I had even asked. But finally he walked over to me, and I felt his featherlight touch on the back of my head, his fingers weaving into my hair. It was such an unusual thing for him to touch me casually, and I found that there was a lump in my throat. "I don't know, love," he said. "The only thing I know for sure is I live here. Vegas and Utah are both easy trips. But Phoenix is my home."

I looked up at him, hoping to see something in his eyes that would help, but he had his walls firmly in place. I could see nothing through them. "Do you want me to stay?"

"Please don't try to make this about me. Whether you go or stay, it needs to be what you want."

"You're not helping. Tell me what *you* want."

"I want you to choose what feels right." He took his hand from my hair and moved across the room, away from me, like he always did. "I can't help you, Jonny. You have to figure this out on your own."

I HAD a lunch date with my father, and although I invited Cole, he declined. I met my dad at the restaurant. He talked about basketball and about taking me to a game in a week or two if I was in town. He talked about having to wait three weeks to see his doctor and how the barber he had been using for the last ten years had retired and about the fact that his office wanted him to take a vacation, but he didn't know where to go. And all the while, I was thinking about Vegas.

It took me a while to get up enough courage to say the words. I was pretty sure that I had never said them before. Certainly not since turning sixteen. "Dad," I finally said, interrupting his monologue about whether or not he should join a health club. "I need your advice."

He stared at me for a moment, completely dumbfounded. "Really?" he said at last in amused surprise. "Is the apocalypse upon us?"

I had to smile a little at that. "Not as far as I know."

"Thank goodness. I'm hoping to have sex at least one more time in my life."

What the hell? My father had never, *ever* mentioned his own sex life to me before, and I felt myself blush. I stormed ahead before he could mention it again. "I've told you that my company might be restructuring. It took them months to get it together, but it's down to the wire now, and I have to decide what to do."

"What are your choices?"

"I can move. I have my choice of Utah or Vegas." I didn't even mention Colorado. "Or I can stay and accept a demotion."

"Utah or Vegas? That's not much of a choice."

"I know."

"It's simple, Jon. Do you want to move?"

"No."

"Then don't."

My whole life, and he boiled it down to one question? It just wasn't that easy. "I've worked so hard, Dad," I explained. "I've been with this company for nine years now. I worked myself up from the ground floor. Do you really think I should let them demote me?"

"It's not 'letting' them do anything, Jon. It's your decision." He was quiet for a moment, watching me, waiting for me to respond, but I didn't know what to say. I felt exhausted and beaten. I wished I could go home and crawl into bed and sleep until it was all over.

"Jon," he said at last, "it seems to me your choice boils down to this: your happiness or your pride. You can let your pride rule. Forfeit your life here to chase your next promotion. Or you can forget all that and do what makes you happy." He shrugged. "I want you to stay. But it can't be about me."

I couldn't even look at him. I kept my eyes on the table and said, "I don't think I want to leave Phoenix."

"What does Cole think?"

I closed my eyes, tried to block out the chaos in my head and in my heart. "He won't say."

A moment of silence, and then he said quietly, "That's good."

"How is that good, Dad?" I asked in annoyance. "It doesn't help me one bit."

"He's not using your feelings for him, or his for you, to make you do what he wants. He's trying to let you choose for yourself." He shrugged. "I think that's admirable."

"I don't want to leave him," I said, and a weight I hadn't quite known was there lifted from my shoulders. It was such a relief, just to say it—to finally admit out loud that he was a factor.

"Are things that serious?"

"No," I said. "Not yet. But I feel like I'm on the right path, Dad. And I haven't felt that way in a long time. I want to be able to see where it leads." He looked away from me, looking at some point over my left shoulder. "Is that so wrong?"

He sighed, and met my eyes again. "No," he said gently. "It's not wrong. If you were staying only for him, I might say it was foolish. But this is your home, Jon. I…." He had to look down at the table again to say it. "You're all I have left, Jon, and I don't want you to go. But I know you can't stay for me either. If you stay, stay for *you*. But the important thing is if you *leave*, then leave for *you* too. Don't throw away your life here simply because they say you should."

"I don't know how to decide."

"Quit thinking about it so much. You're trying to make this about logic, but some things can't be quantified. I know that's counterintuitive for you, but"—he shrugged—"my advice is 'stop thinking'. Pick the option that *feels right*."

"That's exactly what Cole said."

He smiled, shaking his head. "I think I might like that fruitcake after all."

TO MY surprise, Cole wasn't waiting for me when I got home. I had fully expected that we would spend the rest of the weekend together—we usually did when we were both in town.

I called him on his cell phone, and his voice when he answered was wary. "Hello, love."

"Are you coming back for dinner?" I asked.

"I don't think so."

"Then tomorrow?"

"No."

"Cole, are you mad? I'm sorry if—"

"Honey, I'm not mad."

"Then what?"

"You have to tell Marcus your decision on Monday?"

"Yes," I said, unsure what that had to do with dinner tonight.

"If you like, I'll be waiting for you when you get home."

"Why can't I see you tonight?"

"Because I can't help you, love. I know you want me to. But I can't. You need to decide what's right for you."

"But Cole—" I said, feeling like he had abandoned me, but he interrupted me.

"Whatever your decision is," he said quietly, "we'll work it out."

I sighed. I still wished he would say more, but I also felt better hearing those final words. We would work it out. "Okay," I said.

"I'll have a glass of wine waiting, and I'll make the Bolognese. I know how much you like it." That made me smile. It *was* one of my favorites. "We haven't had dessert in an awfully long time, love," he said, and it was good to hear that mocking tone back in his voice. "You're not getting out of it on Monday."

I laughed. "Why in the world would I want to?"

I RATTLED around my house all afternoon, and most of Sunday. Finally, around four, I called Julia.

"I'll buy beer and pizza if you'll keep me company," I said after she answered.

"An offer I can't refuse," she said, laughing. "I'll be there in an hour."

We sat in my living room with the beer and pizza on the coffee table between us and talked. She told me about her husband's job and her kids—the oldest was in the drama club, and the youngest played soccer, and the middle one didn't seem to do much of anything. She talked about her brother Tony in California, who couldn't seem to stay faithful to any man and then couldn't understand why they left him. She asked about Cole and about what shows we had seen recently and about work. And finally she asked, "So what's bothering you?"

"What makes you think anything is?" She didn't even bother to answer. She finished her beer and opened another one. So I told her my dilemma. "And all Cole or my dad will say is that I should do what feels right," I concluded. "And I have no idea what to do."

She sat there looking at me for a long time. I started to squirm a little under her obvious scrutiny. "Here's what I know, Jon," she said at last. "We've been talking for the last three hours. And every single time you say Cole's name, you smile." And as if I had to prove her right, I did it again. "And every time you say 'Vegas'"—I felt the smile leave my face—"you stop." She shrugged. "It's that simple." She put down her beer and stood up to leave.

"You're going?"

"I have to get home, Jon. But thanks for dinner."

"You're welcome."

"Let me know what you decide."

She left, and I sat there thinking about what she had said. It was so ridiculously simple, and it seemed like a foolish thing to base my decision on. But she was right. The thought of moving to Vegas had kept my stomach tied in knots all weekend. Every single time I thought about it, it made me wince.

I leaned back on the couch. I closed my eyes. And for the first time, I really thought about the alternative. I quit worrying about the stigma of accepting a demotion, and I thought about *the job*.

As a *Junior* Liaison Account Director, I would be working from our Phoenix office to support the guys who were still in the field. It would mean phone calls, but mostly during business hours. It would mean less pay, but not significantly. It would mean less travel.

I stopped there for a moment.

Not just *less* travel, but almost no travel at all.

And that knot in my chest started to ease.

I would be home almost all the time. I could actually use my show tickets instead of giving them all to Julia. I could spend more time with my dad. Not only would that make me happy, it would make *him* happy, and that was important to me. And not traveling would mean a return to a *normal* life. Not living out of suitcases half the time. Maybe I could even get a cat again.

And Cole?

I felt myself smile.

Yes. And Cole would be there too, hopefully waiting for me when I got home.

I thought about the way I had felt on Friday as I unpacked. How good it felt to be home again after so long with Cole in the kitchen cooking dinner. I remembered thinking so clearly that it simply felt *right*.

Julia, my dad, Cole—they had been telling me all along. It really was that simple.

Monday morning, I drove to work feeling good. I told Marcus my decision. He was surprised, but he assured me it wouldn't be a problem. It would still be several weeks before the change took effect, and until then, I would still be traveling like always. But now, I saw a light at the end of the tunnel. It looked like salvation.

After work I went home where Cole was waiting, barefoot in my kitchen. I told him my decision, and although he turned quickly away to hide his reaction, I saw the relief there on his face.

I didn't care about dinner. I turned off the stove. I took his hand and led him to the bedroom….

And everything about it felt *right*.

Date:	January 24
From:	Cole
To:	Jared

It seems Jonathan won't be moving after all. I can't tell you how relieved I was to hear him say the words. And the fact that I was relieved frightened me.

I WAS surprised when only a week later, Cole informed me that he was leaving town. I had returned home from work like always to find him cooking in my kitchen. We had a nice dinner, and then I did the dishes and caught up on some work while he read on my couch. And then we went in the bedroom and made love. And it wasn't until afterward, when we were lying in the dark, on opposite sides of the bed like always, that he told me.

"I'm leaving for New York tomorrow."

"You're *what?*" I asked, stunned. "Why?"

"It's just time, love. That's all."

"How long will you be gone?"

"I don't know really. A week, I suppose. Maybe two."

I resisted the urge to ask bitterly if he would be seeing Raul while he was there. "We've only had a few nights together since before Thanksgiving," I said, trying not to sound like I was whining. "Do you have to go now?"

"I really do, love," he said, but there was something strange in his voice. I wished once again that I could see his face. He always waited until the lights were out to bring these topics up.

"Is everything all right?" I asked him.

"Of course," he said, but I wasn't sure I believed him.

I GOT up the next morning and went for a jog. When I came home, he was gone. That was it. He didn't even say goodbye. I tried not to be hurt. I tried not to be angry. I did my best not to imagine him with Raul. I partially succeeded at the first two, but at the last, I failed miserably. I told myself over and over again that I was being an idiot. There had never been any pretense that our relationship was exclusive. I had known about his other lovers from day one. So why did I care so much now?

We had been seeing each other for approximately nine months. In the first two or three months of that time, I had still seen other men occasionally. Cole had been out of town a lot, and I never knew when he would return. It hadn't been a big deal. But at some point over the summer, I had quit wanting to see anybody else. It wasn't that I ever made the decision to be exclusive with him. It wasn't out of any false sense of faithfulness. It was only that what I had with him was good. It was comfortable and exciting and so much more fulfilling than the casual flings I had been making do with up until then. I simply didn't have any desire to look elsewhere. I always knew he would be back eventually, and I chose to wait. It was that simple.

But now I reminded myself that I had other options as well. I could go to a club. I could go to the bathhouse. There was no reason to think I couldn't have sex with somebody else if I chose to. It would do me good to get out there and get laid—pick up some anonymous stranger and fuck each other's brains out. I knew it was exactly what I needed to take my mind off of Cole. Every time I jacked off in the shower, I told myself, "Today I'm going to have sex with somebody who isn't him."

I never did.

I refused to call him, because I didn't want to seem desperate. He never called me either. That was fairly normal for him when he was gone. Still, every time the phone rang, I couldn't help wishing that it was him.

He had been gone a week when Marcus informed me that I was going to Vegas the following Monday. He estimated I would be there seven to ten days. As ridiculous as it was, it created a bit of a dilemma for me. I felt that it was only polite to let Cole know where I was. On the other hand, it seemed obvious that he was trying to distance himself from me, and giving him updates on my whereabouts seemed pathetic. On my second day in Vegas, I broke down and sent him a text message. It said only, "In Vegas." Nothing more.

The week was long. I was beginning to realize how much I hated Vegas. And how much I hated my clients. And how much I hated my job. I began to anticipate the day my demotion would take effect and I would be able to stay home. We worked late on Friday and agreed to meet again early the next morning. It was after eight by the time I got home.

I knew the minute I walked into my condo that something was strange. I couldn't put my finger on what it was. Only that it felt different. It felt... *right.* I stopped just inside the door and looked around. And then I saw all the pieces, and everything fell into place. A wine glass on the coffee table, a book with a French title on the couch, shoes by the door. And I tried to tell myself that the happiness I felt at seeing them was only because it would make my last few days in Vegas more fun. There was nothing more to it than that.

He was just taking off his shirt when I walked into the bedroom. His back was to me. And though I may have wanted to, I could not deny the way my pulse skipped a beat when I saw him. "What are you doing here?" I asked, and he jumped.

"Good lord, love, don't sneak up on me like that!" He turned away from me, and I knew it was so I couldn't see that he was blushing. "I was getting ready to take a shower."

"I thought you were in New York."

"I was," he said, still not looking at me, "and I know I should have called. It's terribly inappropriate of me to barge in on you like this."

I crossed over to him and wrapped my arms around him from behind. He was stiff in my arms, but he didn't push me away. I buried my face in his silky hair and breathed in that scent I loved so much.

"You don't care if it's inappropriate or not," I said, "and you know I don't mind. And even if I *did* mind, it wouldn't stop you. You'd probably do it just to annoy me." He still hadn't relaxed in my arms, but he hadn't pushed me away yet either. I kissed the back of his head. "How long are you staying?"

"I don't know yet. As long as you're here, I guess. I...." He stopped, sounding hesitant, which wasn't like him at all. "I wanted to see you," he finally said, and it almost sounded as if he was surprised at his own words.

"Thank God," I sighed, "because I haven't missed you one bit."

"I got in a couple of hours ago. I thought you'd be here. I was worried maybe you'd gone out, to the bathhouse, or...." He let his words trail away, as if he hadn't meant to say them at all.

I debated telling him that I wanted nobody but him, but I feared it would only make me sound ridiculous. "We had to work late," I said instead. "It's not going well. I have to be back in by seven tomorrow."

He turned in my arms and looked up at me flirtatiously, although his cheeks were still red. "New York was no fun at all."

I leaned down to kiss him, lightly sucking on his lower lip. "What about Raul?" I asked, trying hard to keep my tone light.

He put his arms around my neck. "Like I said, love," he whispered against my lips. "No fun at all."

I kissed him, and he let me. He tasted like something fruity and sweet, and I realized it was probably five-dollar wine. It only made me want to kiss him more.

I felt his hands fumbling at my belt, and I gently pushed them away. I took his face in my hands and kissed him again, making sure not to push too much, to allow him to decide how deep it went. But I wanted to keep tasting him. He kissed me back for a moment, but then I felt his hands at my belt again. I grabbed his wrists and pinned them behind his back. His eyes when he looked up at me were huge and wary.

"Are you really so impatient, or are you trying to make me hold you down again?" I asked.

He strained against me, his breath shaky. "Yes."

I couldn't help but smile. I held his wrists tighter and bent to kiss him lightly. "Yes to which?" I asked in a whisper before biting gently on his lower lip. He moaned and let himself go limp against me. I shifted both of his thin wrists to one hand. I used the other to unbutton his pants. I slid my hand inside of them, rubbing his swollen dick through the silky fabric of his briefs. "Well?" I whispered against his lips. "Which is it?"

He made a ragged sound that was almost a laugh. "Both."

I pushed him roughly back onto the bed and with one quick motion pulled my tie from around my neck. I climbed on top of him, using my weight to hold him down, and pulled one of his arms toward the headboard.

"A tie?" he asked, although his voice was thick and breathy. "Isn't that rather cliché, love?"

I secured the knot around one wrist, looped the tie around one of the posts on the headboard. "It may be," I told him, "but it's very effective." I grabbed his other hand and brought it toward the headboard. I knotted the other end around his wrist. There was about a foot of fabric between his hands, where it looped around the frame of the headboard, so he had some slack to move around in, but it would keep him from being able to rush me.

I stood up and got rid of the rest of my suit as quickly as I could. He watched me in silence, his eyes wide and apprehensive, but the bulge in his pants told me he was turned on as well. I pulled them off of him. It was incredibly arousing, looking down at him, knowing that he was restrained and that I could do whatever I wanted to him, within reason of course. The crazy thing was I didn't want to do anything rough or domineering. I only wanted more time to touch him and to kiss him. I wondered how many other people had to restrain their partners in order to have more foreplay.

I moved on top of him so I could look down into his wide eyes. "Now," I said, my voice thick with arousal, "what should I do with you now that I have you tied down?"

He wrapped his legs around me, pulling me down against him. "Fuck me," he whispered, and I laughed.

"You're too impatient. That's what got you into this, remember?" I teased.

"Please," he said, grinding against me.

"Not yet." I kissed his neck and his ear. I caressed his hip. I loved the way it seemed to fit against my palm so perfectly. I let my hand wander up his side and heard him catch his breath. I traced his ear with my tongue. I kept my touch light as I slowly moved my hand up to his nipples. I caressed them for just a moment—until he moaned a little, grinding himself against me—then I moved my fingers back down, back over his hip. I slid my hand underneath him. That was another part of him that felt perfect in my hands, and I pulled him tighter against me and heard him whimper a little in response. "Still no requests?" I asked him.

He opened his eyes and looked up at me, and I froze. What I saw there worried me. He looked afraid.

"Is everything okay?" I asked, suddenly serious.

"Yes," he said, although his voice shook.

"Do you want me to untie you?"

He shook his head, just barely. "No."

"I will," I said, and started to reach for the tie, but he tightened his legs around me.

"No," he whispered. "I want you to kiss me." I hesitated, still wondering what had caused that look of trepidation in his eyes. "Please," he said. "Like last time."

For better or worse, I couldn't find it in me to argue. I loved kissing him. Ever since that day on the floor of his living room, I couldn't get enough of it. I did as he asked, slowly teasing each of his lips, alternately sucking on them and kissing him gently. Like before, I spent a long time doing only that while we ground against each other. The effect it had on him was undeniable. By the time I worked around his mouth, his lips were red and swollen, and he was arching against me, making sounds that were driving me wild. Just rubbing against him as I kissed him and hearing his breathless cries had me close to orgasm far too soon.

I started to move down, thinking I would use my mouth to bring him off, but he tightened his legs around me. "No," he said. "Not that way."

"Okay." I leaned down to kiss his neck some more. "Do you want me to fuck you now?" I whispered in his ear.

"I don't care," he said, "as long as you're here." And by "here," I knew he meant as long as I was in a position to keep kissing him.

I didn't want to move on to anal sex. It wasn't that I didn't enjoy sex with him. I most definitely did. But with him, sex was generally just sex. It rarely felt intimate. I wanted this to be different. I reached into the drawer by the bed and found the lube. Unfortunately, that presented me with a bit of a problem. I didn't want to break contact with him to do this. I felt like I would somehow lose something if I did. I wanted to keep him how he was now, allowing me to touch him and explore him, rather than pushing me right to sex. I did my best to keep kissing his neck and his lips as I used one hand on the tube. I was ridiculously grateful that it had a flip top and not a screw cap, and I finally managed to squeeze some out onto my fingers, although I somehow got it all over his hip in the process.

"What in the world are you doing?" he asked in breathless exasperation, and I laughed.

"Just wait," I said. I went back to kissing him, nibbling on his lips. His moans were louder now, his legs tight around my hips as he ground harder against me. "Let go of me," I said quietly, and he made a hissing sound.

"No."

I kissed him again. "Yes."

He moaned, and I couldn't help but laugh at the mixture of arousal and frustration I could hear in that one small sound. But he let go.

"Good," I whispered. I was still between his legs, but instead of having them around me, they were spread wide with his knees bent and his feet on the bed. I pushed one leg down so that it was flat on the bed and moved so that it was trapped between my legs. That was completely self-serving. It allowed me to grind my own aching erection against his thigh as I kissed him. Then, I put my slick fingers against his entrance and pushed gently.

He moaned, and his eyes drifted closed. I kissed his neck as I teased him, rubbing my finger in small circles around his rim. And then slowly, very slowly, I pushed into him. He gasped, arching against me. "Oh my God," he moaned, and I pushed in a little further. He started panting hard, pulling against the tie that bound his wrists, pushing toward my hand. He was too far gone to kiss me anymore, and I went back to nibbling at his red, swollen lips.

"Like this," I told him quietly as I pushed further, moving slowly in and out of him, massaging his tight shaft. "I want to make you come just like this."

"Oh God, love, please hurry," he panted breathlessly.

The urgency in his voice almost sent me over the top. I gave up on being slow or gentle. I wrapped my other arm tight around him. I bit down on his neck. I shoved my fingers in the rest of the way, found that spot inside of him, and pushed, grinding myself against him as I did. He cried out, loud enough that the neighbors probably heard him. Not that I cared. His body tightened around my fingers, and he cried out a second time, and I came hard, holding him tight against me as the waves washed over us both.

We were shaking, breathing hard, and for once, I got to just hold him. He usually pulled away from me so quickly, and I was content to be able to be able to spend more time touching him and smelling him. I was so happy to have him there with me. Even still shaking from my orgasm, all I could think of was how glad I was that he had come back from New York. I started to kiss his neck, and he said shakily, almost laughing, "My wrists."

I laughed too. I had completely forgotten that he was still tied up, and I reached up to undo the knots. I only got to untie one of them. As soon as he was free, he pushed me away, and I tried not to be too disappointed. That was his way—to put his walls back up now that the sex was over. He sat up quickly on the edge of the bed with his elbows on his knees and his head in his hands, hiding his expression from me. I wrapped my arms around him and was surprised that he let me. He was trembling, still breathing hard, and I kissed the side of his head.

"Everything okay?" I asked.

"Yes," he said shakily. He laughed just a little, although it was a nervous sort of laugh. "I'm a mess."

"I'll get you a towel." I went in the bathroom for one. I wiped myself off quickly and then handed it to him.

"Thank you," he said quietly, his voice still shaky. But he didn't look up at me.

I wanted so much to touch him more. I sat down next to him on the bed and took his other arm, the one that still had my tie knotted around it. I undid the knot. There was a red mark underneath it, and I lightly massaged his wrist and hand. "Was it too tight?" I asked him.

"No," he whispered.

I leaned over to kiss his wrist, as if I could take away the pain, and heard his breath catch. It didn't sound like arousal. I lifted my head to look at him, and he turned quickly away from me, pulling his hand free to cover his face.

"What's wrong?" I asked, suddenly alarmed. I had thought his quiet, shaky behavior was only a reaction to his orgasm, but now I wasn't so sure. I was terrified that I had hurt him or pushed him further than he intended to go.

"We shouldn't be doing this," he said, so soft I barely heard him.

Nothing could have surprised me more than that. "What do you mean?

He shook his head but still would not face me. "Don't you see?" he asked, his voice torn. "Don't you see how terribly dangerous this is?"

"Do you mean me tying you up? I won't do it again if—"

"That's not what I'm talking about."

I was baffled, and worried. I put my hand on his shoulder but he flinched away from me. "Then what—" and right then, at the absolute worst possible moment, my phone rang. "Shit!"

"It's okay," he said quietly. "You're here to work."

"Are you all right? Did I hurt you?" It rang again. "Cole, I'm so sorry. Whatever I did to upset you—" Another ring.

He sat up straighter and wiped his eyes, but he still wouldn't face me. "You didn't," he said, although it was obviously a lie. "Don't worry, love, really." *Ring, ring.* "Go do what you have to do. I'm fine." His fingers found mine and squeezed for only a second, and then he stood up and walked into the bathroom, closing the door behind him.

I answered my phone. I hoped it would be something quick and simple, but it wasn't. I was on the phone for more than thirty minutes, and I worried the entire time. I heard the shower running, and I heard when he came out. Although I was still on the phone, I went in the bedroom. I took his arm and gently turned him toward me. I had to carry on my conversation with my client, but I felt like if I could just see Cole's eyes, I would know if we were all right. They were a little bit sad, but he smiled up at me reassuringly. I put my arm around his waist and he allowed me to pull him close. I buried my nose in his damp hair, breathed in that scent I loved so much. I wished I could say something to him, but my client was still talking.

He let me hold him for a moment, but then pushed me away. It was playful but firm, and I reluctantly let him go. He climbed into bed and pulled the covers up to his chin. By the time I managed to get off of the phone, he was sound asleep on his own side of the bed.

When we had first started seeing each other, I had been relieved at the fact that post-coital cuddling was not part of our arrangement. But more and more lately, I found myself wanting to bridge that gap—to reach across that expanse of crisp, clean sheets between us. I never did, though. I was sure that, as in all other things, he would push me away. Tonight, more than ever, I wished that I could hold him as I fell asleep.

He was still sleeping when I got up and went to the fitness room for my morning jog. He was in the kitchen when I got back. I took a quick shower and got dressed before finding him.

"I knew you had to leave early," he said, "so I didn't make breakfast."

"That's fine." I was watching him, trying to find some clue as to what had happened last night. I stepped closer to him. "Cole, about what happened—"

"It's fine, honey, really," he said, and he sounded completely sincere. Looking into his eyes, I saw nothing but his usual mocking nature.

"I won't do it again," I told him. "I prom—" But he stepped forward suddenly and put his fingers against my lips.

"Don't," he said. "That's not a promise I want you to make."

"Are you sure?"

He smiled up at me. "I enjoyed myself immensely, I assure you."

I breathed a sigh of relief. "Okay."

"Go," he said. He hesitated for a second, and then he stood on his toes and kissed me. "I'll see you tonight."

It was the first time he had ever kissed me goodbye.

Date:	February 20
From:	Cole
To:	Jared

I know that you are terribly upset with me, and I don't blame you. I've been ignoring you and refusing to answer your questions. The truth is, I couldn't decide what to tell you. I didn't want to lie to you, Sweets. We've known each other too long, and you deserve better than that. But I didn't want to tell you the truth either, because that would mean facing it myself. And I just wasn't ready to do that.

Am I ready now? No, not really, but it must be done. I'm most of the way through a bottle of wine, and right or wrong, I must admit that it helps. It also helps that you're hundreds of miles away. If I had to face you when I said these things, I wouldn't be able to do it. If I had to look in your eyes right now, I would smile and tell you that you're mistaken. I would tell you that Jonathan and I are casual lovers. I would tell you that he's only an uptight accountant who's good in bed, but nothing more. I would tell you that he means no more to me than any of the other men I share my bed with when I feel so inclined.

But the truth? The truth is, Sweets, somewhere along the line, it all went wrong. I started wanting to see him more. I started enjoying our time together out of bed as much as in. I let my guard down. Somewhere, somehow, I let myself start to love him.

I should never have let things go this far. I have learned the hard way that my lifestyle is not conducive to long-term relationships. I cannot stay in one place, Sweets. I just can't, no matter how much I may want to. And the minute I give in and leave town again, it will be the beginning of the end. I know that.

As for Jonathan, he does not love me. He finds me entertaining, and possibly amusing, but not much more. The truth is, I'm glad. Because it's one thing for me to lie to myself. It's another thing altogether for me to lie to him.

In a few weeks, I'll be leaving. I should have left already. I'll fly to Paris and I'll stay there until I'm no longer dying to see him again, and he'll find a new lover and the universe will make sense once again. But for now, I'll allow myself a little more time with him, because the truth is, Sweets, he makes me happy in a way that nobody else has in a very long time. But I know it cannot last. Soon, I will let him go. He does not love me, and I hope he never will.

SOMETHING changed between us after that, but I couldn't put my finger on what it was. When we were in bed together, everything felt different. There was a level of trust and longing between us that I hadn't experienced in a very long time. Maybe not since Zach. I tried not to think about what it meant, mostly because I was pretty sure I was the only one who was feeling it. Out of bed, he still pushed me away more often than not when I tried to touch him or kiss him. He still kept his walls between us. The difference was that where he used to be mocking and carefree, now he seemed sad. And the fact that he kept himself behind those walls, where I could not reach him, made me ache for him. I yearned for more. But I had no idea what to do to change it.

A few weeks later, the restructuring was finally put into effect. I returned from my last week-long trip to LA on a Friday night feeling absolutely giddy. It was like being a kid again and having that last day of school before summer vacation. Starting the next Monday, I would be a *Junior* Liaison Account Director (and it was Cole's mocking voice that I heard in my head when I thought about it). Any trepidation I had held over accepting a demotion was gone. I was so relieved to be home for good.

I called Cole before I even left the airport.

"Hello, love. Are you home?"

"Finally. Did you miss me?"

"Not at all."

"I didn't miss you either. Can I come over?"

He was quiet for a moment, and then he said, "It would be a wasted trip, love. I'm already at your house."

"Good," I said smiling. "I'll be there in twenty minutes."

For once, I didn't find him in the kitchen. He was actually sitting on the couch reading when I got home. I had a ridiculous urge to lie down on the couch and put my head in his lap, but he stood up before I could decide whether or not to follow through.

"I didn't have time to cook," he told me, "but I ordered take-out. It should be here soon."

"That sounds great. How did you know I would be home tonight?"

"I tried to call you, and it went to voice mail, so I knew you had to be on the plane."

"I'm impressed," I said, and he winked at me.

"You should be, love."

I reached out and took his hand, trying to pull him over to me, but he resisted. I pulled harder, but he still didn't cooperate.

"Come here," I said in exasperation.

"Why?"

"Because I want to show you how much I didn't miss you."

He smiled at that and relented. He let me pull him close and put my arms around him. He was a little bit stiff in my arms, but I didn't mind. I put my nose into his hair, just so I could smell that ridiculous strawberry shampoo. It was a smell that had somehow become simultaneously erotic and comforting to me. I felt silly for it, but it was such a part of him and of *home* now that I found myself missing it whenever I was away.

I tipped his head back so I could see his face and his beautiful full lips. He didn't exactly relax, but he allowed me to kiss him. His lips were soft and sweet, his breath shaky, and like always, I wanted only to sink deeper into him. I pulled him tighter against me, and to my surprise, he put his arms around my neck. He sighed, and his lips parted, and then—he really, truly kissed me back. It was something that he still did only rarely, and I lost myself in the sensation of it: his body against mine; his mouth, sweet and fruity; his arms tight around me; his lips soft yet insistent. I abandoned all thought and reveled in *him.*

Until the doorbell rang. It was the first time ever that I found myself wishing that delivery was slower.

"That must be our food," Cole said as he pulled away from me. And there was something strange in his voice when he said it, but I didn't have time to figure out what it was. He was bringing in bags of Chinese food, and then we were sitting down to eat. He was unusually quiet all through dinner. He kept his head down so I couldn't see his eyes. I kept waiting for him to say something, to laugh, to make fun of me for something, but he didn't. He seemed… sad.

"Is anything wrong?" I asked.

"Not at all."

"Are you sure? It seems like something is bothering you."

He was quiet for a minute, and then he surprised me by answering my question with a seemingly unrelated question of his own. "The weekend of April second—would it be at all possible for you to take Friday off?"

"I'll see what I can do. Why?"

"I was considering a few days away."

"Are you asking me to go with you?"

"Is that not what I've just been saying?"

Only in a very round-about sort of way, but I knew better than to argue with him. "I would lov—"

He held up his hand to stop me. "Before you answer, sweetie, let me warn you: I won't be any fun at all. I'll be cranky and moody and sulky and *dreadfully* temperamental. You have to promise me that however badly I may behave, you won't hold it against me."

"Are you going to tell me *why* you'll be cranky and moody and sulky and temperamental?"

He smiled at me, but only barely. "Eventually. Maybe."

"But you want me to come?"

And again, he looked down at the table so that the fall of his bangs blocked his expression from my sight. "Very much."

"Then I will," I told him, "but I'm paying my own way."

That made him look at me again, and he rolled his eyes. "Sweetie, really. That's completely unnecessary, and it will only make the reservations more complicated."

"Then I'm not going."

"Don't be such a killjoy, love. You just said you wanted to."

"Not if you're going to insist on paying. You know how much I hate it when you do that." I knew he still didn't understand why my pride prevented me from letting him pick up the tab everywhere we went, and he probably never would.

He debated for a moment. "Fine," he said, "I'll buy the tickets, because I want to surprise you. But you can buy all of our meals, if it means so much to you—"

"It does."

"—and we'll split the room. Is that sufficient?"

"It is."

"Thank goodness," he said with exaggerated relief. "Good grief, sometimes I don't know why I put up with you."

NOW that I wasn't traveling and had a predictable schedule, we fell into a comfortable pattern. Monday through Thursday, he would be waiting for me when I got home, and the weekends were always spent at his place. I realized then that he never traveled any more either, and I wondered when exactly he had stopped. I wondered if it was because of me. I knew better than to ask him—he would say it had nothing to do me, whether it was the truth or not.

The weekend of our mystery trip drew closer. I was unbelievably curious, but he refused to tell me where we were going. He told me only that I would need one suit and that the weather would be moderate. Friday came, and I picked him up on my way to the airport. He had told me he would be moody and sulky. I hadn't really believed him, simply because I had rarely if ever seen him be anything other than his usual flamboyant, mocking self. But in the weeks since then, he hadn't quite been himself. And today seemed worse than ever. He was silent all the way to the airport. Finally, when we got to the baggage check counter, he handed me my ticket.

"New York?" I asked in surprise as I looked at it. "Your house in the Hamptons?"

"Not this time, love." He didn't seem inclined to say more than that, and the lady at the counter was asking for our tickets and our IDs. She checked Cole's first. "Have a nice trip, Mr. Davenport," she said as she handed it back to him.

I turned to look at him in surprise. He had his head down, and I knew by now that it was to keep me from seeing the blush on his cheeks. "'Davenport'?"

"What about it?"

"Why did she call you that?"

"Because it's my name!"

"I thought—"

"Good lord," he snapped at me, "don't make a fuss." I realized then that the woman at the counter was watching us, listening to our conversation with a suspicious look on her face, and I decided to drop it. For the moment at least.

I finished checking my own bag and followed him through the security line, which was relatively short, to my surprise. I kept waiting for some type of explanation, but he was making a point of not looking at me.

"Cole," I finally said in exasperation after we had made it to our gate and were sitting in the waiting area, "you're really not going to tell me why she called you Mr. Davenport?"

He flipped his hair out of his eyes and gave me that look that meant I was being an idiot, and an annoying idiot to boot. "I *did* tell you. She called me that because that's the name on my license."

"I thought your last name was Fenton."

He turned away from me again, letting his hair block his expression. "It is."

"Are you intentionally being cryptic?"

"Are *you* intentionally being obtuse?"

"Fine," I said, although I was fighting to keep from laughing. "Don't tell me."

We sat in silence for a minute. Maybe two. Finally he sighed dramatically, and I turned to find him watching me warily. "My full name is Cole Nicholas Fenton Davenport the Third."

I burst out laughing before I could help myself, but cut it short when I saw the obvious embarrassment on his face. "Umm…. Wow."

"It's terribly ostentatious, isn't it?"

"It really is."

"You can see why I don't choose to introduce myself as such. It makes me feel pretentious."

"It makes you *sound* pretentious."

He rolled his eyes at me. "You're not helping, love."

They called for first class boarding, and I ignored it out of habit, but Cole stood up. I looked up at him in surprise. "Are you coming?" he asked.

"Are we flying first class?"

"Good lord, of course we are," he said, and I had to hurry to gather my things and catch up with up him.

"I've never flown first class," I admitted as we found our seats.

"I've never flown coach."

He got a blanket down before he even sat down. He wrapped it around himself and curled into the window seat with his head against the wall, looking out at the tarmac. I suspected it was driving him crazy that he couldn't take his shoes off. "Is everything okay?" I asked him.

"Fine," he said quietly. "I warned you that I would be temperamental on this trip."

"I don't mind," I told him. "I'm just not sure if I should try to cheer you up or leave you alone."

"I'm not sure either, love. But I'm glad you're here."

The simple confession touched me. It was so unlike him to say anything genuine. I wished that we weren't on an airplane with a line of people filing past us. I wished I could wrap my arms around him and make him smile. I settled for reaching over and putting my hand on his leg. He put his hand on top of it, allowing his fingers to tangle with mine. "I'm glad too," I said.

The flight from Phoenix to New York took nearly six hours. He hardly spoke for the first half. I read a magazine and left him alone. We were three hours in when he asked suddenly, "What was your mother's name?"

I turned to him in surprise, but he wasn't looking at me. He was still looking out the window, and his bangs hid his expression from me. "Why do you ask?"

He was silent for a bit, and I was starting to think he wasn't going to answer. But finally he sighed and turned to look at me with wary eyes. "I've been reading the cards." For half a second, I thought he was talking about some kind of fortune telling thing. But then I remembered the recipe box. I hadn't thought about it since the day I gave it to him.

"Yes?" I prodded gently.

He looked so unsure of himself. It was unusual for him. He looked down at his lap, letting his hair hide his eyes from me again. "I feel like I know her," he said softy. "I know it sounds silly, but I do. I know what she looked like, from the picture at your house. And I learned a great deal about her from the cards."

"Like what?"

"I know that she loved garlic. I know that her favorite dessert was pumpkin bars, and she liked key lime pie, but she hated anything with coconut. I know that she took the green peppers out of every recipe—"

"Because I didn't like them," I said in surprise, but he kept talking as if I hadn't spoken.

"—and that she put sour cream and onion flavored potato chips on top of her tuna casserole. I know that she mixed cottage cheese into her goulash, and used half hamburger and half spicy Italian sausage for her meatballs, and that she never made pie crust from scratch. I know that she made beef stroganoff more than any other recipe—"

"It was good, too."

"—and that she was allergic to shellfish. I know she didn't like chicken enchiladas or green chili, but she loved cilantro, and I know that her favorite soup in the world was ham and beans."

"You got all of that from a box of index cards?"

He turned away from me to hide his blush. "I could tell which ones she used by how worn the cards were. The ones that are clean were never used. The ones she used often are almost illegible. And she made notes." It amazed me to learn that not only had he kept the recipe box, he had looked at it. And more than that, he had *studied* it. He had used it to piece together a picture of my mother that even I had never quite seen before. His voice, when he continued, was little more than a whisper. "I feel like I know her better than I know my own mother. The one thing I don't know," he had to pause for a moment then, "is her name."

I reached over and took his hand, and although he didn't look at me, he gripped my fingers tight. "It was Carol. Carol Elizabeth Kechter."

"Carol," he said quietly, almost like a prayer. And then he turned to me with a smile. "Thank you."

WE GOT to New York and found a cab, and Cole named a hotel.

"We're not staying at the Waldorf?" I asked him jokingly.

He didn't even look at me. "We can, if you like."

"Cole?" I waited for him to meet my gaze. "I was kidding. Anywhere is fine."

"The one I chose is on Broadway. It will make our trip to theater infinitely easier."

"Broadway?" I asked, knowing that I sounded like an excited kid, but unable to contain myself. "Are we going to a show?"

"Did I not just say that, love?" he asked, but he smiled at me when he said it, if only a little. "Why else would I bring you to this godforsaken city?"

All I could do was laugh with joy. I reached across the cab and put my hand on the back of his neck and pulled him toward me. He didn't push me away like he often did, but he didn't exactly cooperate either. He stared resolutely straight ahead, and I ended up kissing his temple. "Thank you," I told him.

"You're welcome," he said quietly, and I could tell my excitement cheered him up a little.

We got to the hotel and checked in. Over the years, I had stayed in hundreds of motel rooms, but none like this one. It was huge, with a giant window looking down at the lights of Broadway. The bed was deep and soft and wonderfully inviting after a long day of traveling.

"I can't believe you brought me all the way to New York just to see a show," I said to him, and he smiled.

"I hoped you would be pleased. I would have liked to take you to Paris, but it's not very convenient for a weekend trip. I wanted it to be something that you would enjoy even if I was being terribly moody. "

I hesitated for a moment, not wanting to upset him, but I finally asked, "Are you going to tell me why we're here?"

He turned away from me, looking out the window. "Because," he said, his voice so quiet I had to strain to hear him, "tomorrow's my birthday."

And suddenly it all made sense—his comments about being terrible company but still wanting to have me with him. He had all the money in the world, but nobody to spend his own birthday with. Nobody but me. I crossed over to him. He still had his back to me, and I wrapped my arms around him from behind. "Happy birthday," I whispered in his ear.

He didn't answer me with words, but for the first time ever, he truly relaxed in my arms. He seemed to sink into himself, and he leaned back against me with a sigh. It felt so natural and so perfect. It felt *right*. I put my face into his silky hair, breathing in that scent I loved so much.

"Would you rather go out to eat for your birthday, or should I order room service?"

"I don't care, love. First, I'm going to shower." He turned his head so he could look up at me. "Do you want to join me?"

We had never showered together before. It was one of those casual intimacies he seemed to avoid, and his sudden invitation surprised me. I was tempted for a moment, but there was something else I wanted to do more. "You go ahead," I told him.

I called the concierge as soon as I heard the water turn on. She laughed but said she would take care of it. Then I called room service. All that was left after that was to wait. I thought again of him in the shower, wondering if we would have enough time. I gave in, deciding to risk it, but just as I walked into the bathroom, the water turned off.

His shower must have been scorching hot, because the bathroom was thick with steam. It smelled like soap and strawberries, and I found it incredibly arousing. "You're late," he said jokingly as he stepped out of the tub. His skin was beaded with water. His light brown hair looked almost black, wet and stuck to his head.

"I changed my mind."

He reached for a towel, and I stepped in front of them, blocking his access. I knew it was cruel. He was soaking wet and starting to get goose bumps. But I really didn't want him to dry off yet. "Is there a reason you're making me stand here freezing, love?" he asked.

"Yes." I took his hand and pulled him toward me, and he came. I leaned close to him and gently kissed his neck, just below his ear, and he shivered. The water droplets on his skin tasted sweet on my tongue, and I wondered if it was my imagination that they tasted like strawberries. I followed their trail, kissing and licking down his neck to his collarbone, then along his collarbone to tiny pool of water in the hollow of his throat. I let my tongue caress him there, and he sighed and leaned back against the countertop behind him.

I moved lower, chasing water drops down his chest. I got on my knees and followed them over his stomach to his groin. Once there, I took the slender tip of his cock in my mouth, gripping his ass tight with both hands. I swirled my tongue around his head.

"Oh God," he moaned. He grabbed the back of my head. His fingers knotted in my hair, and he pushed me further down his shaft. He held me there for a moment before starting to move. I let him lead, let him use his hand in my hair to guide me up and down. He moaned again, sort of a soft sigh. I loved the sounds he made as he got off.

My own erection was wedged painfully into my jeans, and I reached to unbutton them. In one quick movement, he pulled out of my mouth. He pulled hard on my hair so that I got to my feet, and he kissed me insistently. He let go of my hair, and he started to unbutton my pants. I put one arm around his waist, pulling his still-wet body close. My other hand wrapped around his erection. He was breathing hard and moaning. His slender fingers slid into my pants and—

Knock, knock, knock.

We both froze. "Good grief, what dreadful timing," he said breathlessly, and I laughed at what an incredible understatement it was. "Who could that be?"

"That," I said as I disengaged myself from him and started to button my pants back up over my erection, "is probably our dinner." I answered the door with my clothes half-wet and sticking to my body and an embarrassing bulge in my pants, but the room service guy was either oblivious or used to it. He had the item I had requested from the concierge, and I gave him a generous tip. He was gone by the time Cole came out of the bathroom with a towel around his waist.

"What did you order?" he asked.

"Hamburgers."

He smiled. "And the wine?"

I took it out of the bucket and handed it to him. His cheeks turned crimson, but he smiled. It was a bottle of Arbor Mist Blackberry Merlot, and given that I had to pay extra for somebody to run out and buy it, it was probably the most expensive five-dollar bottle of wine ever.

"It's a red," he said mockingly. "Why on earth is it on ice?"

"They probably figured anyone who drinks this stuff doesn't know enough about wine to know the difference."

"Probably." He stepped up to me and put one arm around my waist. "Thank you."

"Don't thank me yet," I said as I kissed him. "After we eat, I'll finish giving you your real present."

We ate dinner and drank his cheap wine, and then finished what we had started after his shower. And like always, when it was over, he moved to the other side of the bed, not touching me, and turned out the light.

I was just drifting off to sleep when I felt the featherlight touch of his fingertips on my wrist. It was something he had never done before, and it made me smile. I opened my eyes. It was dark in the room, and he was nothing more than still shadow across from me. His fingers came to a stop, lightly resting on the back of my hand. I turned it over, thinking I would hold his hand, but when I moved, he pulled quickly away.

Was it possible that he hadn't meant for me to know? Had he assumed I was asleep? It made my heart ache that he was so determined to keep these walls between us when neither of us wanted them. How many nights had I lay sleeping while he secretly reached out to me in the dark?

I slid my hand slowly across to him and gripped his slender fingers. I tried to pull him toward me. He resisted, pulling against me. Maybe I was wrong. Maybe the contact had been accidental. Or maybe he just wasn't ready to allow anything more. I pulled again, to no avail. I tried to swallow disappointment. I should have known better than to try. It wasn't his idea, so of course he was resistant. I was about to let go of his hand when suddenly, to my surprise, the resistance stopped. I hesitated, unsure if I should try again or not. Finally, I pulled one more time, just barely. And with a quiet sigh he slid across that expanse of clean white sheets and into my arms.

His face was against my neck, one arm around my waist. Our legs tangled together. I tried to ignore the lightness in my chest, the quiet racing of my pulse. I told myself there was no lump in my throat. He didn't speak, and I didn't either. I wrapped my arms around him, buried my face in his soft hair, and held him tight.

BY THE time I woke the next morning, he had moved away from me again. I kissed the back of his head as I got out of bed and headed for the shower. Although it was early based on Arizona time, in New York it was much later than I usually woke, and I decided to let myself slack on the jogging today.

When I emerged from the bathroom, I found him awake. He was standing at the window wearing only his briefs, looking down at the busy street below.

"Doesn't your mother live in Manhattan?" I asked as I pulled on my own briefs.

"Yes," he said quietly, not looking at me.

I waited for him to say more, but he didn't. I walked over to stand next to him and saw the wary way he looked at me out of the corner of his eyes. "Are we going to see her while we're here?"

He didn't answer me—just continued staring resolutely out the window. The curtains were open, but the sheers were closed. He found the opening in the center of them and tangled his slender fingers into the fabric. He leaned his forehead against the smooth glass of the window, allowing his hair to fall over his eyes, and pulled the sheer fabric around him, so that it was between us.

"Are you going to call her?"

He didn't look at me. The soft sunlight through window and the thin fabric made glowing patterns on his caramel skin.

"Cole?" I prodded gently.

He sighed in exasperation, although I was pretty sure it was feigned. "I already did, darling."

"And?"

"I'm afraid she's terribly busy. She doesn't have time to meet with us."

She was busy? Too busy to see her only son on his birthday? "Has she remarried?"

"No."

"And she doesn't work?"

"Of course not."

"So," I said, knowing that I should probably shut up, but unable to make myself do it, "what exactly is it that has her so busy?"

It took him a second to answer me, but he said quietly, "I'm sure I don't know, darling."

"She doesn't even have time for lunch?"

"Apparently not."

The quiet resignation in his voice was painful to hear, and I regretted having pushed him so far. "I'm sorry," I said quietly.

He let go of the curtain, letting it fall back to the window. "Please don't feel sorry for me."

"Why not?"

He shrugged. "It's all terribly cliché, isn't it? 'Poor little rich boy'." He pulled away from the window a little, although he still didn't turn toward me. I could see him only in profile, and his hair still blocked his eyes from my sight. His voice was quieter, different than normal in some way I couldn't quite pinpoint. "Everything about me is a cliché."

And then it hit me what was different: his affectation was almost gone, the sing-song pattern of his speech undetectable.

This was a part of him I had caught glimpses of but never actually seen. It was as if some force field that normally surrounded him had disappeared, and instead of being strong and confident, I saw that he was terribly fragile. I knew he had no intention of letting me see him this way. If he realized that the walls were gone—that I could actually touch him—he would pull back, push me away, slam the walls back into place by cocking his hip out, batting his eyes at me through his hair, winking at me flirtatiously, and calling me "darling."

I wanted more than anything to grab him and hold him and make everything good for him, but I wasn't sure how to even reach him without having him push me away. I was afraid even to speak. I slowly put my hand out. I was sure that when I touched him, he would crumble to dust beneath my fingers or vanish in a toss of his perfectly cut hair.

I put one fingertip on his bare shoulder. He didn't make any indication that he felt it, but when I slid it slowly down his arm, his eyes drifted closed, and his breath caught in his throat. I moved closer. I was moving slowly, quietly, desperate to connect with this secret part of him—to somehow own it and make it mine. I put my hand on the small of his back, and he turned his face toward me.

I could see everything in his eyes at that moment. He was fighting tears. He was desperate for something, yet unable to ask for it. He was ashamed of himself for being vulnerable but too tired of pretending to cover it up.

I kept my voice low and quiet, lest I scare him away. "Cole, there is nothing cliché about you."

He closed his eyes. His breath was shaky. I put one hand on his cheek, used my other arm to pull him toward me. His eyes opened, and they were moist with tears and full of uncertainty.

He looked into my eyes. He said one word, quietly, only a whisper. But what he said was, "Jonathan."

Only my name and nothing more. And yet it was everything. He had never said it before—not once. It kindled a tenderness in me that was undeniable. It touched me in a way that nothing else ever had before. It made me realize with a sudden, painful certainty that my desire to own him was completely misguided. It was too late. I was his in every way, and until this moment, I hadn't quite known it. I wondered if he knew it. I wondered if he cared.

I pulled him tight against me and kissed him. I had kissed him many times, but never like this. Never with my heart in my throat and my hands shaking. Never with the need that I felt now. I wanted to taste every part of him. I wanted somehow to touch him the way he had touched me.

His lips were soft and warm and insistent. He wrapped his arms around my neck and kissed me with a desperation he had never shown me before. I halfway carried him to the bed and pushed him back onto it. We still had our briefs on, and the lube was on the floor on the other side of the bed, and I didn't care. I didn't want to stop touching him long enough to change any of those things. I didn't want to risk losing what we were both feeling at that moment. I only wanted to keep feeling his skin against mine, keep tasting his damp cheeks beneath my lips, keep hearing his trembling breath in my ear.

I pushed against him, and he wrapped his legs around my hips, holding me tighter. We rocked together, kissing and holding each other, allowing only the gentle friction between us to bring us to climax, and afterward my cheeks were damp too. I buried my face in his neck, and he wrapped his arms around me, making quiet hushing sounds in my ear.

I wasn't sure when it had changed from me comforting him to him comforting me. I wasn't sure if it mattered.

Somehow I knew that everything had changed. We had crossed some threshold, broken through some boundary we had never intended to breach. I wondered if we could go back. I wondered if he would want to.

Date: April 3
From: Cole
To: Jared
What have I done?

AFTER the intensity of what had happened, it seemed like the whole world should have somehow shifted in its orbit, but of course that wasn't the case. We lay there for a few minutes holding each other, but soon reality set in. Particularly reality in the form of both of us now wearing wet underwear that was quickly beginning to dry.

"I suppose it would have made too much sense to do that before I showered," I commented, and he laughed as he pushed me off of him. I cleaned myself off and got dressed. There was a coffee shop in the hotel lobby, and I went down to get bagels ("Don't you *dare* bring me a donut, love") and lattes. It took longer than I expected. When I got back to the room, he had already showered and dressed. He was sitting on the bed, typing on his phone. I knew he often used it to check his email, and I was curious who was talking to, but I never asked. I suspected he wouldn't have told me.

Whatever walls had come down between us earlier, they were back in place now. His eyes were wary. I knew it was only his way, but I didn't want to let him pull away from me so easily. I wanted to be able to touch him again. I put the food down on the table and went to him. I pushed him back onto the bed so that I could climb on top of him.

"What do you want to do today?" I asked as I started to kiss his neck.

He turned his head, tipping his chin back to give me better access, but otherwise he didn't respond. He didn't put his arms around me. "Whatever you want to do, love."

I brushed my lips lightly over his ear. "It's *your* birthday," I said quietly.

"I suppose that's true."

I moved to his lips then. Even I couldn't quite understand my fascination with them. Yes, they were soft and beautiful. Still, I wasn't sure why I was so drawn to them. I kissed his bottom lip softy, teasing it with my tongue. His eyes drifted closed, and I felt one of his hands on my side. He was finally relaxing again. "Whatever you want to do," I told him.

He smiled a little, and opened his eyes to look up at me. "You'll laugh at me."

"I won't laugh."

"You will."

"I promise that I won't."

"Okay," he said as he put his arms around my neck. "I want to go shopping."

He was right. I laughed before I could stop myself. "Are you serious?"

"I told you you'd laugh," he said, but he was smiling, and I was glad I hadn't offended him.

"I'll do anything you ask," I said, and I meant it.

For the entire day, I simply followed him. I had been to New York once before, many years ago, and didn't really know my way around, but he seemed fairly familiar with it. He had picked a hotel close to the theater we were going to later, but it was a few blocks from the main shopping district on Fifth Avenue. We decided to take a cab to the far end and walk back. It turned out his style of "shopping" wasn't as painful as I might have expected. He mostly window shopped—

unless it was a gallery. We went in every single gallery we encountered.

He couldn't seem to decide how he wanted to behave around me now. For a while, everything would feel normal between us. He kept up an almost constant monologue as we walked, talking about the people he saw and last trips to the city and the style of the jackets in the store window and whatever else happened to cross his mind. He could be wickedly funny when he wanted to be, and he was good at making me laugh. Slowly, his guard would start to slip. He would flirt more and touch me more without seeming to realize it. And had we not been on a busy city street, I thought I probably could even have kissed him at those times without him pushing me away. But eventually he would realize that his walls were down, and in the blink of an eye he would be distant again, still talking but not making eye contact and certainly not allowing any physical contact between us. What confused me the most was that it seemed to make him sad to do it. I couldn't understand why he felt the need to do it at all.

It was after eating lunch that we wandered into another gallery. It was a private gallery of photographs, mostly taken outdoors but blown up huge, some as big as couches. We had moved fairly quickly through most of the other galleries, but he lingered longer in this one.

The gallery was one large room filled with cubicle-style white walls, creating seemingly random corridors. It turned the entire space into a maze and us into mice. It was quiet as a tomb. I felt like I needed to whisper. I stood very close to him so I could speak softly and have him hear me. He was relaxed at the moment and actually leaned closer to me. "Are you going to buy one?" I asked him.

He shook his head. "No. But they're nice, aren't they? I like the one that's underwater. It's very serene, don't you think?"

I knew which one he meant. It appeared to have been taken in fairly shallow, crystal-clear water. Sand and starfish filled the bottom of the frame, and the shimmering surface of the water could be seen at the top. "That's not the word I would use."

"Oh?" he asked, looking up at me in amusement. "What word would you use?"

"Claustrophobic. I feel like I have to hold my breath." He laughed at that. Even his soft laugh seemed loud in the stillness of the gallery, but he didn't seem as self-conscious about it as I was. "I like the ones with the snow better," I told him. "Especially the one with the aspen."

He shivered a little. "If I were to buy anything, it would go in the bedroom up in the Hamptons, and I can't have snow hanging in the bedroom. It will make me cold."

I laughed. "That is the most ridiculous thing I've ever heard," I said, although in truth, I was starting to imagine him in this bedroom I had never seen. He smiled back, and I had a feeling he knew my thoughts were wandering. He leaned a little bit closer to me—close enough that I could smell his hair. I put one hand on the small of his back and brushed my lips over his ear. "Would it be too predictable for me to offer to keep you warm?"

He laughed again, but he didn't pull away. "Yes, but you can offer anyway. I'm quite tempted to take you up on it."

I pulled him a little bit closer. "Are we almost done shopping?" I whispered. "Because I would love to take you back to the hotel and—"

"*Excuse me.*" The voice was loud and startled us both. I automatically pulled away from Cole, looking over to see who had disturbed us. It was a man in a suit, probably in his fifties, and the look of disapproval on his face was obvious. "Is there something I can help you *gentlemen* with?"

I felt my face turning red. I wasn't usually one for public displays of affection, and I was embarrassed that I had let my hormones get the best of me. I was actually about to apologize. But then I glanced at Cole, and I saw that not only did he not look apologetic, he looked positively annoyed. He flipped his hair out of eyes, his head cocked back a little bit in that way that allowed him to look down his nose at just about anybody.

"Honey, I assure you, we don't need *your* help with anything."

The man—his name tag said "Frank"—bristled noticeably. "This is a *gallery*—"

"I *know,* honey," Cole said, and I had a feeling he had intentionally used the pet name again just to annoy Frank more. "I'm not blind." He actually put one hand on his hip, and cocked his hip out, and I suspected it was all Frank could do to maintain his composure. "My partner and I are trying to decide which piece will look best in our bedroom." He turned to me, and I was trying not to look too startled at being referred to as his partner. "Isn't that right, muffin?" He winked at me. "Which do you think? The snow or the water?"

"I don't know," I stammered, trying not to laugh at his over-the-top behavior. "It's really your call. *Muffin.*" And I could tell that tickled him to no end.

"Perhaps," Frank said curtly, "you'd like to see the *price list* before you decide?"

"Excellent idea, honey," Cole said. "Why don't you run along and fetch that for me? We'll wait right here."

Frank had obviously expected the mention of a price list to send us on our way, and being told to "run along and fetch" didn't seem to be sitting well with him either. But he was professional enough to do his job, even if he couldn't quite manage to hide his biases as he did it.

"Of course," he said, with a forced smile. He walked away, leaving us alone again for the moment.

Half of Cole's affectation dropped away as soon as Frank was out of sight. "What a pompous ass," he mumbled. "Now I suppose I'll have to buy something." He turned to me. "Maybe we can compromise and get one of the above-water seascapes."

"It's your house and your money," I said. "Get the one you like." But I wasn't actually thinking much about the pictures. I was thinking about him.

I remembered months before when I had taken him to the theater, and we had fought afterward about his flamboyance. I remembered thinking that I had seen him turn the levels of it up and down. Yet for some reason, I hadn't ever realized exactly what it was that triggered it. At the time I had thought it odd that it would be worse when we were away from home. After all, it made more sense to me to be low-key when we were in public.

Why had I never realized before that, more than anything, his affectation was a defense mechanism? The more uncomfortable he was, the more he added to it, like pieces of armor. The gestures and the attitude, all just used to put more distance between himself and whoever it was that was threatening him. That was why, when we were at home, it all seemed to fall away. Because he was comfortable there and he didn't need it. But when he really had his guard up, as he did now with Frank, it was amplified. And that night with my father, and the next evening at the theatre, my own disapproval had probably only made things worse.

Frank reappeared then with the price list. Cole took it and started looking it over. I glanced at it over his shoulder and tried to keep my jaw from dropping when I saw the prices. "So tell me, honey," Cole said to Frank as he looked at the list, "do you work on commission?"

Frank looked uncomfortable with the question but said, "We're paid a flat salary, but I do receive a bonus for anything I sell, yes."

"And is there anybody else working today?"

Frank's cheeks started to turn a little bit red, and for the first time, he started to look a little bit worried. It apparently hadn't occurred to him that his attitude could come back to haunt him. "Allison is here is well."

"Why don't you go find her for me?"

"I'm afraid she's busy at the moment," Frank said, but even I could tell he was lying.

And then Cole did something that surprised even me. He yelled out, "Allison? Are you here, sweetie?"

"Sir!" Frank snapped. "*Please* keep your voice down. This is a *gallery*!"

"Honey, I *know*. But I asked you nicely to go and get her for me, and you refused."

There was a frantic bustling from the front of the gallery, and then a young woman stumbled around the corner and into view. She was only in her twenties, red-faced and flustered. "Yes?"

Cole gave her his best smile and walked over to shake her hand. "Allison, darling, it is *so* nice to meet you." He took her arm and steered her back toward the place where the underwater picture was hung. "I'd like to buy this picture over here."

She glanced at Frank, and she actually looked a little bit afraid of him. I suspected he wasn't a fun coworker. "Is Frank helping you?"

"No, darling," Cole said in feigned dismay as they disappeared around the corner. "Frank has been absolutely no help at all!"

Frank's cheeks were red. There was an obvious pulse pounding in his temple. And I had to bite my cheek to keep from laughing at him as I followed Cole and Allison to the front of the gallery. And so Cole acquired a picture he never really wanted for his bedroom in the Hamptons. He arranged to have it shipped there, saying only that Margaret would know what to do with it.

"I can't believe you did all that just to annoy poor Frank," I said as we left, and he laughed.

"What's the point of having money if you can't have fun with it, right, love?"

We slowly worked our way back to our hotel on foot. By the time we got there, it was time for dinner, and after eating, we changed and went to the theatre. The play was *La Cage aux Folles*.

"I wasn't sure which show to pick," Cole said, winking at me, "but this one seemed oddly appropriate." I hadn't ever seen it, although I knew the story. I couldn't even pronounce the title. Cole, being fluent in French, thought it was a perfect reason to laugh at me once again. I didn't mind.

We went back to our room after the show, and he stretched out on the bed with the room service menu while I changed out of my suit. He was on his stomach, with his back to me.

"Would it be terribly cliché to order the strawberries and champagne?" he asked.

I climbed on top of him so I could kiss the butterfly on his neck. "I think it's a great idea."

So we drank champagne and fed each other strawberries and slowly undressed as we caressed each other. When our clothes were gone, I pushed him back on the bed and kissed his neck. He hadn't shaved that morning, which was unusual for him. It took a couple of days for it to start to show on him, but now he had the tiniest bit of cinnamon-colored stubble along his jaw. "Happy birthday," I said.

"Thank you for coming," he said quietly.

"Thank you for bringing me."

"I hate having to spend my birthday alone."

"I don't blame you," I said.

He shrugged a little, seemingly lost in thought. He had one arm around my waist, and the slender fingers of his other hand were tangled into the hair on my chest. Looking down at him, I found myself thinking that he was the most gorgeous man I had ever seen. The brown in his hazel eyes was light, almost exactly the same color as his hair. But there was that hint of green in them too. He had delicately fine features, which somehow contrasted beautifully with the stubble on his jaw. And then of course there were his lips, which always drew my eye.

How could I love him this much? And more importantly, when exactly had it happened? Because I could no longer deny that I was completely head-over-heels in love with him. Finally admitting it to myself, once and for all, was almost overwhelming. I had forgotten how it felt to be in love like that. It was frightening, and exciting, and exhilarating, all at once. It was something I hadn't felt since....

Since Zach.

I pulled my mind away from him, instinctively, almost before I had followed the thought to its end. Not because it was still painful to remember him, but because I didn't want to taint *this*, what I felt *now* with Cole, with memories of that past life. Zach and I had been young, and in many ways, we had been thoughtless. Even cruel. But *this*? This felt new and pure and fragile. It felt sacred.

It felt like a second chance.

And I knew without a doubt that I had no intention of letting it pass me by. I wanted to tell him right now how I felt. I wanted him to know how much I loved him. I wanted him to know that he never had to spend another birthday alone again.

"Cole," I said, but before I could finish, he put his soft fingers on my lips. His eyes were wide and a little bit scared.

"Shhh," he said. "Don't say it, Jonny."

"But—"

He shook his head. And then he kissed me. He pulled me close, his arms tight around me. His lips were soft and warm, and his mouth was sweet from the fruit we'd eaten. He wrapped his legs around my hips, and in that moment, he became my whole world. I wanted to pour everything that I was feeling into him.

We took our time. The urgency of this morning was gone, and now there was only tenderness. I kissed him, feeling his thin body underneath me, his skin soft against mine. I tried to caress every part of him with my hands or my lips or both. His touch was light and gentle, but his fingers dug painfully into my shoulders as I pushed into him. And then there was only him in my arms, his legs around me, our breath mingling, and the building pleasure of our bodies locked together. And through it all, the knowledge that I loved him more than I ever would have believed possible.

Afterward, he was silent. He let me hold him far longer than he usually did. I was just drifting off when he started to move to the other side of the bed. "Please don't," I said sleepily, holding him tighter so he couldn't get away. "Stay here." I could sense him debating for just a second, but then he sighed—not in frustration or exasperation. It was a sound of contentment. He relaxed again in my arms, and I curled up against his back. And for the second night in a row, I went to sleep smelling strawberries.

Date: April 5
From: Cole
To: Jared

I am a fool, and a coward. I'm not sure which is worse.

ONCE his birthday was past, the overall melancholy that had shrouded him for the two weeks leading up to our trip disappeared. And yet he still wasn't quite happy. At least not all the time. I, on the other hand, could not remember having been happier. Not for a very long time, at any rate. I loved him. I loved everything about him. Every moment we were together thrilled me. He was flighty and bright and beautiful and stubborn, and I marveled at how much fuller my life felt now with him in it.

I was also happy that he seemed to accept now that our relationship had changed. He quit trying to keep his walls between us. He let me touch him more. He let me kiss him. He laughed more. And most of the time, he seemed to be as happy I was. But then there would be moments when it was as if the sun had suddenly gone behind the clouds. That laughing light in his eyes would suddenly dim, and he would seem sad.

"What's wrong?" I asked him once when it happened. We were in bed, still not quite breathing steadily again after making love, and as I looked down at him, thinking that I loved him more than I could ever put into words, that sadness had come into his eyes.

He was hesitant to answer, I could tell, and I suspected he was debating whether to deny that anything was wrong at all. But then he said, "I'll have to leave soon."

"Okay," I said, pulling him close and kissing him. Of course I didn't want him to go, but it had always been his nature to not stay in one place for too long. "I won't miss you at all," I told him. He sighed, but he didn't say anything else after that.

My father called a few days later to invite Cole and me to dinner. I was still reluctant to put them at the same dinner table again, but my dad insisted. "Jon, you can't divide your life in half and keep the two of us apart. If this is a relationship you're serious about, and I'm pretty sure it is, then I think the fruitcake and I will have to get used to each other."

"Fine," I relented, because as usual, he was right. "How about Saturday?"

"Perfect."

"But not a restaurant. He'll want to cook."

"Even better."

"And Dad?"

"Yeah?"

"Don't call him a fruitcake."

For only a moment, there clouds in Cole's eyes as I told him about dinner with my dad. But just as quickly, they were gone and he smiled. "Anything you want, love."

We had to go shopping on Saturday afternoon to buy what he needed for dinner. "I'm nervous about this," I confessed as we got out of the car and started walking toward the store. "It didn't go well last time."

"It won't be like that again," he assured me.

"How do you know?"

"Because you trust me now," he said, as if that made all the difference. Had I not trusted him before? I wasn't sure what he meant, but I was used to feeling that way around him, and I decided to let it go.

"What are you making?" I asked him as we walked into the grocery store. "You could make the cioppino again. He liked it so much last time he practically licked the pot clean after you left." Of course that made me think about why Cole had left early that night and the horrible fight we had the next evening after the show. "I'm sorry," I said. "I was so—"

"You were forgiven a long time ago, love," he said, interrupting me. "But I love that you're suddenly so repentant. And I'm not making cioppino."

"What are you making?"

"It's a surprise," he said, in that voice that told me I wouldn't get any more info out of him, even if I begged. "Should we get bread here or at that shop up the street?"

"Let's just get it here. We should buy a pie or something too," I told him. "He likes dessert."

"We could have strawberries for dessert," he said, picking up one of the little plastic containers of fruit and smelling it. "They're perfectly ripe. You can tell just by the smell. Here."

He held the container up to my nose. The smell of strawberries was associated with him so strongly in my mind, and upon smelling them I immediately thought of how it felt to have his thin body underneath me, to be inside of him, to have my nose buried in his cinnamon-colored hair.

And suddenly, I had a raging hard-on.

What the hell? I was in the middle of the grocery store! I turned toward the racks of produce to hide my predicament from anybody who might be looking my way. I closed my eyes and tried to think of baseball. Or mowing the lawn. Or anything but the way he smelled, and the sounds he made when—

"My goodness, love," he said, interrupting my decidedly too-erotic thoughts. "Do you have a strange fruit fetish I don't know about?"

I glanced over to find his eyes on me, and not surprisingly, they were full of laughter. "It's you," I whispered in embarrassment.

"Me?"

"Your hair." He still looked a little bit confused, and I had to say, "It smells like your hair!"

I saw the comprehension in his eyes. I could also see how much it pleased him. "Strawberries," he said. "That's very interesting. Anything else?"

I felt my cheeks turning red as I thought again about his hair—the color this time, rather than the smell—and his skin. "Cinnamon," I admitted quietly. "And caramel."

Now he *really* looked amused. "All that's missing is the whipped cream."

And *that* of course brought a whole new set of images to mind. And those images did absolutely *nothing* to alleviate the tightness in my groin. "You're not helping," I hissed at him and he laughed.

"I wasn't trying to, love." He stepped closer, stood on his toes a little so he could whisper in my ear, "Too bad you're stuck here. If we make it home in time, I might let you have dessert first."

"*Still* not helping."

"Would this be a bad time to tell you how much I've been thinking about your ties lately?"

"Oh my God," I moaned, and he laughed. I pushed him away, which only made him laugh louder. I grabbed the basket from him. If I carried it strategically, it would cover the embarrassing bulge in my pants. "Can we hurry this up?"

"Anything you want, love," he said in amusement. He turned and headed further into the grocery store, and I followed behind. I figured wandering through the aisles behind him would help take my mind off of sex. As long as we didn't encounter any more strawberries. Or cinnamon. Or caramel. Or whipped cream.

Yeah, this was going to work.

Especially since he was in front of me, and I could see that butterfly on the back of his neck and the curve of his back where it arched into the soft globes of his ass. I was driving myself crazy, and he was laughing at me the entire time.

We finally had everything he said he needed, *plus* the strawberries—we had to go back to the produce section to get them, which didn't help—and we each carried a bag of groceries back to my car, which was parked near the back of the lot.

"You're absolutely cruel," I told him as we put the bags in the back seat, and he laughed again. We got in, but before I could start the car, he took my keys from me. "What are you doing?" I asked.

He leaned over and put his lips against my ear. One of his slender hands went to the buttons on my jeans. "I'm making up for being cruel," he whispered, and I felt his tongue move over my ear.

I had been partially erect for most of our time in the store, and that was all it took to get my full attention. Still, we were in a parking lot. At the grocery store. "We can't do it here," I said in a hoarse whisper, and his laughter was soft in my ear. He had my pants undone already, and his hand slid inside of them, caressing me. After the torment in the store, it felt unbelievably good, and my breath caught in my throat. But I was still worried about being seen. He pulled my briefs out of the way, exposing my erection. His soft fingers slid over the end, where wet beads were forming.

"Honey," he said softly, "you're always so uptight. Just this once, try to *relax*." And then, before I could answer, he put his head in my lap, sucking me deep into his warm mouth.

The world seemed to spin. I was torn between the pleasure of what he was doing to me, and the anxiety of being caught. I glanced around the parking lot. There wasn't anybody too close to us, and the people I *could* see weren't looking our direction. But what if the people parked next to us were the next ones out of the store? And then—then he did *something* with his tongue, and I was no longer capable of caring. I could not possibly stop him now.

I had a white-knuckle grip on the steering wheel. I closed my eyes, and I thought about the smell of strawberries. And the image of whipped cream on his dark skin. And the feel of having his thin body underneath mine. All of the desire I had felt for him as I followed him through the store, I quit fighting it. I let it fill me and reveled in the release he was giving me. "Oh Jesus," I moaned, and he sped up, moving his head up and down on my shaft. I could tell by his soft moans that he was almost as turned on as I was, and that made it more intense. Nothing turned me on as much as hearing him get off. I wished I could somehow do something for him, but in the tight space of my front seat, it would have required a level of flexibility I definitely wasn't capable of. He had one arm around my waist, and his fingers were digging into my back in a way that was almost painful. He was using his other hand to hold my pants out of his way. I pushed it away so that I could hold them myself, freeing him to use that hand in other ways. He immediately used it unbutton his own pants enough that he could slide it inside. He wasn't quite stroking himself, but he ground against his own hand as he sucked me, and his moans got louder.

I was so close already, and part of me was still worried enough about being caught to want it to happen quickly. But mostly I just wanted to keep feeling his warm, wet mouth sliding up and down my length. Mostly I just wanted to keep hearing the frantic sounds he made as my own breathing sped up. In the end, of course, I had no real control over it anyway. I felt myself peaking. I hung on tight to the steering wheel with my free hand so I wouldn't be tempted to push his head down when it happened. His soft lips moved over my head again, and that was all it took. I came hard, felt his fingers digging into my back as I did, and knew by the guttural sound he made around my cock that he was climaxing too.

I opened my eyes, still breathing hard. There was one person walking past the front of my car, looking at me suspiciously. It was a woman, probably in her sixties, wearing a muumuu and flip-flops, with curlers in her hair. I put one hand on Cole's head to keep him from sitting up right at that moment, and I waved with my other hand, grinning like an idiot. Her cheeks flushed red, and she quickly turned away, shuffling to her car in the next row.

And then, before I could help myself, I burst out laughing. I couldn't believe how good it felt. Not just the blowjob, although that was part of it too, of course. But all of it—it was so liberating: being with him, trusting him, and letting myself relax. And laughing. The laughter felt almost as good as the sex. He was right. I needed to learn to let things go once in a while.

I took my hand away from his head, and he sat up. He put his lips against my ear and asked in a teasing whisper, "Better?"

"Oh my God," I gasped as my laughter finally started to fade. "*Yes!*"

"You should relax more often," he teased.

"I think you might be right."

He kissed me once on the cheek, then pulled away from me and started digging in the glove compartment. "I hope you have napkins in here somewhere. Otherwise I'm going to be stuck to my pants by the time we get back to your place. We may never get them off."

"That would be rather unfortunate," I told him, still smiling.

He smiled back and winked at me. "I'm glad you think so, love."

MY FATHER arrived early. I hadn't even set the table. "Dinner's not quite ready yet," Cole told him as they sat down at the table, "but Jonny can get us some wine, right, love?"

My dad looked a little bit nervous, I suspected because Cole was so obviously sending me out of the room so they could be alone, but I did as he requested. I went into the kitchen and opened the wine and got three glasses out of the cabinet.

"I need to take some time off this year," my dad was saying as I came back in from the kitchen.

"Really?" I asked, surprised. "Dad, you never take vacation."

"I know. And that's why my PTO bank is maxed out. They're telling me I *have* to take some time off."

"What are you going to do?"

He shrugged. "I haven't decided," he said. "I'd like to travel, but it's so expensive, and I'm not sure where to go—"

"Oh, honey," Cole jumped in. I kicked him under the table for calling my dad "honey." He gave me a dirty look, but didn't slow down. "You just have to know the right people, and now," he batted his eyes jokingly at my dad, "you do! I don't know if Jonny's told you or not, but I have homes all over the place. You can use any of them you want. Where would you like to go?"

"Well," my dad said with obvious discomfort, "I'm not sure—"

"How about Paris?"

"Paris?"

"Of course, honey. Who doesn't love Paris?" He leaned forward in his chair, tucking one bare foot underneath him. It brought him a little closer to my dad, like he was about to tell him a secret. "I usually spend half the summer there, and Christmas too, of course. I have a condo there that is completely adorable. Really, it's more convenient than any hotel, and it's free, so that's even better, isn't it? Just tell me when you want to go and—"

"Cole," I said, but he ignored me.

"—I'll call Alain and let him know you're coming. It's rather small, but unless you're planning some kind of soirée, it should suit you fine. Now, the lady next door has a bichon frisé that will bark its fool head off any time you walk past her door, which is terribly annoying, but don't let it worry you. And don't let any of those magazines in the bathroom scare you. Just toss them under the sink—"

"Cole," I said again, but he still ignored me.

"—before you open them, or you'll be in for shock. It has a full kitchen of course, so you don't even have to go out, which is infinitely cheaper than restaurants every night, I'm sure. I'll give you Alain's number, and you can call him and let him know what you want him to buy, and he'll have everything ready for—Wait! Do you speak French?"

My dad looked like he was barely managing to keep up with Cole's monologue, but he said "No."

"Well then, you better not call Alain, honey, because his English is *terrible*. I think it's all an act because he doesn't like Americans, but if we're not careful, he'll fill the kitchen with Spam. You let me know what you like to eat and I'll make sure the kitchen's—"

"Cole!"

This time he didn't ignore me. "*Good lord*, Jonny!" he said, turning to me in exasperation, "*What* is so urgent?"

Now that I had his attention, I realized I didn't actually know what to say. "You can't bribe my father with use of your condo in Paris."

"Whyever not?"

My dad made a snorting sound—I was pretty sure he was trying not to laugh—and ended up covering it by coughing.

"Because," I stuttered, "it's not appropriate."

Cole pretended to be surprised—I knew him well enough to tell that he was faking—and turned back to my father with his "I'm innocent" face on. "Paris is out, love. Sorry. Jonny seems to think it's terribly pretentious of me to even offer it. How about the Hamptons? I have a house there too. And with summer on the way, it might be the better choice anyway. The pool will be ready any day now, I suspect, and my lawn is beautiful. Flowers everywhere. And my gardener—"

"Cole!" I said again. He didn't answer, but he reached over and gripped my wrist in his slender hand. He squeezed just a bit, giving me a quick look out of the corner of his eye as he continued to talk, and I had a feeling it was his way of telling me to shut the hell up.

"—well honey, I'm pretty sure you won't find him as intriguing as I do, but there is a lovely widow who lives next door. I think her name is Martha, but don't quote me on that. She finds me *horrifying*— it's actually rather amusing. Sometimes I think about dressing in drag just to see her run screaming back into her house. But you? I have a feeling she'll like you just fine. She's not much of a cook—at least that's what Margaret tells me—but she does make *fabulous* lemon meringue pies." My father was smiling now, looking a little less stunned, but obviously unsure how seriously he should take Cole. "Do you golf?"

"Not really."

"Thank goodness. I don't even know where the nearest course is. Do you fish?"

"Why?" my dad asked, and he really was smiling now. "Do you?"

"Heavens no," Cole said. "Just look at me, honey. Do I look like a fisherman to you? Can you even imagine me trying to bait a hook?" He gave a dramatic shudder and—

My dad laughed. Not like the nervous chuckles from earlier. It was a true, from the stomach laugh. I looked at Cole, worried that he would be offended, but Cole was laughing too.

And I realized then what an idiot I was.

At our first dinner together, I had been so worried that my father would laugh at Cole and that Cole would be offended, or that Cole would embarrass himself in front of my father. I spent the entire meal wondering why Cole was being so over-the-top and trying to shelter each of them from the other's derision. I saw now that Cole did not need my help in any way. Not only that, he didn't want it. He had his own way of putting my father at ease, and if it involved my father laughing at him, he didn't care in the least. My clumsy attempts to interfere had only made things worse.

"—and it's a bit of a drive, but honey, they have *the best* lobster bisque I have *ever* tasted—"

And at that moment, I loved him so much, I wondered how he and my father couldn't feel it pouring out of me. He was still talking, and I leaned over and kissed him. He didn't cooperate at all—he didn't even stop talking, and my kiss landed somewhere around his left temple, but I didn't mind. My dad blushed a little, but he was laughing at something else Cole had said, and he didn't look away.

"He skis," I said in Cole's ear, and this time the surprised look he gave me was genuine.

"Oh good lord, Jonny, you're only telling me this now?" he asked, pushing me playfully away. "You could have saved me a great deal of time by stating that up front, you know. George, honey, I have to tell you, you did a *terrible* job raising Jonny. Now listen, I have a condo in Vail—"

I got up and went in the kitchen to get the dishes we would need for dinner, leaving them to talk—or, to be honest, leaving Cole to talk my father's ear off. Cole followed me in a few minutes later, and I grabbed him as soon as he walked by. "I'm sorry about last time."

"You're forgiven."

"I was so worried he would offend you, or you would offend him—"

"I'm not that easily offended. And if people can't laugh, they can't relax, love. He can think I'm foolish all he wants if it means he's comfortable with you and I being together." He stopped short at that, and his eyes started to get that sad look again.

"You're amazing."

He smiled a little. "I really am, love. The annoying thing is you're only now figuring it out."

"I think I lov—"

He stopped me again with his fingers on my lips and a hint of panic in his eyes. "Don't say it," he whispered, shaking his head. And then he kissed me. He wrapped one arm tight around my waist and the other around my neck, pulling me hard up against him. It was a more aggressive kiss than I was used to from him, and it was unbelievably arousing. It was deep and passionate. It was the kind of kiss that would normally have led us straight to the bedroom. That is, it would have if my dad hadn't been there. And if he hadn't chosen that very moment to walk into the kitchen.

"Hey Jon, do you—Oh shit!" He turned around and walked right back out, and Cole let go of me, laughing.

"It's okay, George," he called out as he turned back to the pot on the stove. "You can come in now. I promise to wait until you're gone to rip Jonny's clothes off."

I was surprised, once the food was on the table, to see that it was not a meal he had ever made for me before. It was beef stroganoff with egg noodles. My dad was oddly quiet as he put the food on his plate. Cole didn't seem to notice. He was standing next to my dad's chair, opening another bottle of wine. I took a bite, and it was so wonderfully familiar. It hit me all at once.

"This is my mother's recipe," I said, and Cole smiled at me.

"It is," he said, and I could tell he was pleased that I had made the connection.

It was such a simple thing, and yet I couldn't believe how one small bite brought back the memory of my mom. And of countless family dinners, all of us at the table together. It felt like suddenly she was there with us again, in spirit at least. "It's perfect," I said. "Dad, did you—" But I stopped short when I looked at him. He was still staring at the food on his plate, and there were tears on his cheeks. "Dad—" I started to say again, but Cole had turned to look at my dad at exactly the same time.

"Oh George," he said in dismay. "I'm sorry. I'm so, *so* sorry!" And looking at Cole, I could see how horrified he was at having caused my father to cry. "It was a terrible idea! I don't know what I was thinking! I should have realized. I should never have surprised you like that. Let's go out instead," he said, reaching to take my father's plate away. "We can go to that new place down the street—"

Before he could finish, my dad stood up. He turned to Cole.

"George," Cole said again, "I'm so sorry."

My dad reached out and grabbed the front of Cole's shirt.

I stood up from the table, thinking my dad might actually be about to punch him but knowing I would never get to the other side of the table in time.

And then—he pulled Cole toward him and wrapped his arms around him, hugging him tight. "Thank you," I heard him say hoarsely.

If it weren't for the fact that my dad was crying, the whole thing might have been funny. Cole was completely stiff in my father's arms, and the look on his face was bordering on absolute terror. He seemed to be looking at me for help. One of his arms was pinned to his side by my father, but his other arm was loose, and he was waving his hand frantically in my direction, like I might be able to rewind the whole incident and play it back without the awkward hug at the end. It was all I could do not to laugh at his obvious distress.

My father finally let go of him. He stepped back to his chair and sat down, as if nothing strange had happened at all. "Originally," my dad said as he dried his eyes with a napkin, "this was my mother's recipe. But Carol did something different to it."

Cole still looked a little bit shaken, but he managed to say, "She added sherry to it."

My dad looked up at him in surprise. "Is that all?" Cole nodded. My dad laughed, shaking his head. "My mother never forgave her for that." Whatever emotions had overtaken him momentarily, he was back to being himself and was digging in to his plate of stroganoff enthusiastically.

Cole looked at me, obviously still a little upset, with a mute question in his eyes. "It's really good," I told him, and he relaxed again, if only a little.

"I wanted to surprise you. I should have realized—"

"It's fine," I told him.

"Okay," he said shakily. "I'll just... I'll get us some butter," he said, and disappeared into the kitchen.

We didn't need butter. I knew he just wanted a minute to get his bearings back. "He didn't mean to upset you," I said to my dad. "He's looked through the box a lot. You wouldn't believe how much he learned about Mom from reading her recipes."

"I think it's great, Jon," he said. "And she would have thought it was great too. I think she would have liked him."

"You really think so?"

"I'm sure of it, actually," he said. He gave me a smart-ass grin. "Your mother's the only person I've ever known who actually enjoyed fruitcake."

Date:	May 9
From:	Cole
To:	Jared

I fear that what I'm doing is wrong. I think, just possibly, it's even cruel. I'm living a lie, and I hate myself for it. I'm allowing Jonathan to think this can last, when I know that it can't. It was never my intention to deceive him. It's only that things were so good in New York, and when we got home, it was terribly easy to allow it to continue. It felt so natural to keep seeing him, even though I feared I was only delaying the inevitable.

I've never been in one place for this long, and that petulant child inside of me is starting to get restless. He is demanding, as he always does, that I go somewhere—anywhere—and I know from experience that I cannot deny him, no matter how much I may wish to. He has always been in control, and it's only a matter of time before I must heed him.

I know that when I leave, it will be the beginning of the end. I know it with every fiber of my being. I know Jonathan senses that something is wrong, too. I could try to explain it to him, but in the end, it won't make any difference. He won't understand. He won't believe me. We'll spend our last days together arguing. He will swear that we will make it work. He will promise me the moon. He'll even try to give it to me, I'm sure. But it won't matter. It will end as it always does, with him tiring of my restlessness, and moving on.

So I choose to keep quiet. I choose to allow us both to be happy for as long I can. Is it wrong for me to do that? Is it wrong for me to stay until that terrible voice in my head becomes so loud I can no longer ignore it? Is it wrong for me to let him love me?

Don't answer that.

The truth is, I can do nothing else. I love him too much.

IT WAS a Wednesday morning when I arrived at the office to find a note saying that Marcus wanted to see me right away. Now that I wasn't traveling, I didn't have reason to meet with him as often as before, but it still wasn't unheard of, and I didn't think much about it as I made my way upstairs to his corner office. I knew something was wrong though, when I walked in the door and saw his face. His normal joviality was gone, replaced by a solemnity that made me nervous.

"Thanks for coming so quickly, Jon. Close the door behind you." That wasn't an unusual request either, and I tried to tell myself not to worry. I did as he asked and sat down in my usual seat, across from him.

"Is something wrong?" I asked.

He wasn't even looking at me. He was looking at some point over my head. He stared at it for a moment, and I made myself count to five. And five again. And finally, he took a deep breath, and looked at me.

"Jon, we're letting you go."

The room spun. My world collapsed. I had to remember to breathe. It was like one of those carnival rides where the floor falls out beneath you. There was a roaring in my ears. I felt a terrifying sense of vertigo. "You're *what?*"

"The company is struggling, Jon. We're barely in the black. Moving the Senior Liaison Account Directors out of state helped, but not enough."

"You told me that nobody would lose their jobs! You told me—"

"I know what I told you, Jon," he said, "and I thought it was the truth. I had no reason to suspect otherwise."

"What happened?"

"Monty's trying to cut costs. The board only decided on Monday."

"Why *me?*"

"It's not just you. It's all of the Junior Liaisons. Ten of you total." He sighed, looking down at his desk and rubbing his head. "I was the one person on the board who didn't vote to downsize. But it's my department, so I'm the sucker who has to tell ten people today that they're out of work." I put my head in my hands and tried to breathe. Tried to stay calm. This wasn't Marcus's fault. I truly believed that. He had never been my enemy. But I couldn't fight the rage that was welling up inside of me. "I'm telling you first, Jon, because you have seniority. We're prepared to offer you one month's severance—"

"*One month*? I've been here for nine years!"

"Jon," he said firmly, and there was a bit of an edge to his voice now, "I'm sorry. None of this is my decision. You have to know that."

I took a deep breath and made myself say, "Fine."

He sighed again. "One month's severance, plus any unused vacation time." That helped, actually. I had quite a lot of that.

I stood up. "I assume this is effective immediately."

He went back to looking at his desk, rubbing his forehead. "Yes. The personnel department has all of your paperwork ready. You can stop there first." I got his door open, but he stopped me before I walked through. "Jon, I have nine of your colleagues coming behind you." I knew what he was trying to tell me—nobody wanted to hear about being laid off through the grapevine. He was asking me to be low key about it.

"Yes, sir," I said.

He stood up and came out from behind his desk. "I'm sorry, Jon," he said, shaking my hand. "I really am."

All I could say was, "I am too."

I cleaned out my desk. I started out trying to be subtle, but one at a time, my co-workers were returning from their own meetings with Marcus. By the time five of us were cleaning out our desks, the rest could pretty much guess what was coming. Some were despondent. Some were angry. One actually seemed relieved. And me? More than anything, I felt betrayed.

It was two o'clock when I got home, and my house was empty. I wasn't sure if I was disappointed or relieved to not have to tell Cole yet what had happened. I threw my tie and jacket on the floor. I kicked off my shoes. Then I lay down on the couch and stared at nothing.

How could this possibly happen? That was the one thought that kept circling in my brain, over and over again. *How could this happen?* I had worked my ass off for that company for nine years. In that time, I had never said no. I had hardly taken a day of vacation. I had been the model employee. And this was how they repaid me? With one month's severance pay, a handshake, and an apology?

Would it have been better if I had never accepted the demotion? I would be in Vegas or Utah, but I would still have a job. My gut reaction was to think yes, it would have been better to move. But then I thought about the last few months with Cole, and I knew I had made the right choice. I would not have traded my time with him for anything.

Which brought me back to my original question. I had done what was right. So *how* could this happen? I chased it around in my brain, over and over and over, and I got nowhere. I was by turns completely furious and terribly despondent.

I had no idea how much time had passed. I only knew that I was starting to get hungry. More than hungry, actually. I was starving. I hadn't eaten lunch. A glance at my watch showed me that it was almost four. I wasn't sure if I should call Cole or if I should just get shit-faced drunk.

I was still trying to decide when he found me.

I hadn't moved from my position on the couch, and the door was behind me, so I couldn't see him. But I heard his key in the lock, and I heard him come in. I heard the crinkling of paper which told me had been at the store. "Hey, love," he said. "Why are you home so early? Are you sick?" I didn't answer at first. He came into view, looking down at me in concern, with a brown paper bag in one arm.

The words came easier than I expected. "I lost my job."

"Oh no!" He dropped the bag of groceries on the coffee table and sat down on the edge of the couch next to me. "What happened?"

I couldn't look at him. The sympathy in his eyes was painful, and I kept my eyes on the ceiling. "They're downsizing. They cut my whole department."

"Jonny, I'm sorry. I'm so, *so* sorry." He took my hand, holding it between his. "I don't know what else to say that won't sound trite."

"It's okay."

"Tell me what you want me to do, love."

"Just…." I wasn't even sure myself until the words came out of my mouth. "Leave me alone for a bit."

There was a moment of stunned silence, and then he said, "Okay. I can go home." He stood up, but I gripped his hand tight, so that he looked back down at me. I was able to meet his eyes this time.

"No. Not for that long. Just give me a few more minutes."

"Okay." He sat back down, looking concerned, still holding my hand. "I was planning to make dinner. Should I still—"

"That would be great."

"It's Cornish hens with scallio—"

"What about the wine?"

"It's a Zinfandel."

"We're going to need two bottles."

"Okay." He leaned down and kissed me. His lips were soft and a little hesitant and so sweet that it brought a lump to my throat. He pulled away to look into my eyes. "Anything you want, Jonny."

The dinner was fantastic, but I wasn't nearly as appreciative as I should have been. I let myself get ridiculously drunk and passed out in my bed while he cleared the table. The next morning I was hung over and completely miserable for the entire day. He was infinitely patient. He stayed by me the whole time. He was unusually quiet. And not once did I see the clouds in his eyes.

Date: May 18
From: Cole
To: Jared

I have found hope in his misery. Does that make me a terrible person? I know he is devastated, and yet, all I can think is that now, we can stay together. The answer is so clear. If only he will accept it.

I SPENT a couple of weeks being miserable. I snapped at everybody. I didn't jog or shave. I was sullen and angry, and any intelligent person would have stayed far, far away. Cole, on the other hand, proved to be a glutton for punishment. He was there the entire time, making meals, putting up with me, still making love to me when we went to bed at night.

After two weeks, I was able to accept that sulking would get me nowhere. I made myself straighten up. I worked up my résumé for the first time in nearly ten years and started looking for a job. Still I was hostile and jaded. I had gambled away a portion of my life, banking on a payout, and been shit on instead. My attitude was far from stellar.

Finding a job proved to be impossible. Lots of companies were downsizing, and the market was flooded with men and women of all ages scrambling for the few positions that were still available. I had a handful of interviews, but it seemed that if I wasn't under-qualified, then I was over-qualified. It was hard to accept that there was nothing I could do. The entire process was unbelievably frustrating.

On top of that, things between Cole and me were hot and cold, and I had no idea what to do about it. I was absolutely crazy in love with him. There was no other way to put it. And at times I thought he felt the same way. We spent most of our time together. We rarely argued, and if we did, it never lasted. The sex had reached an all-new level of intensity that left me breathless. We would have periods where everything seemed perfect.

And yet, more and more, I saw those clouds in his eyes. More and more, as I tried to pull him close, he would push me away as he had done in the past. He seemed sad and restless. I tried to ask him about it a few times, but he would just give me a strained smile and say, "It's your imagination, love." All I could do was hope that he wasn't lying.

I returned one afternoon from an interview that had not ended on a promising note to find him sitting on my couch. His back was to me, and at first I thought he had curled up in the corner of the couch to read, as he often did. But when the door closed behind me, he jumped. He turned toward me for only a moment, probably on sheer impulse, before turning away to cover his face with his hands. But in that moment, I saw what he was trying to hide from me—that his eyes were red and wet with tears.

"Hi, sweetie," he said, standing up, but not turning to face me. He was wiping his cheeks. "How did the interview go?"

"Terrible." But I didn't care about that. "What's wrong?"

"Nothing! I just nodded off. I guess I'm tired. I shouldn't have fallen asleep, though. I'll start dinner. Are you hungry? I was going to make—"

"Cole," I said, interrupting him, because I knew he was lying. I knew that talking a mile a minute about inane bullshit was his primary method of avoidance. "Tell me what's wrong."

"Nothing, love. Really."

"I don't believe you."

"I was so tired, but I'm better now. Just give me a minute...." His words trailed off as he went into the kitchen, trying to escape, but I followed him. He was pulling things out of the fridge, still refusing to look at me.

"Why are you lying to me?" He froze, and hung his head. "Are you angry at me? Have I done something to upset you?"

"No," he said, shaking his head, and his tone sounded sincere.

"Then what?"

He covered his eyes with his hands, and I knew he was fighting not to cry again. "I need some time," he said shakily, "to get myself together. I can't face you like this."

More than anything, I wanted to pull him into my arms and hold him, but when I reached for him, he flinched away from me. It was painful, being kept outside his walls. I wished they were tangible so I could tear them down with my bare hands. "Please," he whispered, pleading. "We'll talk after dinner, Jonny. I promise. But I need you to give me some space right now."

"Okay," I said, not because I wanted to. It broke my heart to have him push me away again. But I knew that honoring his wishes was the only thing I could do. I changed out of my suit, and after debating it for a while, I decided to join him in the kitchen. I tried to help him cook most nights now. I knew nothing, and mostly I just got in his way and drank wine, but it was still fun. Tonight was no different. Although he was awkward with me at first, once he realized I wasn't going to push him, he relaxed, and when I put my arms around him from behind, burying my face in his hair, he actually leaned back against me and sighed as I kissed his neck.

I was a little bit curious about what he would have to say after dinner, but I wasn't concerned. Most of the time, he seemed happy with me, and I wasn't worried. We ate, and I wasn't surprised when he didn't say anything immediately afterward. I did the dishes while he read on the couch. When I came out of the kitchen, he took me into the bedroom, and we had sex that I truly would have classified as earth-shattering. When it was over, he moved to the other side of the bed, not touching me. And then, lying in the dark, he finally spoke.

"Come to Paris with me."

I wasn't sure what I had been expecting, but that certainly wasn't it, and I actually laughed. "Are you serious?"

He didn't laugh with me. "Yes."

"Why?"

"Why not?"

I realized then that, although I didn't understand why or how, this was connected to whatever it was that had had him in tears on my couch earlier. Whatever this was, it meant a great deal to him. I quit laughing and thought about what he was saying. Paris? "I would love to, Cole, someday, but—"

"I mean now, love. *Soon.*"

"I…." I still couldn't quite believe that he was serious. "I can't."

He was silent for a moment, and as usual when he started these conversations in the dark, I wished that I could see his face. "Why not?" he finally asked.

"I have to find a job. My severance will be out soon. I have some vacation pay coming after that, but—"

"Once you find a job, you'll be stuck here, love. You won't get vacation time for months. If we're going to go, this is the time to do it."

He was right about the vacation time, of course. It would probably be a full year before I was afforded a single week of vacation time. Maybe a short trip wouldn't be too irresponsible. I would still have time when I got home to find a job. "I could go for a few days—"

"No, Jonny." He turned toward me and rolled so that he was lying on top of me, looking down at me in the dark. I wished I could see what was in his eyes. "I'm not talking about a few days. I'm not talking about a quick trip, and then back to Phoenix." He stopped, as if he had to gather his courage. "I'm asking you to come to Paris with me indefinitely."

"Cole, I don't have that kind of money. Two weeks, maybe. Max. But—"

"Jonny." It took him another second to say the next words, but when he did, I realized why he had been so hesitant. "You don't need money."

My first instinct was irritation, as it always was when he talked about money. But hot on its heels came anger, and I tried to beat it back. But my voice was harsher than it should have been when I answered him. "You want me to allow you to support me?"

Another moment of silence, and then, "Yes."

"No."

"I have plenty, love. It's nothing to be ashamed of. And then, when we come back in four months, or six—"

"*Six months?*"

"—you can find a job then. We could—"

"No!" I said, louder, and he stopped short. He pulled away from me, almost as if I had slapped him. "No," I said, gentler this time. "I can't do that, Cole. Let's go for two weeks. I can spare that—"

"And then you'll be working again, and we'll never get anything more than that," he said, and I could hear him fighting to sound normal, although I suspected he was near tears again. I didn't understand. I couldn't see how this could mean so much.

"Cole…." What could I say? "I just can't. I'm sorry."

He was silent. And then, in the darkness, I saw him nod. "I understand," he said with quiet resignation.

"Really?" I asked, not wanting him to be upset.

"No," he said. "Not really. But it's what I expected you to say." He moved off of me, but to my surprise, he didn't move back to the other side of the bed like he so often did. He cuddled up next to me with his head on my shoulder, and I wrapped my arms around him.

"Cole," I said, wanting to tell him how much I loved him. But he seemed to anticipate me, as he always did, and his soft fingers fell on my lips, quieting me.

"Shhh, Jonny. Don't say it." He moved his hand away, wrapped his arm around me and snuggled closer. "Goodnight."

He didn't mention Paris again. And if over the next two weeks I saw clouds in his eyes more often than not, I did my best to ignore it.

Date: June 19

From: Cole

To: Jared

I understand addiction now. I never did before, you know. How could a man (or a woman) do something so self-destructive, knowing that they're hurting not only themselves, but the people they love? It seemed that it would be so incredibly easy for them to just not *take that next drink. Just stop. It's so simple, really. But as so often happens with me, my arrogance kept me from seeing the truth of the matter.*

I see it now though.

Every day, I tell myself it will be the last. Every night, as I'm falling asleep in his bed, I tell myself that tomorrow I'll book a flight to Paris, or Hawaii, or maybe New York. It doesn't matter where I go, as long as it's not here. I need to get away from Phoenix—away from him—before this goes even one step further.

And then he touches me again, and my convictions disappear like smoke in the wind.

This cannot end well. That's the crux of the matter, Sweets. I've been down this road before—you know I have—and there's only heartache at the end. There's no happy ending waiting for me like there was for you and Matt. If I stay here with him, I will become restless and angry. It's happening already, and I cannot stop it. I'm becoming bitter and terribly resentful. Before long, I will be intolerable, and eventually, he'll leave me. But if I do what I have to do, what my very nature compels *me to do, and move on, the end is no better. One way or another, he'll be gone. Is it not wiser to end it now, Sweets, before it gets to that point? Is it not better to accept that this happiness I have is destined to self-destruct?*

Tomorrow I will leave. Tomorrow I will stop delaying the inevitable. Tomorrow I will quit lying to myself, and to him.

Tomorrow.

What about today, you ask? Today it's already too late. He'll be home soon, and I have dinner on the stove, and wine chilling in the fridge. And he will smile at me when he comes through the door, and I will pretend like this fragile, dangerous thing we have created between us can last forever.

Just one last time, Sweets. Just one last fix. That's all I need.

And that *is why I now understand addiction.*

HE WOKE me in the dead of night, his soft hand gripping my arm. It was something he had never done before, and it took me a minute to even figure out what had happened.

"Cole?" It was pitch dark in the room. I could barely make out the shape of him, lying in front of me. His face was nothing but shadow. "Is something wrong?" He didn't answer, but moved quickly into my arms. He was never hesitant about sex, and I knew if he had woken me for that purpose alone, he would be pursuing it already. This was something else, and it troubled me. Everything about it was wrong. He was too still, too quiet, too stiff against me. "What is it?" I whispered.

He wrapped his arms around me. He was trembling, and his lips were soft against mine. "Just one more time, love," he whispered.

It was slow and gentle, and I found myself wanting to touch every part of him. He was quiet the whole time, his breath shaky, his soft, slender hands urging me on, his legs tight around my hips. And when I kissed him at the end, I tasted tears.

I stopped then, wondering if I was mistaken. I brushed my fingers over his cheeks and found them wet, and his breath caught in his throat. "Tell me what's wrong." But he didn't. He just shook his head. He buried his face in my chest, and he quit fighting. Whatever it was that was bothering him, he gave in to it, crying quietly, shaking from the force of it, and I had no idea what to do. I held him tight until he fell asleep, his cheek still damp upon my chest. Long after his breathing had slowed, I lay awake, my chest aching with a sense of foreboding. I told myself it was nothing. I told myself it would be fine.

It was nearly five by the time I fell asleep. When I woke up two hours later, he was gone.

MY FIRST thought was only that he had gone to the store. He almost always made breakfast. I was probably out of eggs or bacon. Or maybe he had decided not to cook today, and he would be back soon with bagels and lattes. I went for a jog, expecting to find him in the kitchen when I got home. But he still wasn't there. I wondered about it, but I wasn't worried. Not yet. It wasn't until I was in the shower that I thought about what had happened in the night. How still he had been. His tears on my lips. His quiet whisper.

"Just one more time, love."

And I knew then, in an instant, that something was wrong.

The trepidation I had felt as he lay sleeping in my arms grew into absolute dread. I called his house, but he didn't answer. I called his cell phone, and it went to voice mail. I dressed as quickly as I could and drove to his house.

His eyes, when he answered the door were sad and a little bit red. He turned quickly away. "Would you like some wine?" he asked with forced casualness. As if this was okay. As if the ground was not shaking beneath my feet.

"It's not even nine o'clock yet."

"I know what time it is, love. I'll mix it with orange juice if it makes you feel better about it."

"I've been trying to call." He was silent, staring resolutely away from me. That seed of dread in my chest was blooming into full-blown panic now. "Is something wrong?" I asked.

"No," he said, although his voice was strange. Strained. A little too quiet. Nothing followed except tense silence, and he still wasn't looking at me.

"I don't know what's happening here, Cole, but you're scaring the hell out of me. Please tell me what's going on."

It took him a second to answer. One second, and a deep shaking breath, and then: "It's quite simple, darling. I'm leaving."

That panic I was feeling exploded then, cutting off my air, squeezing my chest, threatening to choke me. My heart was pounding, and I had to grab on to the back of the couch, just to keep the world from spinning away while I stood there in numb shock. "You're leaving me?" I finally managed to ask.

"I'm leaving Phoenix."

Breathe.

I made myself breathe. Made myself count to five. Made myself think.

Leaving Phoenix did not necessarily mean leaving me. It didn't have to mean that we were over.

"How long will you be gone?" I made myself ask.

"I don't know yet, darling."

"Where will you go?"

"To the Hamptons for now. Maybe Paris later."

In a flash—only a heartbeat—my panic was gone, replaced by something much worse. Something ugly. "To Raul? Is *that* where you're going?"

"No," he whispered, and I could hear the tears in his voice.

"Am I not good enough for you?" I snapped, and I saw how hard it hit him. I saw his shoulders start to shake under the weight of my indignation.

"That's not it," he whispered, and my momentary anger melted away. I was left with nothing but pain and confusion and the unwavering conviction that I could not lose him.

I closed my eyes. I fought back the tears that were burning behind them. I tried to swallow the lump in my throat. How could this be happening? If it was hurting him as much as it was hurting me, and I was pretty sure that it was, then why?

"Cole?" I said, opening my eyes, and he finally turned to me. His cheeks were wet, and I could see in his eyes that I was not wrong. He was so close to falling apart. "Cole," I said again, pleading this time, "talk to me."

"I have to go," he said, his voice breaking on the words.

I crossed over to him. I took his face in my hands and tried to look into his eyes, but he closed them tight against me. I kissed the tears from his cheeks. "Then go," I said. "But tell me you're coming home to me eventually. Please tell me this isn't over."

"It has to end," he said.

"Why?"

He took a deep, shaking breath, and when he opened his eyes again, they were swimming with tears. "Jonathan," he said. It was his real voice—not the lilting cadence he normally used, but the quiet one underneath it. It wasn't any lower than normal. It was still slightly feminine. But it was different—softer, and full of fear. And that one word, only my name, hurt me more than I would have thought possible, because it meant that he was deathly serious. "If I told you that I would see nobody else while I was gone, would you believe me? Would you take me at my word? I may be gone for two months or four or even six. You know how I've lived in the past. If I told you now that I would have no other lovers but you, would you have faith in me?"

I wanted to say yes. I wanted to say that I would trust him. But would I? Six months with him on the other side of the country or halfway around the world. Would I trust that he was alone all those nights?

"And what about you?" he went on, his voice a strained whisper. "Four months from now, when I'm still not home, will you wait for me? Or will you find somebody else to share your bed?"

"I don't know," I admitted, and his tears started to come faster.

"*I do*." He pushed my hands away, turned away from me to wipe his eyes. "Either you'll assume I'm being unfaithful and you'll be bitter and angry, or you'll get tired of waiting for me and you'll find somebody else. Either way, one day I'll come home, and you'll be gone."

"You don't know that it would be that way."

"I *do* know, Jon. That's how it always works."

"You told me you hadn't ever tried."

"I lied. And I can't go through that, Jon. Not again."

I took his arm and turned him toward me. "I don't want this to end, Cole. Please don't do this. I lov—"

"*Don't* say it!" he whispered, putting his fingertips against my lips to quiet me. There was something like panic in his eyes. "Please don't say it," he said again, pleading.

"Cole—"

"We should never have let it go this far."

"I don't want you to go, Cole. I don't want this to be over. Please don't do this. I can't believe that there are no other options."

His tears were coming faster now, but he didn't make a move to hide them from me or to wipe them away. "There's one other way," he said. "Do you want to hear it?"

"Of course."

"You won't like it."

"You don't know that."

He didn't believe me, I could tell. But he took a deep breath and said, "Come with me."

"Come with you where?"

He hesitated just a second, then said, "Everywhere."

I had to think for a bit about what he was saying, and once it dawned on me, I felt anger stirring in my breast. I let go of him and took a step back, and I saw in his eyes that it was what he expected. "You mean forget about working and just travel with you?"

"Yes," he said.

"We've already talked about this once, Cole. I will not follow you around like a kept boy and live off of your charity."

"It's not charity, Jon."

"It will look that way to everybody else." My voice was getting louder.

"It doesn't matter what other people—"

"How could I even hold my head up, Cole?"

"If I were straight, everybody would expect me to support my wife. How is this—"

"A *wife*?" I snapped, yelling now, and he winced, but I couldn't stop. "Is *that* what you want?"

"You misunderstood. I only meant—"

"And shall I have dinner waiting for you when you come home, too? Or is that still *your* job? Shall I call *you* the wife, then?" He winced at that, and I knew I had hurt him. But I was too angry to take it back.

He stepped closer to me, although his expression was wary. "I have a life that most people envy, Jon. I can go anywhere. I can do anything. I have more money than I can ever spend." He put one trembling hand against my cheek. "All I want to do is share it with you. All you have to do is say yes."

I loved him. God, I loved him so much I wondered how my chest didn't burst open from the force of it. But I couldn't imagine doing what he asked. I couldn't imagine knowing that I had nothing of my own, knowing that I was dependent upon him for absolutely everything.

"I can't live like that." I tried to make my voice gentle, but I might as well have slapped him. His breath caught in his throat. He closed his eyes and turned away from me, but not before I saw what he was trying to hide from me. He was ashamed. "Cole—" I started to reach for him, but he flinched away and held a hand up to stop me.

"You asked me once why I act the way I do. This is why, Jon. Because being flamboyant and eccentric is exactly what's expected of me, and although people may laugh, they have a certain amount of respect for my ability to not care about what they think. But if I let that go, Jon, this is all that's left. I'm a fool, and I'm a coward. And I'm *weak*. And that's the one thing a gay man is not allowed to be."

"I don't underst—" But he held up his hand again to stop me.

"I'd like you to leave now." His voice was torn. It was almost his real voice, soft and quiet, yet choked with tears. But I could also hear the cadence of it changing again; the small lilt being forced back in. He kept his back to me and crossed over to the table. He picked up his wine and downed all that was left in the glass.

"Can we talk about this, Cole? Please?"

"There's really nothing left to say." It was still another moment before he turned to face me, but when he did, the affectation was there. His walls were firmly in place. He leaned back against the table and cocked his head to the right so his bangs fell away from his eyes. There were still tears on his cheeks, but his eyes were dry. "My plane leaves in five hours. I think you know where the door is, darling."

Date: June 22

From: Cole

To: Jared

It's over. I finally did it. I feel certain that it was the right decision. I just wish it didn't hurt so much.

I miss him.

I WOKE an indeterminate number of days later to somebody ringing my doorbell. I had absolutely no idea what day it was. A glance at my watch told me that it was four o'clock in the afternoon. I was still in bed. I pulled the covers over my head and tried to go back to sleep before I could think about whatever it was that had reduced me to this state.

The doorbell rang again. I didn't want to answer it.

It was too late, though. The truth hit me hard, just like it did every time I surfaced: Cole was gone. That was why I was lying in bed with an empty hole in my chest, wishing I could slip back into oblivion. Whoever was on my front porch, waking me from my self-induced stupor, I knew it couldn't possibly be him. And there was nobody else in the world I wanted to see.

It rang again.

Whoever they were, they were persistent. And I was already awake. With a groan, I dragged myself out of bed. I found a pair of sweats and a T-shirt on the floor and put them on. I glanced in the mirror on the way to the door.

I was a mess.

There was really no other way to put it. I hadn't shaved in three days. I hadn't been out running in longer than that. I ran my fingers through my hair, trying to make it lie flat. I was trying to remember if I had ever showered yesterday.

The doorbell rang again.

"I'm coming!" I yelled, and gave up on the idea of my hair. It was going to take more than a comb to disguise the fact that I was falling apart. I finally made it to the door and opened it.

It was Julia. She had a casserole dish in one hand and a six-pack of beer in the other. "For Christ's sake, Jon," she said as she pushed past me into the house, "go clean yourself up while I put this in the oven."

"Julia, I'm really not in the mood—"

"Not in the mood to do anything but hide in your house and wallow alone in your misery?"

"Exactly."

"Too fucking bad. You can resume your pity party with me, *after* you've made yourself human again."

I didn't have the energy to argue. I showered and put on jeans and a clean shirt. I debated shaving, but then Julia called out, "It's ready!"

I wandered out of the bedroom and sat down at the dining room table. "When was the last time you ate?" she asked as she put a bowl of something unidentifiable in front of me.

"I don't know," I admitted. "It must have been yesterday."

She tousled my hair like I was a child. "Eat," she said. "I'll put some laundry in for you."

"You don't have to do that."

"I know, Jon. Shut up and eat."

I looked at whatever was in the bowl. I tried not to think about the last time somebody had cooked for me. I tried not to think about sautéed pasta with lobster or cioppino or what wine went with each one. I looked at the empty chair on the opposite side of the table and tried not to wonder where he was or what he was doing. I felt myself wanting to cry again, and I pushed it down, fought it back, and made myself take a bite.

It was good. It was chicken and rice, and I wasn't sure what else, but by my third bite, I realized I was starving. I finished the entire bowl and went into the kitchen for seconds. Julia was there, working on the dishes.

"You really don't need to do that," I said as she put more of the casserole in my bowl.

"I won't be making a habit of it," she said as she handed it to me. "I'm just here to get you back on your feet."

She emerged from the kitchen as I was finishing the second helping of chicken-mush. "Come on," she said, handing me a beer, and I followed her into the living room. She opened a beer for herself and put the rest of the six-pack on the coffee table in between us. "Tell me what happened," she said as she sat down in the armchair opposite from my spot on the couch.

Having to say the words made a lump form in my throat, and I had to count to five three times before I could myself say, "He left me."

"What did you do?" she asked.

"Why do you assume it was my fault?" I asked defensively.

"Because he's the one who left."

Fair point. I opened the beer and downed half of it at once. It wasn't even a micro-brew. It was some kind of weak mass-produced crap, and I wondered if a six-pack was enough to help me forget again. Just for one more night.

"Well?" she said, and I sighed.

"I honestly don't know. We didn't fight. Everything was fine. More than fine. It was…. It was…." And I had to stop before I started to cry again. I finished the beer while I got myself under control again. "He had to leave town," I finally said, as I opened a second one.

"So he's coming back?" she asked in confusion.

"No. At least, not to me."

"I don't understand."

"Neither do I."

"Bullshit, Jon. Tell me."

I finished the second beer too. I was starting to regret having eaten so much. On an empty stomach, two piss-poor beers might have at least been enough to give me a buzz. "He's too restless to stay in one place, but he assumes that if he's traveling, and I'm here, it will end. He says I'll get tired of waiting or that I'll doubt him."

"And so he left?" she asked in disbelief.

"Yes." I opened a third beer, telling myself I would make this one last. "I guess he decided it was better to end it now than to stick around and watch it all fall apart."

"And there aren't other options?"

I almost laughed. "That's exactly what I asked him."

"And?"

"And he said the only other option was for me to go with him."

"Well," she said with obvious indignation, "why the hell didn't you?"

"I can't afford to live the way he does, Julia."

"And what was his answer to that?"

"He said he would support me."

"So what exactly is the problem, Jon?"

"The problem," I said in annoyance, "is that it's absurd! Just because he has money, I'm supposed to swallow my pride and follow him around like some kind of pet?"

"So let me get this straight. He loves you so much that he offered to support you, just so the two of you could be together."

"I guess so. But—"

"But you're too proud to say yes."

"How could I even face myself in the mirror every morning?"

"Is it really so disgraceful," she asked with a surprising amount of venom in her voice, "to be supported by somebody who loves you?"

"To be unwilling to support yourself when you're perfectly capable? Yes, it's disgraceful. And absolutely humiliating."

She slammed her beer down on the coffee table and stood up. "Fine!" She started looking around on the floor for her shoes.

"Why are you mad?"

"I had no idea you thought so little of me, Jon!" she said, not looking at me. Her sandals had somehow ended up under her chair, and she bent down to retrieve them.

"You? I thought we were talking about me!"

"My husband chooses to support me financially. Does that make me a disgrace, too, Jon? Should I feel humiliated?"

Oh shit. I couldn't believe it hadn't occurred to me that she would take my words personally. I felt like there was a giant cliff right beneath my feet and I was wobbling, trying to figure out which way I had to lean to avoid falling off. The problem was she wasn't giving me enough time. "That's different, Julia."

She turned to face me. She had one sandal on, and the second one in her hand. "Why?"

"Because you're a woman."

I knew immediately, based on the look on her face, that that was the way wrong answer. "Excuse me?" she said, her voice going up in volume. "What did you just say to me?"

"No. I mean, you're not a woman! I mean, you *are* a woman, but not like a regular woman!" Her eyes got bigger, and I was almost surprised I wasn't being vaporized by the rage burning in them. "Wait, that's not what I meant!"

She pointed her sandal at me like some kind of weapon. "You're an asshole."

"Julia, I only meant that it's not the same thing at all! Not because you're a woman, but because you're a... a...." I stopped short, feeling myself tipping over the edge of that cliff.

"A *what?*" she hissed. The word that had popped into my head was "housewife," but I wasn't sure if I should say that or not. Was "housewife" a politically correct term? I was racking my brain, trying to think of a better word, but I was too slow. "A *breeder*, Jon?" she asked, her voice like ice. "Is that the term you're looking for?"

"What? *No!* I wasn't going to—"

"Bullshit!" she said advancing on me, with her sandal still in her right hand. "You think you're so much better than me? Is that what you think?"

"*No!*"

"Well, fuck you!" she yelled, and she smacked me hard on the arm with the sole of her sandal.

"*Ow!* Julia, what the hell? I never said any of those things!"

"You think your stupid pride is more important than love? Then you deserve to be miserable." She finally put on her second sandal, and I breathed a mental sigh of relief that she wouldn't be able to smack me with it again. She grabbed the remainder of the six-pack off of the table with one hand, reached out with the other hand and pulled my half-full can out of my hand. "You're an idiot," she said. And then she left.

I sat there for a minute trying to figure out what the hell had just happened. And then I gave up and went back to bed.

I DIDN'T allow myself to sink back into the pit Julia had pulled me out of. The next morning I got up and made myself go for a run, for the first time in a week. Afterward, I showered and shaved, then went down the street where I picked up donuts and coffee for two.

I was a little nervous knocking on her door. I was halfway expecting her to start beating me with her shoe again. But when the door opened, she looked apologetic.

"I'm glad to see you've joined the land of the living again," she said.

"Thanks to you." She shrugged. "How about a donut?" I asked her, and she smiled a little.

"Sounds good."

"Julia," I said, once were sitting down, "I'm sorry."

"I'm sorry too."

"I didn't mean to offend you."

"I know."

"I only meant that it was different because you work too—maybe not for pay, but I know it's not easy doing what you do."

She shrugged again. "I'm not asking for sympathy, Jon. I have a good life. Don't get me wrong—sometimes it feels like I'm juggling with one hand tied behind my back. But I know how lucky I am to have the luxury of staying home."

"I swear to you, Julia, I was *not* going to say that word."

"It wasn't you," she said. "It was Tony." Tony, her gay brother who lived in California. "I talked to him two days ago, and *he* used that word. And I was just so shocked, I hung up before I could really say anything to him. I tried to tell myself he didn't really mean anything by it, but the more I thought about it, the more pissed off I got. And then when you started talking about it being disgraceful for somebody to not work—"

"Julia, I'm sorry. I didn't mean it like that."

"I know."

"Have you talked to Tony since then?"

"No." She shrugged. "It's not fair," she said, sounding sheepish. "I'm his biggest advocate. The rest of my family won't even speak to

him. I stand up for him, and what do I get for it? I get called names."
She shook her head, not looking at me. "I don't understand. Neither one
of us can help what we are, and yet for some reason, he feels that I
deserve his contempt simply because I'm not like him."

"I'm sorry," I said again, because I didn't know what else to say.

"If I were to call him a name like that for being gay, he would
never forgive me."

"Julia," I said cautiously, trying to tread carefully, "I'm not trying
to be an asshole here, but I don't think being a straight woman in our
society is nearly as difficult as being a gay man."

She looked at me like I was a moron. "I never said it was, Jon."
Good point. "But I don't think that justifies him being a bigoted
asshole."

I wasn't really sure what to say to that, and I was afraid that
anything I did say would only get me in trouble again. I finally settled
for saying a third time, "I'm sorry."

She smiled at me. "I'm sorry, too."

"Am I forgiven?"

"Yes," she said as she pulled a donut out of the bag. "But you're
still an idiot."

Three days later I had a dinner date with my dad. I had been
avoiding him since Cole had left me. I knew he would ask about it, and
I wasn't sure I would be able to face it.

"I thought Cole was coming," he said as I sat down.

It hurt more than I could believe, but I was ready to say the
words. "He left me."

He didn't say anything for a few moments. He just sat there
looking at me. "I'm sorry," he said at last.

"I know you think he's a fruitcake."

He shrugged. "He is. But that doesn't mean I didn't like him."

"Because he made Mom's stroganoff? Or because he had a condo in Vail?"

"Neither one, Jon," he said gently. "I liked him because he made you happy."

I had to look down at the table. I didn't want my father to see me cry. "Yes," I whispered. "He did."

Date: August 2

From: Cole

To: Jared

Sweets, I know you're probably terribly upset with me. You've been emailing over and over and I haven't replied. It's dreadfully inappropriate, I know, and I hope you won't hold it against me because the truth is, you're the only person I can be honest with. Partly it's because we've known each other so long. But mostly it's because I don't have to face you when I admit to you how terribly, terribly much I miss him.

I've been in New York for the past several weeks. I keep telling myself that I'm leaving for Paris soon, but I can't make myself do it. Somehow, having only a continent between us seems bearable. Having an ocean between us does not.

He's tried to call me many times, but I never answer. I had hoped to avoid him until... until when? I don't know. Until I could think of him without my heart breaking all over again, I guess. But it's not to be. Something has come up, and it seems I will have to face him sooner than I had hoped. I'm sick with fear, just thinking about it. I know he will be strong, and I will be weak like I always am. I hate myself for it.

The thing is, Sweets, this could be the answer. It's not contrived. It's not my doing. It's a happy coincidence, and it could fix everything. If only he will see.

I FOUND a job. It was an entry-level position at a large accounting firm. My salary was half what I had been making before, and I found myself in a pool of hard workers who were ten years younger than me or more. I watched them jockey for position as they tried to decide which of the partners to ingratiate themselves to. They worked overtime, although being on salary, they never got paid for it. They were exactly as I had been, and I found them absurd.

My position did have great potential for advancement, but I discovered quickly that I did not care. Being at the bottom of the ladder, there was very little expected of me, and I was happy to let the younger men fight and beg for the tiny advancements that were handed down. I no longer had to travel. I sold my condo in Vegas and was glad to be rid of it. My phone didn't ring at all hours of the day. I never worked more than forty hours in a week, something I hadn't been able to do in years, and at the end of each day, I went home. When I walked out of the office at five o'clock, I didn't give my job another thought until I walked back in the next day at eight. It was somehow incredibly liberating.

One Saturday, three weeks into my new job, my cell phone rang. It surprised me. Between Cole leaving and losing my job, it hardly ever rang anymore. I was even more surprised when I looked at the screen and saw who it was.

I couldn't even answer at first. My heart was pounding and my palms sweating. My head was spinning with all of the possible reasons he might be calling now. I prayed it was to fix things between us, but I didn't want to get my hopes up.

"Hello?" I answered, my heart in my throat.

He was quiet for a second, but then he said, "It's me." His voice was off, like he wanted to use his normal, lilting cadence but couldn't quite pull it off.

"I know." I stopped short, fighting back tears. There were a thousand things in my head I wanted to say to him: I miss you, I love you, are you home? Please come back to me. I had no idea where to start. "I'm so glad you called," I finally said, my voice shaking. There was just silence. At first I thought he had hung up. I looked at my phone, saw that the call was still active. "Cole?" And then I heard his breath catch. He was either crying or trying very hard not to.

"I don't know," he said in a soft, shaky whisper, "why this has to be so hard."

And at those words, I lost my own battle to keep my tears at bay. "It's hard for me too, Cole. God, I miss you so much."

He took a ragged breath then, and I could almost see him putting his affectation back on, like armor, one piece at a time: the mocking look, the way he cocked his hip out, the way he let his hair fall into his eyes. I was not surprised, when he spoke again, to hear that the cadence of his speech was back. "Sweetie, I need to see you if you can spare a few moments for me."

My heart skipped a beat. "Of course. Are you back in town?" *Please let him say yes.*

"Very briefly."

"Do you want to come over?" *Please let me hold him one more time.*

"That's not a good idea."

"Cole, I can't—" *I can't bear to live without you.* That's what I wanted to say, but he interrupted me.

"Can you meet me at the coffee shop at two? The one near your house, down by the grocery store?"

"Of course," I said, feeling confused. Why were we meeting in a coffee shop?

"Thanks, sweetie. I'll see you then."

I got to the coffee shop before him. The place was empty except for the employees. I ordered for both of us. Cole arrived as they were handing me my drinks. Seeing him again was like a slap to the face. The two hot drinks in my hand were the only thing that kept me from grabbing him and holding him tight. That, and the healthy distance he was keeping between us. He kept his head down a little, his hair in his eyes so that I could not read his expression.

"Chai?" I offered, holding it out to him, and he almost smiled. Almost.

"Thank you."

We sat down at a table but neither of us tasted the drinks I had just bought. I was trying to look at every bit of him, like I could take him all in. As if that would somehow ease the pain I felt at the distance between us rather than making it worse. I was trying to get a sense of what he was feeling. Trying to determine if he was as heartbroken as I was. He did not look at me. He kept his eyes on the table.

"Cole," I finally said, "I miss you." I started to reach across the table to where his hand was resting, but he pulled away.

"Stop," he said, and I froze, my heart aching in my chest. He took a deep breath. "This isn't a personal visit, sweetie. It's a professional one."

I could hardly even follow his words. All I could think about was how much it hurt to see him and have him push me away again. "I don't understand."

Another deep breath. He still would not look at me, and his hands were clenched tight together on the table in front of him. I suspected it was to keep me from seeing how much he was shaking, but I could still hear it in his voice. "I want to offer you a job."

"A job?" I asked stupidly.

"I have an accountant. Chester." He stopped, and he glanced up at me for the first time. It wasn't direct eye contact. It was only a glance through his hair, but I saw the humor there, along with the strain of trying to act casual. "Actually, his name is Warren Chesterfield, and he hates when I call him Chester."

"Which is why you do it."

He went on as if I hadn't spoken. "You know I have money, sweetie, and I'm sure it will not surprise you to learn that I pay no attention to it at all. I have multiple accounts. I don't know how many. I have a stockbroker. Or maybe I have a few. I'm not clear on that either, to tell you the truth. I believe they make more money for me, although I could be wrong. I give money to certain charities on a regular basis. You know that I have several houses and at least one person on staff at each one. My other homes, all but the one here, are rented out as vacation properties at various times of the year, which results in a small amount of income I assume. And of course, I have my mother to support." He stopped for a minute, and I waited, knowing he wasn't done. "All of this has been managed for me by Chester since—well, since before the money was even mine, to tell you the truth. I live my life, I spend what I need, I do what I want, and Chester is there to tell me if anything goes wrong."

He stopped again, and this time I asked, "What does this have to do with me?"

"Three weeks ago, Chester informed me that he is retiring. He's been hounding me mercilessly to find a replacement ever since." He stopped short again, and his voice was quieter when he started talking again. "It took me that long to get up enough nerve to call."

"You're offering the job to me?"

"Is that not what I've just been explaining, sweetie?"

"What does this mean for us?" I asked.

It took him a moment to answer, and he still wasn't looking at me. "It has nothing to do with us at all," he said quietly, and it was like being punched in the stomach. "It's a job. Nothing more."

"Then why me?" I asked. "There are a million accountants out there for you to choose from."

And for the first time, he flipped his hair back out of his eyes, and he met my gaze evenly. "Because I trust you, Jon." Hearing him say my name almost undid me. My eyes closed, and I had to concentrate on just breathing. "It would be very easy for somebody in this position to steal from me, and I know that you won't. It's that simple."

It made sense, and yet I didn't care. I felt like my heart was breaking all over again. I only wanted him. "Cole," I reached over and took his hand, and this time he let me. "I'll do anything you want. Just come back."

His eyes closed, and I felt him trembling. And slowly, very slowly, he pulled his hand away from mine. "Please don't, Jon," he said in a shaky whisper. "Please don't make me cry here." And I realized that was why he had insisted on meeting in a public place: so that he would have to keep his distance, to keep his walls in place. I fought back my own tears, staring at the table in front of me.

"I realize," he finally said, and his voice was still strained from the effort of keeping his emotions in check, "that it may seem strange to think of me as your employer. But I assure you, it won't feel that way. Chester and I probably spoke once or twice a year at best, and then only when he felt I needed to know something. You will be your own boss, really. I won't be looking over your shoulder." I had been so busy thinking about how much I missed him that I hadn't managed to think that far ahead. But now that he said it, I realized it should have occurred to me, and it was good to know that we wouldn't have these awkward meetings often, because this one was more painful that I could stand. "Will you do it?"

I didn't really even have to think about it. "I haven't done any personal accounting in years. I'll have to brush up on it."

"Does that mean yes?"

"How much?" I asked. It felt cheap to ask him about salary, but a job was a job. My new one didn't pay all that well, and my savings account was getting frighteningly low. He took a piece of paper out of his pocket and slid it across the table to me. The number he had written on it surprised me enough that I looked up at him again. It was more than I had been making after nine years at my old job. "This is too much," I said.

And just barely, he smiled at me. "That's thirty percent less than I was paying Chester. You see, love?" And I winced at that pet name. "You're saving me money already. I'll have Chester call you. He'll want to meet with you at least once, I'm sure. He's an arrogant, homophobic asshole, but he's very thorough."

"I'll be expecting his call."

"Thank you."

He stood up then and turned to leave, and without even thinking about it, I reached out and grabbed his hand. "Cole, please don't go."

"I have to," he said, but he didn't pull away.

I couldn't even look at him. I felt my control slipping. I kept my eyes on his slender fingers, trapped in mine. "Cole," I said, my voice shaking, "I can't stand this. I lov—"

But before I could finish, his fingers were against my lips, stopping my words. "Shhh," he said. One of his hands was still in mine, but the other, the one he had used to quiet me moved slowly across my cheek, and I closed my eyes. His fingers went into my hair. I tightened my grip on his other hand, pulled him toward me—and he came. He let me wrap my arms around him. My face was against his stomach, and his hand was in my hair, holding me against him, and any control I had been trying to maintain was gone. I let myself cry, not caring where we were or who was around to see.

"Please don't leave me again. I can't stand being apart. I miss you so much."

For some immeasurable amount of time, it may have been only seconds, or an hour—whatever it was, it was far too short—he held me. "I miss you too, Jon," he whispered at last, "but nothing has changed."

And then he let me go. He walked away, out of the coffee shop and out of my life. Again. By the time I had composed myself enough to look up from the table, he was gone.

Date: August 6

From: Cole

To: Jared

He knows where I am. He knows how to find me. But he doesn't. I love him, Jared, more than I can say. He says he loves me too, but still he let me go.

I HAPPILY quit my job at the accounting firm and submerged myself in my new role as Cole's accountant. It took several meetings with Chester—and Cole hadn't lied. He really was an arrogant, homophobic asshole. But it was also obvious that he was thorough and incredibly honest, and I had to admire him for that.

It took me a bit to brush up on personal accounting and to get a grasp on where all of his money was. There were multiple holding accounts, but only one account that he used actively. It had to have enough in it at any given moment to cover spontaneous purchases or traveling expenses, but not so much that it would be disastrous if his debit card was lost or stolen. There was an account for his mother. Her stipend was deposited into it at the first of each month, and she spent every cent. There were accounts set up for each of the housekeepers at his various homes. I realized then that they did much more than clean. They were more like property managers, and he paid them generously, although he probably didn't even know it. They used their accounts to pay expenses on the properties as needed. One of my jobs was to make sure they had enough to cover those expenses but didn't take advantage of the easy access to his funds.

I realized something else. He really did have *a lot* of money. He was also right when he said that it would have been unbelievably easy for me to steal it and nobody ever would have known. Needless to say, I didn't even consider it.

The weeks went by. There were still days when I missed him like crazy—days when the tiniest things would make me ache for him. I missed dinner together and having him laugh at me and just waking up next to him each and every morning. But there were other days when I could think of him and smile, and that pain in my chest would be almost bearable.

I missed the sex too. The two were not necessarily connected. On multiple occasions I debated visiting the bathhouse, but in the end, I never did. Somehow I felt that finding a new partner, even an anonymous one in the glory hole of a bathhouse, would be the final straw. It would be admitting defeat, accepting the fact that I had lost him forever. I wasn't ready to do that yet.

I found that I could live vicariously through his accounts. He used his debit card for everything. Although it took a couple of days for the charges to come through, I could piece together a picture of what he was doing. I knew at all times which city he was in. I saw when he made a purchase for eight thousand dollars at a gallery in New York, and wondered what exactly he had bought. I saw when he ate at his favorite restaurant in Paris, and I wondered if he had been alone.

I knew it wasn't necessarily healthy, but it helped me cope. It gave me a connection to him, however tenuous.

My days had no discernible rhythm. My time was my own. He had given me a freedom I hadn't had since college, and I reveled in it. I slept late. I donated most of my suits to Goodwill, although I kept every single tie he had bought for me. I wore jeans or shorts, like a regular person. I didn't shave every single day. Sometimes my house felt like a tomb, and I would take my laptop to the coffee shop to work. I still jogged almost every day, but rather than rising at five in the morning to beat the Arizona heat, I often waited until nine or ten at night, after the sun had set.

And finally, nearly a year after he had given me the gift certificate, I went skydiving. It was at once the most frightening and the most exhilarating experience of my life. I wasn't even surprised to discover that Cole was right. I longed to fly.

Six weeks after taking the job, I decided I needed to get out of the house. I took my laptop to a café near my home that offered free wireless. I ordered a Cobb salad and a glass of wine. That was another small but somehow significant sign of my new life: I could have wine with lunch. There was no office to go back to, no client to impress, nobody who could frown on me for it. I smiled as I ordered the Sauvignon Blanc, because I could picture the look on his face if I were to order Chianti.

While I waited for my food, I got online and checked his accounts. I found that two days earlier, he had booked a flight from Paris to New York. It wasn't hard to check the flight number on the airline's webpage. He would be arriving in New York late tomorrow afternoon. I wondered if he would spend his nights with Raul while he was there. The thought made that pain in my chest flare to life, and I pushed it away.

"We already made the reservations!" The statement caught my attention. It came from the table next to me where a young couple was having lunch together. The man was wearing a suit and had a briefcase leaning against the legs of his chair. The woman was fighting tears. It was she who had spoken. She was talking in a forceful whisper, obviously trying to keep her voice down, but unable to keep it completely under control. "We've been planning this trip for months!"

"What do you want me to do?" he asked her. "If I say no, they'll give the account to Connor."

"So let them!"

"Claire, you're being unreasonable. This is the chance I've been waiting for. The chance *we've* been waiting for—"

"The only thing I've been waiting for is our anniversary!"

"Maybe next year—"

"That's what you said last year!"

"You can still go, Claire. You may as well use the tickets."

"By *myself?*"

"Sure. Why not? You'll have fun. Maybe Carrie can go with you—" His phone rang, interrupting him. Claire sat back in her chair and crossed her arms, angrily wiping the tears from her cheeks.

That stupid man actually took the call. "This is Mike."

It reminded me of my first date with Cole, when he had walked out. I had been such an ass, so caught up in the rat race that I couldn't even enjoy dinner. But even with my phone ringing non-stop, he had still given me his number and told me to call.

What if he hadn't been willing to give me that second chance? What if I'd never taken it?

Mike was still talking. "Of course, sir. It's not a problem at all, I assure you."

Claire stood up, grabbed her purse, and walked out of the café.

Mike didn't follow.

And suddenly, with painful clarity, I realized what an idiot I really was. Julia had said it. My father had said it. Why it had taken me until now to realize that they were right, I didn't know.

More than ten years earlier, in an apartment in Colorado, I had packed a bag and walked out the door, leaving my own cat behind—not because I didn't want her, but because I was sure I wasn't really leaving for good. I was sure Zach would beg me to come back. I waited and waited, missing him the whole time.

He never called.

My own failure to act had cost me the man I loved once already in my life. But had I learned my lesson? Apparently not. Here I was, older but no wiser, waiting for Cole to realize that he loved me as much as I loved him. Waiting for him to realize that we were meant to be. Waiting for him to call.

What if he never did?

I was unwilling to admit that we might be over. But if I waited for him to admit he was wrong or to change his wandering lifestyle, I would be waiting the rest of my life.

I made my plane reservation before I even left the café. I went straight to Julia's house when I got home.

"I need you to watch my house for a while. Can you do that?"

"Of course." It had been months since I had traveled anywhere, but she still had the key. "How long will you be gone?"

"I don't know yet. I'll call you."

"Where are you going?"

"I'm going after him."

She smiled at me. "It's about damn time."

THE flight from Phoenix to New York was six hours long. Six hours to contemplate all the ways this could end.

Every minute was an exercise in patience. Pre-boarding made my heart pound. Finding my seat made my palms sweat. The take-off almost caused me to hyperventilate—there was no turning back now. I was given a bag of pretzels (because peanuts were no longer allowed), and a tiny shot of Sprite on the rocks. What I really needed was a Valium, but I was pretty sure the stewardess didn't have those on her rickety little cart.

Every choice I had ever made had led me here, to this airplane. Everything I wanted in the world was at the other end of this unbelievably terrifying cross-country flight. What if it all went wrong? What if he didn't want me?

I rented a car at the airport and headed for his home in the Hamptons. After the nerve-wracking flight, my arrival at an empty house seemed oddly anticlimactic.

Cole had told me his house was small for the Hamptons. It was certainly less ostentatious than many of the other homes in the area, but it was probably still worth at least a cool million. It was a nice ranch-style home with large, open rooms and an unbelievable kitchen that had probably been remodeled to his exact specs. I was surprised to find the underwater picture from our New York visit hanging in the living room. I went in search of the bedroom, and what I found there made me smile. Even though it was summer, there was a thick comforter on the bed. And on the wall was a different photo from the same gallery—a photo of drifts of snow among leafless aspen.

In the back yard, I found a pool surrounded by a small, perfectly manicured lawn and a gorgeous array of flowers.

I also found the gardener.

Cole had said if I saw him, I would understand, and he was right. He was in his early twenties with deeply tanned skin and jet-black hair. He was wearing only canvas tennis shoes and a pair of incredibly short cut-off jeans. He was on his knees, pulling weeds from one of the flowerbeds. His body was strong and muscular and absolutely amazing. He looked up at me with the face of some ancient god, and I stopped short.

"Hey," he said, smiling at me.

I tried to smile back, but failed miserably. "You must be Raul."

"You must be the boyfriend," he said lightly.

"What makes you say that?"

His smile was open and friendly, and he shrugged and turned back to the flowers. "Let's just say I haven't taken care of anything but the lawn for a very long time."

And suddenly I found that I could smile at him after all.

I was in the kitchen doing my best imitation of cooking when I heard Cole come in. I stood there, listening to him rattle around the living room, and tried to get up enough courage to face him. This was what I had come all the way to New York for. I couldn't exactly back out now. I hoped for a minute that he would save me the effort of making a decision by coming into the kitchen, but he didn't. In fact, whatever he was doing, I couldn't hear him anymore at all. I stepped quietly through the doorway into the living room.

His back was to me. He had already taken his shoes off and was standing barefoot, going through the stack of mail Margaret had left for him on the dresser by the door. I knew I should say something, but I found that I couldn't make my voice work. It had only been six weeks since I had seen him last, but it felt like ages. I felt like he should have looked different somehow, but he didn't. His clothes were the same, his hair was the same. The slender lines of his body were the same. I found myself hoping like crazy that he smelled the same too.

I wasn't sure what to say to him, but I was dying to touch him. I took a few slow and hesitant steps toward him. On about the fourth one, the floor creaked under my foot just a bit.

"Margaret, is that you?" he asked. And then he turned and practically ran right into me.

He jumped about a foot backward and bumped into the dresser behind him. The only reason it didn't tip over was because it was against the wall. "Good lord, Jon! You scared me out of my wits!"

"I didn't mean to startle you," I said. I had caught him enough off his guard that he had actually said my name, and I couldn't help but smile. He seemed to realize it at the exact same moment, because his cheeks turned red and he turned quickly away from me.

"How in the world did you know I would be here?" he asked.

"I have access to all of your accounts. I saw the charge when you booked the flight."

"And did you find the door open, or are you perfecting your lock-picking skills?" I could hear that lilting cadence starting to creep back into his voice as he started to put his walls back in place.

"I sign Margaret's paychecks. It wasn't hard to convince her to let me in."

He was quiet for a moment, and when he spoke again, his voice was quieter. "Why did you come?"

I stepped closer to him. He didn't move, and when I put my hands on his arms, he tensed noticeably. I hesitated a moment, not wanting to push him too far, too fast, but I had waited so long. I couldn't stand not to touch him. I stepped close enough that I could put my nose into his hair and smell the strawberry shampoo he used. Such a ridiculously stupid thing, but smelling it almost brought tears to my eyes. It was hard to speak. "I came to tell you that I'm not letting you run from me anymore."

"Is that what I've been doing?"

"Yes. And I was stupid enough to let you. But not anymore. We belong together, and you know I'm right."

"It's a terrible idea, darling," he said shakily. "Really. It will never work."

"It's not a terrible idea, and you know it. You're just being stubborn."

"You'll get tired of me, love, and—"

"Stop!" I said, and was surprised when he actually fell silent. "Ever since we met, we've done things your way. I've always let you call the shots. But I'm not letting you destroy what we have just because you're scared." I felt him start to tremble then, and I wrapped my arms around him. "I—"

"Don't say it!"

"—love you. I want to be with you. I hate being apart. I hate not being able to touch you. I hate wondering where you are and what you're doing. And *more than anything*, I hate not knowing when you'll finally come home."

"I don't like being apart, either," he said in a shaky whisper, "but I can't possibly stay in Phoenix, darling. Not all the time."

"I know."

"What will you do when I leave?"

"I'll follow."

He was quiet for a moment, but when he spoke again, I could hear hope in his voice. "Anywhere?"

"*Everywhere.*"

His breath caught, and he tried to pull away from me, but I tightened my grip around him. He stilled again, but he was straining away from me, his breath ragged, and I knew he was trying desperately not to cry in front of me again. "Let me go," he whispered, but I only held him tighter.

"Stop fighting it, Cole. Stop fighting *me*."

"I hate for you to see me like this," he said shakily.

I put my lips against the birthmark on the back of his neck and felt him shiver. "I don't mind. You don't have to hide from me, Cole. You don't have to pretend. I know the part of you that you let the world see, and I know what's underneath. I know you think you have to keep it hidden, and it only makes me love you more."

He went a little bit limp in my arms then, and I felt him trembling. I could feel that wall between us crumbling down as he finally let go and allowed the tears to come.

"I'm a mess," he said, halfway joking but halfway not. "I'm demanding and temperamental and I'm terribly high maintenance."

I laughed without even meaning to. "Do you honestly think I don't know all that by now?"

"Then how could you *possibly* love me?"

I held him tighter, kept kissing his neck. "How can I *not*?" I asked. It had been so long since I'd been able to touch him. Part of me just wanted to hold him all night. The other part of me wanted only to drag him into the bedroom and tear his clothes off, throw him on the bed and make love to him forever. "Cole," I whispered, "I can't live without you."

"That's rather cliché, isn't it, darling?"

"That doesn't make it any less true. I need you."

"*Why?*"

"To make fun of me when I'm being too serious. To remind me that there are more important things in life than climbing the corporate ladder."

"I'm quite sure you could manage without me, love," he said, and I was glad to hear the term of endearment, because it meant he was giving in.

"Who else is going to make sure that I don't drink Chianti with lobster Alfredo?" I asked, and he laughed. "I love you, and I won't let you stop me from saying it."

It took him a moment and one deep, shaking breath to answer. "I don't want to stop you," he said quietly. "Not really."

That caused a lump to form in my throat. I held him tighter. I put my lips against that butterfly on the back of his neck and said again, "I love you."

And finally, he relaxed in my arms completely. He leaned back against me with a soft sigh of surrender, and I knew then that I had won. "Jonathan," he said quietly, "I love you too."

All of the fear and anxiety I had felt coming here, and the nervousness at seeing him, and the relief of getting to hold him again, and the happiness at *finally* hearing those words and knowing that I had him back—it was all too much. Suddenly I was the one fighting not to cry, and he must have sensed it, because he turned around and pulled me close.

"I haven't missed you at all," I managed to say in a hoarse whisper.

"I haven't missed you either," he said quietly. "Certainly not every single minute of every single day." His arms were tight around me and mine around him. His skin was soft and warm, and his hair smelled like strawberries like it always did. And everything about it felt right.

"Please don't leave me again," I begged, and my voice broke on the words.

"I never wanted to leave you at all, love."

"Then why?"

"I couldn't stay. And you were too proud to come with me."

"But...." I had to stop and think about that, and it helped me calm down. It helped me get my bearings again. He was right. He had asked me twice to come with him. But I was too proud to allow him to support me. And with a regular office job, I would have been tied to Phoenix. I never would have had the freedom to come after him if it weren't for the job I had, working for him. I pulled away enough to see his face. "But you gave me the job—"

"It was sheer luck that Chester decided to retire, but I hoped it would change your mind."

"Why didn't you just say so?"

"I felt like it had to be your idea." He shrugged. "Maybe it was foolish. But I was afraid you would think I was using the job to manipulate you, and I really did want you to take it. I knew I could trust you, whether you came after me or not." He put his arms around my neck and brushed his lips over mine. "I've been waiting for you for ages, love," he said. "I'd almost given up. What on earth took you so long?"

I couldn't help but laugh. "Either I'm an idiot or you really need to work on your communication skills."

He smiled. "I suppose it could be a little of both."

"I met Raul today."

"And?"

"I may have to fire him."

He laughed. It was so good to hear. Already, I felt like we were back to normal. Like everything was perfect. I put my arms around him and I pulled him close. I kissed his neck, and he tipped his head back to give me better access to the soft skin there. "I made you dinner," I said as I kissed him.

"Oh my," he said jokingly. "Is it frozen pizza?"

"I wish I could say it was sautéed pasta with lobster. But it's actually sloppy joes."

"And the wine?"

"I bought the Arbor Mist Peach Chardonnay."

"Well that's just dreadful, darling. The Blackberry Merlot is obviously the better choice."

"They were sold out." My hands were wandering now. I pulled up his shirt just to feel the smooth skin of his back. I pushed him back so he was sitting on the dresser behind him, and he wrapped his legs around my hips and let me push against him. "I know you're probably starving, and I should let you eat. But I can't wait to get these clothes off of you."

"I'm not sure what to tell you," he said. "I am rather hungry, but I'm quite sure I smell your sloppy joes burning. I suspect they're quite inedible by now."

I unbuttoned his pants as I kissed him. I pushed my hand into his open fly, caressing the bulge in his briefs. "There's always frozen pizza."

His breath caught for a moment, and then he said breathlessly, "How about we skip dinner and go straight to dessert?"

"Strawberries?"

"What a perfect choice, love."

"I haven't been able to eat them since you left."

"And do they still have the same effect on you?" he asked with a wicked grin.

"As a matter of fact, they do."

He laughed as he put his arms around my neck and pulled me close. "I'm incredibly happy to hear that."

Date:	September 30
From:	Cole
To:	Jared

Good lord, Sweets, can you please stop being so smug? If you gloat any more I imagine you'll become absolutely unbearable. Tell that big angry cop you live with that I'm sorry I turned his sweet loving partner into such a know-it-all. As if he didn't hate me enough already.

Yes, fine, I admit it, you're right. Jonathan and I are back together, and everything is peaches (and strawberries). The truth is, I've never been happier. And no, I will not thank you for it. You're intolerable enough already!

We're back in Phoenix now, and we'll be here for a couple of weeks, at least. We came back for George's birthday, because I truly believe that nobody should have to spend their birthday alone. I decided to buy him Diamondbacks season tickets. I wanted to get him a clubhouse box, but Jonathan said it was too ostentatious. He said the infield would be sufficient. Well, infield, outfield—what's the difference really? And I figured George might as well be close enough to actually see those men on the field (even if he doesn't fully appreciate them) so I bought a third-base box instead. George was so happy, he practically cried. And Jonathan? Honey, he went through the roof! Well how was I supposed to know that all boxes were off-limits? He really should have been more specific, don't you think? I swear, that man is so aggravating, it's a wonder I put up with up him at all.

Well, anyway, it's nothing to worry about. I'll apologize, and Jonathan will forgive me. Besides, why shouldn't I spend my money on George if I want to? I have a family now. A tiny little family, since Jon and I have only the one real parent between us, but a family nonetheless. I absolutely adore George, and the truth is, I think he rather likes me. And not just because of the box seats.

I have to go, Sweets, but before I do, there's something I've been dying to say. I've never been able to say it before. I could barely even admit it to myself, because it just seemed so impossible.

But not anymore.

I'll tell Jonathan, of course, when I'm feeling brave. I know he'll understand. But I'll say it here first, to you. I want to see how it feels to let the words take form. I want to know what it's like to allow them to become real and true, and to acknowledge that just maybe, someday, this wish will come true too. The thing is, Jared…

I've always wanted to be a father.

MARIE SEXTON was always good at the technical aspects of writing but never had any ideas for stories. After graduating from Colorado State University, she worked for eleven years at an OB/GYN clinic. She quit the clinic at about the same time she started reading M/M romances. At some point in the ensuing months, the static in her head cleared, and her first story was born.

Marie lives in Colorado. She's a fan of just about anything that involves muscular young men piling on top of each other. In particular, she loves the Denver Broncos and enjoys going to the games with her husband. Matt and Jared often tag along. Marie has one daughter, two cats, and one dog, all of whom seem bent on destroying what remains of her sanity. She loves them anyway.

Visit Marie's web site at http://www.MarieSexton.net or find her on Facebook.

Also by MARIE SEXTON

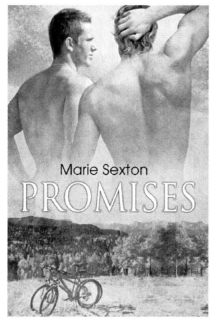

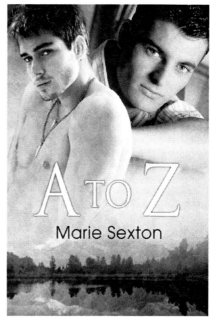

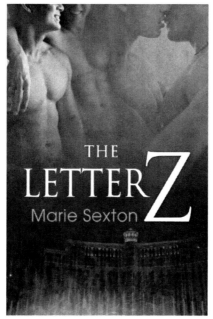

http://www.dreamspinnerpress.com

Lightning Source UK Ltd.
Milton Keynes UK
UKOW021202301111

182955UK00010B/112/P